MERRY MERRY MURDER

When I burst outside the church, the first thing I noticed was the red-and-blue flashing lights. The night was so bright and crisp, the lights seemed to reflect off the very air, making it blinding. It took me a moment to realize that no one was on the sidewalk on this side of the street. All the excitement was happening on the other side, at Andrew's Gifts.

More people spilled out of the church doors behind me, but I barely noticed. My eyes shot to the parking lot, to the empty space where Dad's car had been. Rita's car was gone as well. Nothing had happened to either of them.

But not everyone was so lucky.

Across the street, a stretcher was being carried out of Andrew's Gifts. On it, was a sheet-covered body. And following behind, a grim-faced Detective John Buchannan was barking orders at anyone who'd listen to him.

He jerked to a sudden stop, as if he sensed someone watching. His gaze zeroed in on me standing across the street for a heartbeat before he spun around and marched right back into the gift shop.

That look might have only been brief, but there was no questioning its meaning.

Whatever had happened next door wasn't a mere accident. If my guess was right, it appeared as if someone had been murdered . . .

Books by Alex Erickson

Bookstore Café Mysteries
DEATH BY COFFEE
DEATH BY TEA
DEATH BY PUMPKIN SPICE
DEATH BY VANILLA LATTE
DEATH BY EGGNOG
DEATH BY ESPRESSO
DEATH BY CAFÉ MOCHA
DEATH BY FRENCH ROAST
DEATH BY HOT APPLE CIDER
DEATH BY SPICED CHAI
DEATH BY ICED COFFEE
DEATH BY PEPPERMINT CAPPUCCINO
CHRISTMAS COCOA MURDER
(with Carlene O'Connor and Maddie Day)

Furever Pets Mysteries
THE POMERANIAN ALWAYS BARKS TWICE
DIAL 'M' FOR MAINE COON

Published by Kensington Publishing Corp.

Death by Peppermint Cappuccino

ALEX ERICKSON

Kensington Publishing Corp.
www.kensingtonbooks.com

KENSINGTON BOOKS are published by

Kensington Publishing Corp.
119 West 40th Street
New York, NY 10018

All Kensington titles, imprints, and distributed lines are available at special quantity discounts for bulk purchases for sales promotion, premiums, fund-raising, educational, or institutional use.

Special book excerpts or customized printings can also be created to fit specific needs. For details, write or phone the office of the Kensington Sales Manager: Attn.: Sales Department. Kensington Publishing Corp., 119 West 40th Street, New York, NY 10018. Phone: 1-800-221-2647.

The K and Teapot logo is a trademark of Kensington Publishing Corp.

First Printing: October 2023
ISBN: 978-1-4967-3669-7

ISBN: 978-1-4967-3670-3 (ebook)

10 9 8 7 6 5 4 3 2 1

Printed in the United States of America

1

A mass of colored bulbs and tangled wires sat at the bottom of the battered cardboard box. There appeared to be no beginning, no end. Just a bundle that would forever remain tucked away in the back of the church's closet, never to be used again.

I closed the tattered flaps and shoved the box away.

"Are the lights no good?" Rita Jablonski called over her shoulder. She was standing on her tiptoes atop a step stool to hang garland in the corner of the church. The room was coming together, but without lights, it wouldn't have the same effect.

"No. I'll buy some more in a little while and get them hung up before the party." I didn't know if that mass of Christmas lights worked or not, but there was no way Krissy Hancock was going to spend the rest of her evening untangling them to find out. I had more important things to worry about.

I snuck a glance toward the stairs, but no one was walking up them yet. A peek at the clock told me that the person I was waiting on was five minutes late. A gnawing worry rested in the vicinity of my gut, along with a healthy dose of excitement. Five minutes was nothing, not when planes were involved.

"Are you expecting someone?" Rita climbed down from the stool. She was a short, somewhat stout woman with a penchant for noticing *everything*. "You've been watching the door like a hawk for at least an hour now."

"No." A lie, but it was for a good reason. "I thought I heard something."

"Mmhmm." Rita didn't look as if she believed me, but she let it drop. "I don't rightly know why no one else showed up to help with the decorations. I told the entire group that we'd be here this morning. You'd think at least *one* of them would have shown to lend a hand. You know, gotten into the holiday spirit?"

I nodded absently, only half listening. I opened another box and groaned. The tree—and I use that term very loosely—was in pieces, with most of the fake needles lying at the bottom of the box.

"How old is this tree?" I asked. It smelled like something had used it for bedding. A skunk maybe.

"That thing? Lordy Lou, I couldn't say. I'm pretty sure Norma Fielding purchased it sometime before that Y2K fiasco. You remember that? Everyone got all bent out of shape over nothing."

"So, it's over twenty years old?" Looking at what was left of the tree, I'd believe it.

"That and then some."

I closed the box and, like with the lights, I shoved it away. "I'll get a new tree, too."

"If you say so, dear. It's not like anyone is going to care. If they did, someone from the writers' group would be here, wouldn't you think?" She gave an overly dramatic sigh. "It's not like it used to be, I tell you. No one wants to help out anymore."

"They could be at work or decided to have breakfast first." Though, I imagined that if anyone was going to show, they would have been here by now. "What about Andi and Georgina?"

"They aren't moving around like they used to," Rita said. "You know how it is. You get older and your body starts to break down."

I wasn't nearly as old as Andi Caldwell or Georgina McCully, Rita's gossip buddies and members of the writers' group, but I was definitely feeling my age. It was that or the effects of all the bumps and bruises I'd taken over the last few years.

The sound of the front door opening caused a surge of excitement to zip through me. It quickly died when I heard the voices accompanying the clatter of footsteps on the stairs.

"It makes me sick, honestly." The woman's voice was harsh, almost lecture-like. "Everywhere you look, it's the same. I—" She jerked to a stop as she entered the room. "What is going on in here?" Her eyes fell on me to answer.

"Uh." I glanced at Rita, wilting under the woman's stare. She had to be in her sixties and put every ounce of her aged experience into her withering glare.

"We're decorating, Doris, as you can see."

"Decorating?" The woman—Doris—scowled all the harder. She was wearing a blue dress, one of those large pearl necklaces that looked gaudy on the wrong person, but elegant on others, and a large coat that was unbuttoned, revealing the black hose and blue pumps that served as her legs' only protection from the cold.

"Yes, decorating. It's for the writers' group. We meet here, if you recall."

"Oh, I remember."

I slunk over to the table we'd set up for concessions and started removing the plastic cups from their sleeves, just to have something to do. I didn't know this Doris, and from her tone, I wasn't sure I wanted to. Something about her expression reminded me of the Church Lady from the old *SNL* skit, though I was blanking on the actor's name who'd played her.

"It's a Christmas party," Rita said, though I thought the decorations made that obvious.

Doris laughed and looked back at her companions. There was no humor in it, or in her voice, when she said, "A Christmas party? See this, Agnes?" She shook her head and made a disappointed clucking sound. "This is exactly what I've been talking about. Look at this!" She gestured around the room. "What's missing here?"

A woman dressed much like Doris, but in

cherry red and carrying a handbag with a shiny silver strap, piped up. "True spirit."

"Exactly." Doris turned her glare onto Rita, and then me. "Elves and jolly men in red suits? Really? And don't get me started on the anagram for *that* man. We all know what it is, what *this* represents." She gestured all around her.

There was a murmur of agreement from the other women.

"Were you scheduled for a meeting today?" Rita asked. "I didn't see it on the calendar."

"I don't need to schedule anything on some calendar. We have a right to be here whenever we please."

"So do we," Rita shot back. "And *we* scheduled our party, right along with the time we would need to decorate, just so everyone would know."

Doris gave Rita one of those "if you say so" tight smiles. "We're here, in the *church*, for the right reason. But you can carry on with whatever you're doing. We can meet despite you, isn't that right, Cleo?"

A woman loitering near the back jerked in surprise when her name was mentioned. She gave me a wide-eyed look before nodding rather unconvincingly.

"You go right ahead," Rita said. Her voice was rising with every sentence, but I thought she was doing a good job of keeping her temper in check. "We can share the space, though tonight, we do have this room reserved for the party, so if you plan on meeting, it'll have to be elsewhere."

"We'll see about that." Doris and her gaggle

headed for the far end of the room, well away from our decorating. Cleo ducked her head as she passed, and I'm pretty sure she was mouthing apologies, though it was hard to tell since she wasn't making eye contact, let alone a sound.

"Who is that?" I asked Rita when she came over to join me at the table. And then, before she could answer, I snapped my fingers. "Dana Carvey!"

Rita gave me a funny look. "No, it's Doris Appleton. She's a member of the church. A vocal one. I swear she acts as if she runs the place."

Doris was holding court with the other women. She was talking and gesturing nearly nonstop, and every few seconds, she'd shoot a glare Rita's way.

"I take it you two don't get along?"

"Honestly? That woman only cares about one thing, and one thing only." Rita huffed and walked off without telling me what that one thing was, though I could hazard a guess.

I finished with the cups and decided to start in on the chairs that were to be placed around the room for people to sit during the party. Doris and her crew had borrowed a few, which was fine by me, but it did mean I had to walk over near them to gather the rest.

"Did you see how much he was charging for that garbage?" Doris was saying. "Marked the price right up, then called it a sale. It's exploitation. They've been doing it for years. As soon as Christmas hits, the vultures swoop in and try to make a few extra bucks. They have no concept of what the season is truly about."

"I tried to get a coffee at that coffee shop downtown and was appalled by what I saw." This from a woman I don't ever recall seeing at Death by Coffee, though I'm not always there.

"Exploitation." Doris said, turning to me. "You own that place, don't you?"

My arms were laden with metal folding chairs or else I would have crossed them defensively. "I do. With my friend."

"Can you explain to me, to Annie here, why you are exploiting the holiday season for *profit?*"

"I'm not exploiting anything."

"You're not?" Doris placed a hand near her pearls. I noted the overlarge wedding ring on her finger. It appeared as if everything about this woman was exaggerated. "So, you aren't selling Christmas books or Christmas themed drinks?"

"Well, I am, but—"

"What did I tell you?" Doris shouted over me as she turned back to her cohorts. "Exploitation." She readjusted so she could look directly at me. "You are part of the problem, young lady. You've forgotten the true spirit of the season and are instead looking to capitalize on it for your own greed. It's just like that place across the street."

I had no idea what she was talking about. "What place?" I asked.

"The toy store!" Doris clapped her hands together, causing me to jump. "Have you seen the prices in Andrew's Gifts? And look at what he's selling? Name-brand toys when local businesses are flailing. It's ridiculous. No, it's more than that; it's pure unadulterated greed. It's running rampant in this town, and you and the man that runs that place are guilty of it. Honestly, someone should shut you all down and put an end to this . . . this . . . *travesty* once and for all."

Something rather un-Christmas-like was on the tip of my tongue, but thankfully, the door opened again and the sound of boots on the stairs caught my attention. I knew that walk.

"Excuse me," I said, setting the chairs down right where I'd gotten them. They could wait.

A shadow darkened the doorway and a moment later, a fit, bald man with a trimmed beard that had gone completely to gray stepped into the room, a book in one hand, and a wide grin on his face.

"Dad!" I hurried across the room and hugged him.

"Buttercup." He squeezed. "It's so good to see you."

"You too." Even though I'd known he was going to be there, I felt as if I'd been surprised by him. I breathed deep and memories of my youth flooded in. No matter how old I got, how far away from home I lived, I would never tire of having my dad around.

A gasp came from the other side of the room. I released Dad and stepped back. I might have known he was coming to Pine Hills for a visit, but there was someone else who'd had no idea he was flying in to town.

"Oh, my Lordy Lou!" Rita practically squealed it. "James Hancock? Here?" She took two quick steps our way and then stopped, as if she wasn't sure if she should rush him or wait her turn. "I didn't know you were coming. If I did, I would have . . . I . . ." She started fanning herself.

To say Rita had a crush on my dad was an understatement. She considered herself his number one fan in a not quite, but kind of, *Misery* way. She had yet to kidnap him or lock him up in her bedroom, and I was pretty sure Rita wouldn't go that far, but with how excited she got whenever Dad was in town, it wasn't hard to imagine the thoughts going through her head.

"Hi, Rita," Dad said, crossing the distance toward her. "I brought you something." He held the book out to her.

Rita's eyes were wide as she took it. "Is this *Scars of the Heart*?"

"It is. An early copy, just for you."

Rita clutched it to her chest. "I loved *Victim of the Heart* so much. I'm sure this is going to be even better." She opened the book, hand flying to her mouth when she saw whatever message he'd scrawled inside along with his name. "I will cherish it forever."

Dad gave Rita a hug, one that likely saved her from bursting into happy tears. She'd had a tough time lately, so this little surprise I'd arranged was hitting her hard. Her boyfriend, Johan Morrison, had gotten himself caught up with some shady characters recently and was currently on the run. Rita tried to play it off like she was fine, but every so often, I caught a glimpse of the sadness hiding behind her jovial nature.

"Did you come alone?" Rita asked once she released my dad. Her eyes traveled to the doorway, but no one else was walking through it.

"Laura is here." Laura Dresden was Dad's girl-friend. "Well, not *here*, here, but at Death by Coffee."

Across the room, Doris scoffed. I ignored her.

"Oh." Rita appeared crestfallen for a heartbeat before perking back up. "Well, that's all right. You should both come to the party tonight. It's for the writers' group so I'm positive they'd love to have a real-life author in their midst." She paused. "That's not to say we don't have writers of our own. We do. Just no one of your stature." Her gaze traveled back to her book. "I can't wait to get started on reading this."

"And here, look." Dad took the book from Rita, turned a page, and then handed it back.

She stared at whatever was there, mouth agape, making strange, shocked sounds.

Curious, I moved to look over her shoulder.

To my most loyal fan; the woman who has stood by my daughter, no matter what trouble she'd gotten herself into, Rita Jablonski.

"You . . . You dedicated it to *me?*" This time, the tears did fall.

"Who else would I dedicate it to?"

I had to dab at my own eyes as Rita gushed over the dedication. The rest of Dad's visit could be a disaster, and I'd find it worth it for this one moment. Not that I wanted a bad visit, mind you. But I doubted anything could top this.

"I think I might need to take a break, dear," Rita told me with a pat on my arm. "You should spend a little time with your father. We can finish this up later."

"Sounds good," I said. "I need to get the tree

and lights anyway." Besides, most of the decorating was done. All that was left were the chairs and the tree and lights I still needed to buy and then we'd be finished.

"Laura dropped me off before taking the rental to Death by Coffee," Dad said. "We could walk, but it's awfully cold out there."

"My Escape is just outside." He couldn't have missed the bright orange vehicle, even with his eyes closed. "The store's not far from here, but we can drive anyway." I'd been exercising much more as of late, so I wasn't as out of shape as I used to be, but I still didn't want to walk anywhere in the cold. It had yet to snow, but that didn't mean it wasn't bone-chilling freezing.

"Thank you so much for this, James," Rita said. "I do hope to see you later."

"I'll be here." He winked at her, which caused her to blush, before he turned to me. "Ready to go?"

"Let me grab my coat and I will be." I hurried to the front of the room where Rita and I had dumped our things. I snatched up my coat and purse, threw them on, and then rejoined my dad by the door. "Ready."

"Then lead on, Buttercup."

I glanced back at Rita. She was seated in the recliner she used during group meetings, caressing the cover of the book. I didn't know what she was thinking, but by her expression, I was pretty sure they were good thoughts.

"Don't worry," Dad said. "Your copy is in the car."

Turning away from Rita, I caught a glimpse of Doris glaring at me, as if I'd completely ruined her day by causing the little burst of joy for Rita. You'd think that someone who was concerned with the spirit of the holiday so much would have been thrilled by it.

Oh, well. You can't please everyone.

And honestly? I didn't care one lick about what Doris what's-her-name thought.

I turned my back on her, and headed out the door with my dad, intent on enjoying the holiday however I saw fit.

2

A large cup of coffee sat atop an open book above the door to the bookstore café. The words "Death by Coffee" were spelled out in white froth within the coffee mug. Through the plate glass windows, I could see movement within the store, including a head of purple hair I hadn't seen in months.

Lena? I couldn't be sure, but I thought it might be.

"What is it?" Dad asked as I just about fell from the front seat in my haste to climb out of the car. "What's happening?"

I was too excited—and too choked up—to answer him.

A blast of warmth hit me as I all but ran through the front door of Death by Coffee. Many of the seats were occupied with customers sipping hot drinks. Upstairs, dice rattled across a coffee table where Yolanda Barton sat with a couple of her friends, playing a board game.

And standing by the counter, surrounded by employees, was indeed Lena Allison.

Lena had worked for us from the time we'd opened, right up until she'd left Pine Hills for college. Her hair was a shoulder-length vibrant purple that tapered to black at the tips. It matched her eyeshadow, and the bruise on her left arm that was likely caused by a skateboarding spill. She grinned from ear to ear when she saw me enter.

"Hi, Ms. Hancock." When I narrowed my eyes at her, she laughed. "Okay. Krissy."

"Lena! When did you get back into town?" I hurried over to her and hugged her. Already, this was turning into the best Christmas ever. "I didn't know you were coming back."

"Yeah, it was sort of last minute." She reddened and stepped back. "Surprised everyone at home when I came crashing through the doorway."

I was blinking rapidly in a desperate attempt not to cry. "I see you've met your replacement."

Eugene Dohmer's normally squinty eyes widened and he raised both his hands. "I'm not replacing anyone."

Beside him, Beth Milner laughed, and then her grin turned mischievous. "Right. He's been talking nonstop about how he's far superior to the slacker who'd come before him, and that they might as well rename the place to Eugene's Coffee because he's *so* much better."

Eugene's mouth dropped open as he looked from me to Beth. A faint red was rising up his collar. "I never . . . you're just . . . No!"

I let him off the hook. "It's really good to see

you, Lena. Is Zay here?" Zay was Lena's boyfriend. Or friend who is a boy. I don't know. She'd never actually admitted to dating him, but it was obvious they'd had a thing for one another when they lived in Pine Hills. They'd even left for college at the same time, to the same place, so it would seem strange if they *weren't* dating.

Some of the luster faded from Lena's face. "Zay and I have moved on from one another," she said, almost carefully, as if choosing her words. "He's cool and all, but we found our interests didn't align as much as we'd thought."

"I'm sorry to hear that."

She shrugged. "Nah, it's cool. It was getting harder and harder to pay for food for the both of us, so now that it's just me, I'm managing."

The "barely" was implied.

Now that she mentioned cash flow problems, I noted that her arms were a bit thinner than before, the bones in her face a smidge more prominent. She wasn't starving by any means, but I could tell she wasn't living in the lap of luxury either.

"Vicki and Mason are in California visiting her parents for the holidays," I said, wondering how that was going, even as I said it. Vicki didn't exactly get along with her mom and dad, and since Mason's own contentious father, Raymond Lawyer, and his cantankerous girlfriend, Regina Harper, had gone along with them . . . Yikes. "I'm sure they wouldn't mind if you wanted to step in and snatch a few hours. You know, for old times' sake?"

Lena bit her lower lip, which had started to quiver. "I couldn't . . . Hey, Mr. Hancock!" She sounded almost relieved as Dad and Laura approached. "It's been a long time."

"Lena. It's good to see you. Please, call me James."

"Hi, Krissy." Laura's smile was radiant and was reflected in the gleam in Dad's eye as he looked at her. I could easily have been upset when he'd started dating her, accused her of trying to replace my mom, who'd died many, many years ago.

But he was happy, so I was happy. And, honestly, Laura was good for Dad. He looked younger and fitter than I ever remember seeing him, despite the gray.

"Laura." I hugged her, carefully, so as not to spill her drink. "It's good to see you." I noted the candy cane sticking out of the cup. "How do you like the peppermint cappuccino?"

She stirred the coffee with the candy cane before taking a long drink. "It's fantastic."

"That reminds me," Beth said. "We're running low on the candy. I don't think we'll have enough for more than a day or two."

"I'll pick some up," I said, adding it to my mental list of things to do. "But it might not be until tomorrow."

"You know? I should get going," Lena said, easing away. "I really don't want to intrude."

"You're not intruding," I said. "You're family."

"Yeah, well, my *family* family will be wondering where I've run off to, so I should pop in at home for a bit. I kind of left this morning without telling anyone where I was going." She gave me a sheepish grin as she shrugged on her coat. I noted the wince as she did, telling me the bruise still hurt, and I wondered if she might have more hidden beneath her clothing.

"Think about my offer," I said. "With Vicki and Mason gone, we really are a little short-staffed." Other than Eugene and Beth, all that was left was me, Jeff Braun, and Pooky Cooper, and I was going to be busy with Dad most days.

"I'll think about it." And after a brief hesitation, she added, "Thank you. It would help a lot."

I beamed. "I told you before you left that you'd always have a place here."

More hugs went around and Lena took off. She didn't hop onto a skateboard when she reached the sidewalk, and instead climbed into a minivan that was likely her mom's. I watched her go, a frown forming.

"Something wrong?" Dad asked.

"No." Or, I didn't think so. But that bruise bothered me, especially since Zay wasn't here with her. "Just thinking." I turned to him with a clap of my hands. "So! What's the plan?"

"The plan?" He glanced at Laura, who'd finished off her drink and was crunching on the candy cane. "I was thinking Laura and I could check in to our room and get a little sleep. It was a long, early flight and I'm beat."

My heart sank. "Oh."

"Besides, weren't you helping Rita with the set up for the party tonight?" Dad stifled a yawn. "A party that I won't be awake for if I don't catch a little shut-eye beforehand."

"Yeah, I guess you're right." Though I wasn't happy about it. Dad was in town and all I wanted to do was spend time with him. It felt strange to have him here and *not* be with him.

Or have him not be staying with me.

"You know you don't have to stay at Ted and Bettfast," I said. "I have more than enough room at my place for you." And it had to be strange since someone he knew had been murdered at the bed-and-breakfast. Not that I planned on bringing that up to him, just in case he'd somehow forgotten.

"No, we wouldn't want to intrude," Dad said. "And if Paul decides to stop by some evening, we definitely wouldn't want to get in the way of whatever you two might have planned."

I sputtered, not quite sure how to respond to that.

"Speaking of Paul," Laura said, fighting a grin. "Look who's here."

The door opened and, sure enough, Officer Paul Dalton walked in. He removed his hat, smoothed down his hair, and smiled. "Mr. Hancock. Ms. Dresden." He bowed to each before turning to me. "Krissy? Are you okay? Do you need to sit down?"

"I'm fine." I shot Dad a warning look not to add to his last comment. "I'm just excited that Dad and Laura are here."

Dad and Paul did the man thing and shook hands, as if they were doing business instead of saying hi to what might as well be family. "Please, call me James," Dad said.

"James," Paul amended before he checked his watch and frowned. "I can't stay. I stopped by the church and Rita told me you were here." He sighed. "I know I said I'd come, but I can't make the party tonight. Two of our officers are out sick and, well . . ."

"I get it." Paul's mom, Patricia Dalton, was police chief, which often meant that when someone needed to fill in, Paul got the job whether he wanted it or not. "And it's all right. Dad and Laura are coming, so I'll have someone to talk to."

Laura raised her eyebrows in question. "There's a party?"

"I'll tell you about it later," Dad said, nudging her with his shoulder.

"It's probably better that you'll be there instead of me," Paul said. "I'm not a writer."

Neither was I. Well, I mean, I'd attempted to write a few times years ago, but failed so miserably I'd mostly given up trying. Whatever writer gene Dad had, it hadn't passed down to me.

A round of goodbyes followed, along with another round of hugs and cheek kisses. And then, quite suddenly, I found myself alone. Dad and Laura were headed to Ted and Bettfast to get some sleep. Paul was off to work. Even Eugene and Beth had drifted off to clean up and restock.

I left Death by Coffee, bundled tight against the cold. A look to the sky showed me a blue sky unmarred by clouds, with no hint of a coming snow. We were a week from Christmas and not even a light dusting had fallen. I was beginning to wonder if it ever would.

I turned the heater on full blast as I started my car. A moment later, and I was coasting down the street, trying to decide where to go for lights and a tree. Pine Hills was a small town that prided itself on the businesses being locally owned, not chain.

That meant there was no Walmart. No Target. No one-stop shops at all.

I preferred helping out local shop owners, especially since I was one myself, but there are times when having a place where you could go to grab everything you needed without having to make a half dozen stops was convenient.

Pine Hills was decked out for the holidays. Wreaths hung from lampposts. Removable stickers of snowflakes and reindeer were plastered to windows. If there'd been snow, it would have been postcard-esque.

A sign caught my eye, causing me to slow to a crawl: ANDREW'S GIFTS. I frowned. Almost all the businesses in Pine Hills were named with puns and rhymes in mind. Andrew's Gifts didn't follow that pattern, nor did it have the same joyous decorations on the windows or door like everyone else had. It was so bland, my eyes wanted to pass right over it, which was probably why I'd never noticed it before now.

It was the toy store the woman, Doris, had mentioned, the one right across the street from the church where Rita was waiting for me. Curious, I pulled up to the curb, but I couldn't see much through the window. A few boxed toys. Something that might have been a box of Legos or maybe a board game. Or a brick. It was hard to tell. Leaning in the window was a cardboard CHRISTMAS SALE sign that looked anything but festive.

Maybe he'll have a tree? I shut off the engine. There was only one way to find out.

No bells or sounds came from the door when I

entered Andrew's Gifts, which felt odd considering every other shop in town seemed to have some
sort of warning system that a customer was entering. I was immediately assaulted by large SALE!
signs on nearly every shelf, though the old prices
or how much saved wasn't on display.

I'm not much of a shopper, so I didn't bother
browsing. I scanned the shelves in the hopes of
spotting Christmas decorations, but as far as I
could tell, Andrew's Gifts was stocked full of name-
brand toys, game consoles, and figurines. The only
hint of the season was the single, sad wreath hanging from the front counter.

"Hey! You! Get out of here."

I jerked to a stop, thinking the man was talking
to me, but when I turned, I discovered I wasn't the
intended target.

The speaker was wearing a sweater vest over a
blue button up shirt and khaki pants. Something
about the ensemble gave me the impression that
he worked in Andrew's Gifts, if he wasn't the man,
Andrew, himself. He was making straight for the
entrance, where a guy with long hair, all black
clothes, including combat boots, a skull earring,
and wallet chain, was holding a box with the word
"POP!" on it in large yellow letters.

"I'm just looking around," the long-haired guy
said.

"No, you're not." This from Sweater Vest. "You're
going to steal it."

I expected a retort from the guy in black, but he
just smirked. "You think so?"

"I know so." Sweater Vest snatched the POP! figure from the other man's hand. "I've had enough of your type. If I see you in here again, I'm going to call the police."

"My type?" Black Shirt scowled. "What's that supposed to mean?"

"Thieves. Thugs."

"You don't know me, man. I haven't stolen anything." He reached for another POP! figure.

Sweater Vest snatched it out of his hand, like he had the other. "Get out!" He jabbed a trembling finger toward the door before shoving it into Black Shirt's chest. "I won't hesitate to—" He glanced over his shoulder to where I was standing and cut himself off.

Black Shirt shoved Sweater Vest's hand away. "You'll what?" he said. "Follow me around the store? You can keep your overpriced crap." And with that, he spun and stormed back out the door, smacking the glass so hard with his palms, I was afraid it might shatter.

Sweater Vest watched him go, shoulders heaving. Once he was certain Black Shirt wasn't coming back, he replaced the figures on their shelf, and then headed back behind the counter without so much as a glance—or an apology—to me.

I decided that I'd seen enough—the store didn't have what I was looking for anyway—so I left. When I got outside, Black Shirt was long gone. I climbed back into my car, paid Andrew's Gifts one last look, and then resumed my search for a tree and lights for tonight's party.

3

Misfit wound around my legs, purring like he thought I was about to drop a bag of treats in front of him. The orange cat had turned into Mr. Loveable the moment Dad and Laura had arrived at my house. He had yet to turn off the rumble machine.

"We'll be back soon," I told him as I pulled on a shirt with the words "coffee" and "books" surrounded by a big pink heart on the front. "Then you can love all over Dad as much as you want. He enjoys the attention."

After finding a cheap, fake Christmas tree and some string lights, I'd finished helping Rita set up for the party, and then spent the rest of the day with Dad and Laura—after their naps, of course. We'd consumed well beyond our fair share of coffee and cookies and other not-so-healthy snacks that had Laura warning my dad that they were going to need to spend at least a week doing nothing but running to work it off.

All in all, it was about as pleasant a day as I'd spent in a long time, not counting those spent with Paul. Those . . . well, I wasn't going to talk about *those* days, with Dad or anyone else.

I headed back out to the living room. Misfit trailed behind, doing his best to get underfoot and trip me. "I'm rea—" I jerked to a stop at what awaited me in my living room.

Dad had his arms around Laura in an embrace that would make just about anyone blush. At the sound of my voice, he leapt back from her like she'd suddenly grown spikes. "Buttercup, er, Krissy." He coughed and grinned. "Sorry about that."

"It's fine." And I found I meant it, despite my embarrassment. "But maybe next time, hang a sign up or something to warn me, okay?"

I almost cheered when Dad's face flamed much like mine did when he'd made that joke about Paul stopping by. It wasn't often I could embarrass him.

"Yes, well." He cleared his throat. "I'll consider it."

"We're ready," Laura said, hiding a smile before breaking out in a face-eating yawn. "I don't know why I can't stop yawning."

A flash of worry passed over Dad. "Are you sure you're up for this?" he asked.

Laura nodded. "I'm fine. Just a bit tired." She sniffed and fished out a tissue. "And a smidge stuffy, I suppose."

"If you don't want to go—" I started, but she cut me off.

"No, I'll be okay." She stuffed the tissue back into her pocket. "Let's go."

Dad and Laura were driving themselves at Dad's request. I wasn't sure if it was because they were afraid of my driving, or if they wanted to spend time alone. Probably some combination of both.

I was about to climb into my Escape when someone called out to me.

"Krissy! Do you have a moment?"

I waved for Dad and Laura to go ahead, and then crossed the yard toward my neighbor and friend, Jules Phan, who was making his way toward me. We stopped where our yards met.

"Sorry to bother you on your way out," he said. His white Maltese, Maestro, was tucked under his arm, squirming to be let down, but Jules kept a firm hold on him. "I just wanted to let you know I have a fresh shipment of candy canes at the store for you. You can pick them up tomorrow or I can deliver them to you; whichever serves you best."

"Perfect timing," I said, holding my hand out for Maestro to sniff—and lick. "We were getting low. I'll pick them up tomorrow morning, if that's okay?" The candy canes we used for the peppermint cappuccinos at Death by Coffee came from Jules's candy store, Phantastic Candies. It was a good way to help another local business.

"Tomorrow is perfect. I'll be there all day." Jules shivered, despite his large, thick coat. "It's frigid out here." The tip of his nose and his cheeks were both bright red. "Maestro didn't even want to come out to do his business, it's so cold. I sometimes wish he was a cat so he could use a litter box."

Maestro barked and shook his head, little legs pumping as if he could already feel the grass beneath his feet and was intent on running as far and as fast as he could.

"I didn't mean it like that," Jules said, kissing the dog atop the head. "I'll let you go before we both freeze our butts off. Besides, I've got to get this rascal back inside before he manages to slip free."

"You be good." I rubbed Maestro behind the ears. "Tell Lance I said hi." The latter was for Jules, though I suppose Maestro could have passed the message on in his own way.

"Will do. He's inside mixing us something to warm us up." Lance Darby was Jules's significant other, and was a master of mixing all sorts of drinks, alcoholic and non-alcoholic alike. My mouth watered, but I didn't have time to pop in for a taste.

"Enjoy that," I said. I was only mildly jealous.

"Oh, I will." Jules winked, clearly meaning more than him only enjoying his drink.

And then, with a mutual, good-natured laugh, we parted.

A handful of cars were already in the church parking lot when I got there, including Dad's rental. I pulled up beside him and got out, thinking he and Laura had already gone inside. One look at the car, however, told me otherwise.

A hand swiped across the steamed-up window and a second later, the car door popped open.

"Hey, Buttercup we were just wa—"

I held up a hand. "I don't want to know."

"But—"

"Nope. Not listening." I started for the church doors, and then, because I didn't want to seem rude, waited there for Dad and Laura to make their way over to me.

Laura flashed me a smile and a wink on her way past, while Dad just scurried past me, into the church. Once they were inside, I paused to look toward Andrew's Gifts. Like much of the town, the store closed shop relatively early, so the lights were off, and the place empty.

I turned away and went inside.

"James!" Rita caught sight of us the moment we were up the worn stairs, which were printed with bible verses, and through the door. "I'm so glad you made it." She hurried over, leaving her friends, Georgina McCully and Andi Caldwell, sitting alone together. She came up short when she spotted Laura. "Oh. Well, you too, of course." She turned to me. "Krissy! Did you know Lena Allison is back in town? And she's *here!*"

Lena, sensing our attention, waved from across the room. She was talking to one of the other writers' group members, a man I hadn't seen in quite a while, Adam. He looked dead on his feet, as if he'd spent a long couple of days working without a break. I knew nothing about him, other than he was a member of the group, not even his last name.

"Yeah, I saw her at Death by Coffee earlier. Actually, I think I'm going to go over to talk to her now.

Will you three be okay if I leave you alone together for a few minutes?"

"Go on," Dad said. "We'll be fine."

"I've already started *Scars of the Heart,*" Rita said, dismissing me without a word. "I must say, I already think it's the best you've ever done."

I left them to discuss the book and headed over to where Lena and Adam were chatting. Adam was middle-aged, and seemed disinterested in what Lena had to say, but then again, he always looked that way. When I reached them, he muttered something completely unintelligible and wandered off to the drink table.

"I didn't mean to scare him off," I said, watching as he poured himself a drink. He sipped it slowly, head bobbing to the light music playing from a speaker Rita had set up.

"It's not you. When I first came over to talk to him, he looked panicked, like he was afraid I might bite." She grinned. "Little does he know . . ."

At the door, two more people entered. Haley and Wendy were newer, college-aged members of the group. I'd only met them a few times, and briefly at that. They saw Adam and made a beeline for him. For the first time since I'd known him, he perked up.

"Looks like someone has a crush," Lena said, watching them.

"Yeah, but on which one?"

"Probably both. You know how men can be."

I glanced over at Dad, who was trapped between two women himself. Rita was talking his ear off, while Laura stood stoically by his side. Every so

often, she'd reach out and touch him on the arm.
I don't know if she was giving him strength, or if
some inner jealousy was seeping out and she was
looking to remind Rita that James Hancock belonged to her.

Whatever her reason, it was endearing. To me,
at least. Rita didn't seem to notice.

"Do you think Chief Dalton will show?" Lena
asked. There was an odd tone to her voice that
made me wonder if the question had something to
do with her injuries, rather than mere curiosity.

"I doubt it," I said, deciding not to pry. "Paul
was going to come with me tonight but got called
in to work because a couple of officers are sick.
She's probably pulling a double or triple shift
right along with him."

"That sounds like her. I think she lives in her
uniform."

I started to laugh, taking it for a joke, but then
paused. Had I ever seen Chief Dalton out of uniform? Now that I thought about it, I wasn't sure I
had.

Lena rubbed at her arm, wincing slightly as
she did. "I miss everyone. College is great and all,
but . . ."

I opened my mouth to ask her about her bruise
when a group of women entered. Doris Appleton
was leading them.

"Uh-oh," I muttered, watching as she looked
around the room, nose held high in the air. She
glared hard at Rita and sniffed in derision.

"Who's that?" Lena asked.

"Someone who's not a fan of the writers' group."

Rita caught sight of Doris and stiffened. She said something to Dad and then marched over to where Doris and her group still stood.

"I think I might need to go over there," I said, not sure what good it would do. But standing back and watching would help no one, Rita especially.

"I'll pass," Lena said. "She doesn't look like a nice lady."

"She's not." I crossed the room, but stopped a few feet back, not entirely sure I really wanted to get involved.

"You're ruining the sanctity of the church." Doris raised her voice so she could be heard by those nearby, though she tried to make it appear as if she was talking solely to Rita. "Events such as these should not be allowed."

"We're not hurting anything," Rita said. "In fact, our group has brought more people into this church than yours ever has."

Doris scoffed, looked back at her crew, who all grumbled in unison. "Right." She glanced around the room, eyes lingering on Lena. "Just because you invite the riffraff, doesn't mean they deserve to set foot in a holy place such as this."

Okay. That was enough for me. I marched over to join them. "These are good people," I said. "We're just here to relax and have some fun, not cause any trouble."

"This isn't a place for *fun*." Doris sneered the word. "This is a house of worship and what you're doing here is against everything we stand for."

I opened my mouth to retort, but Rita cut me off with a stern look.

"Doris Appleton, you have no idea what you are saying," she said. "I know you and I don't get along, but that doesn't mean you have to put down my friends."

"Your friends do not belong here." Doris glared hard across the room at Georgina and Andi, who'd remained seated since I'd gotten there, hurting no one and doing nothing to earn the reprimand. "I will find a way to get this little group of yours removed. Your presence is insulting to the rest of us, isn't that right, Agnes?"

There was a beat of silence. The woman with the tiny handbag—Agnes, I supposed—didn't appear to be in attendance.

"You go ahead and try." Rita was practically trembling with rage, something I'd never seen out of her in my life. "We have every right to use this space, the same right as you do."

"And perhaps I wish to use it now." Doris pushed past both Rita and me and wandered into the room a few feet before stopping. "Then again, it needs to be cleaned first." She turned right back around and headed for the door. "I think it's time I worked with the town's leadership to bring real faith back to Pine Hills. We need to get rid of groups like these, get rid of businesses that exploit *my* faith for their own profits." She shot me a dirty look, before turning away. "Let's go."

Doris and her crew stormed out with a chorus of "Amens" and "Heathens" though I noted Cleo remained silent, despite her following Doris around like a lost puppy.

Rita's hands were bunched into fists and her entire body was stiff as a board. I could almost *hear* her teeth groaning under the pressure she was putting on them.

"Don't worry about her," I said. "She's all talk. She can't do anything."

Rita took a deep breath, let it out in a huff. "I'm not worried, dear. I'm just . . . angry." She looked around the room, at her writers' group. They were all still watching, Dad and Laura included. "She's ruined the night."

"No, she hasn't." I kept my hand out of her line of sight as I made a "get on with it" gesture to the rest of the room. Everyone hopped back to mingling, though they kept shooting glances our way.

"I honestly don't know what I did to upset that woman," Rita said. "She's had it in for me from day one and hasn't let up since. I mean, I understand she is a woman of faith, but doesn't she realize she's supposed to love and care about everyone? Not just her little group of followers?"

"Some people are like that." And I'd met my fair share of them. "Come on, let's get back to the party. Forget about her."

"I can't." Rita wrung her hands together before patting my arm. "You go ahead and have fun. I think I'm going to go ahead and call it a night."

"But the party's just started."

"I know, dear. I've lost the heart for it." And with that, Rita gathered her things and left.

"What was that all about?" Dad asked once she was gone.

"I guess there's some town drama I'm not privy to." But two other people in the room might be. "Be right back."

"Actually, Buttercup, I think we're going to head out." He motioned to Laura, who'd joined us. "I'm beat and still haven't recovered from the trip."

"Me too," Laura added. "It was nice to get out, but I think it best if we do most of our partying tomorrow."

"Are you sure?" I felt bad, like I'd abandoned Dad and Laura while I'd dealt with Rita and Doris. "This will only take a sec and then we can spend the rest of the evening together."

"I'm sure." Dad shot a quick glance at Laura, who looked exhausted. "I'd rather you have fun with your friends without worrying about us."

Laura managed a smile that vanished into another yawn before she asked, "Breakfast tomorrow?"

"Sounds great. I'm meeting a friend in the morning, but should have time for breakfast first."

"We can meet at Death by Coffee and you can tell us all about what we missed." Dad leaned forward and pecked me on the cheek. "I'll see you tomorrow, Buttercup."

"See you then."

They turned away and headed for the door.

I watched them, frustrated, yet there wasn't anything I could do about the night. The day had started out great, but had devolved as it stretched on. And now, with Laura, Dad, and Rita gone, the party was looking like it might fall apart before it even began.

I spent the next few minutes making sure Rita hadn't left anything behind in her haste to leave. I imagined the decorations would be fine if left overnight, but I wasn't so sure about her speaker. I made a mental note to grab it on my way out, just in case, and then decided to make the rounds.

I took a moment to speak to a few other members of the group before I walked over to where Andi and Georgina sat, chatting animatedly with one another. The two older women were notorious gossips, and would be a good source of information when it came to whatever problem Doris had with Rita. They saw me coming and both straightened in their chairs.

"Andi," I said, coming to a stop in front of them. "Georgina."

"Hello, Krissy. It's been a goodly long while since you've been to group," Georgina said, patting at her white cloud of hair. "A good long while."

"I was starting to wonder if we'd ever see you again," Andi added, squinting at me like she was having a hard time seeing me.

"Sorry about that. I was curious—"

I never got to finish the thought or ask my question.

"Something's going on outside!" Haley, who must have stepped out at some point because she was wearing her coat and was standing at the door, pointed back the way she'd just come from. "The police are here."

My heart sank straight through the floor before ratcheting up in speed.

Rita.

Now, I didn't truly believe Rita would have gone and hurt anyone, but she'd been so *angry.* Could she have gone outside and confronted Doris?

Would the women have gotten into it enough that the police had to be called?

Or could it be Laura? She'd looked awfully tired when she'd left. What if she was sick, not just tired, and had collapsed the moment she'd stepped outside?

Or worse, what if it was Dad? He wasn't as young as he used to be.

I was moving before I realized I was going to. It started as a quick walk, but by the time I hit the stairs, I was running. I kept thinking that I was going to step out into the freezing cold of winter and would find someone I cared about lying motionless on the sidewalk.

When I burst outside the church, the first thing I noticed were the red-and-blue flashing lights. The night was so bright and crisp, the lights seemed to reflect off the very air, making it blinding. It took me a moment to realize that no one was on the sidewalk on this side of the street. All the excitement was happening on the other side, at Andrew's Gifts.

More people spilled out of the church doors behind me, but I barely noticed. My eyes shot to the parking lot, to the empty space where Dad's car had been. Rita's car was gone as well. Nothing had happened to either of them.

But not everyone was so lucky.

Across the street, a stretcher was being carried out of Andrew's Gifts. On it, was a sheet-covered body. And following behind, a grim-faced Detective John Buchannan was barking orders at anyone who'd listen to him.

He jerked to a sudden stop, as if he sensed someone watching. His gaze zeroed in on me standing across the street for a heartbeat before he spun around and marched right back into the gift shop.

That look might have only been brief, but there was no questioning its meaning.

Whatever had happened across the street wasn't a mere accident. If my guess was right, it appeared as if someone had been murdered.

4

I stirred my peppermint cappuccino with a rapidly dissolving candy cane. I watched the swirls, a faint frown on my face. Around me, Death by Coffee was hopping, yet Dad and Laura had yet to arrive for our planned breakfast. I was trying hard not to be worried, but after what I'd seen last night, it was difficult not to be. About Laura and Dad. About Rita.

About the body.

So far, all I really had was speculation. Someone had died. I assumed it was the shop owner, Andrew, but it could have been an employee. It could have been a thief. Or someone the cops were chasing, someone who'd tried to hide within the store and . . . what? Had a heart attack?

While Buchannan's expression might have made me think "murder," it could very well have been a natural death and he'd only looked at me like that because the detective was thinking of murdering *me*.

"Krissy?"

I looked up to find a large redhead with a wide, gracious smile, half-leaning over me. Behind her, looking all the world as if she wanted to be anywhere but there, was a wiry teen.

"Yolanda? Avery? It's good to see you both."

I'd met both Yolanda Barton and Avery Mills at a party for women seeking help for their troubles. Some just needed support, like my friends, Shannon and Trisha, who'd been very pregnant at the time. Others were dealing with more personal issues. Abuse, addiction, loneliness, and so on.

"You too," Yolanda said. "I thought it was you when we came in, but I wasn't sure."

"It's me." I managed a smile that quickly morphed into a yawn. "Sorry. I didn't get much sleep last night."

"Is it because of the . . ." She glanced around the dining area and then lowered her voice as she finished with, "*murder?*"

I nodded, wondering if she knew something concrete, or if she, like me, was merely guessing. "I saw the police outside the scene last night."

Yolanda slid into the chair across from me. Avery hesitated, and then sat next to her. I noted that there were no visible bruises on her and hoped that meant that whoever had given her the last one was out of her life. It also made me think of Lena and *her* bruise. I almost turned in my seat to check behind the counter, where Lena was working with Jeff.

"I *know!*" Yolanda said. "I didn't see them or anything, but I heard all about it from a friend who was driving by. Said they saw the body even. I was told that they had to carry him out bit by bit." She shuddered.

"It wasn't that bad." Not that I'd actually *seen* anything. "I saw the stretcher." I paused. "Did your friend say who it was?"

"Yeah!" Her eyes got big. "It was the guy who owned the place, Andrew Carver. I talked to him like two days ago."

"You knew him?"

Yolanda nodded solemnly, then shrugged. "I suppose not all that well. I went in to check out his board games, but they were priced way too high. I asked him about it, casually mentioning that I'd just bought one of the games somewhere else a few weeks back for half the cost. Let me tell you, the guy got angry with me for bringing it up. He told me that if I didn't like his prices, I could shop elsewhere."

"So, she did." Avery almost smiled when she said it.

"I could order the same games and have them shipped to my house for less than he was asking. It was crazy." Yolanda's eyes widened again. "Do you think that's why he was killed?"

"Someone didn't like his prices?"

"Yeah? I mean, it was pretty bad. And it's Christmas and everything. People are already short on cash and when they go out to buy stuff, to find everything marked up so high? It sucks."

It did. It made me wish I'd paid more attention to the prices when I was in the store, just so I could have seen it for myself.

Then again, I'd been distracted by an argument. An argument that very well could have been a prequel to murder.

I was about to ask Yolanda if she knew anything about a long-haired, black-clad guy causing trouble when the door jangled and Dad walked in. Alone.

"Hey, Buttercup," he said, using my nickname without considering how embarrassing it was to have him call me that in public. I suppose I was mostly used to it by now, but when someone smirks, just like Avery did then, it's hard not to want to crawl beneath the table and hide.

"Oh! You're expecting someone." Yolanda popped up from her chair and offered it to Dad. "We'll get out of your hair."

Dad held up his hands. "I don't want to interrupt anything."

"You're not," Yolanda assured him, urging Avery to her feet. "We've got to run anyway. Right, Avery?"

Avery shrugged, refused to meet anyone's eyes, and then slunk off toward the counter. Yolanda gave us a thousand-watt grin and then followed her.

Dad watched them go before he sat down, eyebrows raised in question.

"They're friends," I said. "New ones." And then, because I was curious. And worried. "Where's Laura?"

Dad rubbed at his face. He looked tired. "Still at Ted and Bettfast. She wasn't feeling too great this morning and didn't want to drag us down."

"Oh no, is she sick?"

He paused, shook his head. "I wouldn't say *sick*, but I think she's run herself a bit too hard lately and just needs a day where she doesn't do anything. I know we planned on breakfast but . . ."

"No, if she's not feeling good, she should rest. And if you want to spend the day with her, I'm not going to be mad. We have all week."

Dad dropped his hands heavily onto the tabletop. "I feel like I'm abandoning you."

"You're not. Besides, like I told you last night, I have morning exercise plans with Cassie." Plans I was beginning to dread. It was far too cold to go running, but that was what she wanted to do.

"I know, but still . . ." He sighed. "Maybe we can meet up later? I'll monitor Laura and see how she's feeling and then decide if she should come with me. Right now, she just feels tired and has a headache and the sniffles, so it's not like she's hacking up a lung or anything."

"Later would be great. I'm going for my run in . . ." I glanced at my watch, "forty minutes. After that, I'll be free."

Silence fell. Dad sat across from me, visibly torn.

"Go," I said, shooing him with my hands. "Be with Laura. I'll check in with you later."

He made a pained face.

"Go!" I stood and helped him to his feet. "I'll be fine."

The door opened as a new guest entered, making Dad's exit a thousand times more difficult.

"Oh, my Lordy Lou!" Rita made a beeline straight for us. "Can you believe what happened? And to happen right across the street from us! I can't believe I missed it!" She paused. "Well, I don't mean that I wanted to see a man murdered, but I wish I would have been there. Maybe I would have seen something that would help the police figure out who did it."

Dad looked to me. "Someone was murdered?"

"Yes!" Rita cut in before I could speak. "In that shop across the street from the church. From what I heard, there's no question that someone killed him. Surprised him in his very own place of business!"

I tugged gently on Dad's arm, hoping to get him moving, but he didn't budge.

"And you knew about this?" Dad sounded hurt.

"Kind of, not really?" It came out like a question. "I mean, I knew someone had died, but I don't know the details." I glared at Rita, hoping she'd get the hint to drop it until Dad left. "I'm sure the police have it covered."

Rita snorted. "Like they always do." She rolled her eyes. "But now with the both of you in town, I can't imagine this *not* getting solved. Maybe you could find inspiration for your next book, James!"

That made Dad smile. "Maybe."

"Laura," I reminded him. "Tired and feeling grungy. She's in need of comfort. We can talk later." Though I hoped the police had the murder—if that was really what it was—solved by then and we could resume a normal Christmas holiday together without talk of death.

Who was I kidding? At this point, *not* having someone get murdered would be *ab*normal.

Dad looked like he was considering sitting right back down, but thought better of it. "You're right," he said. "I should check in with her. Maybe hearing about a little town drama will perk her up."

I didn't see how, but I was happy to go along with it if it meant he was going to go. "Can't hurt to try." I escorted him to the door. "I'll call you later, okay?"

"You do that, Buttercup. And if you hear anything . . ."

"I'll be sure to let you know."

Dad left and I turned to find Rita standing behind me, hand on one hip, foot tapping on the floor.

"Now, why'd you go and do that?"

"Do what?" I asked.

"Send him away like that? You know your father loves mysteries and what do we have here? A mysterious murder right here in Pine Hills."

"Yes, but I also want my dad to be safe." He wasn't as young as he used to be, and a murderer is a murderer. I'd met quite a few of them in my time, and they didn't much care for people poking around in their lives.

"Well, I suppose that's understandable." Rita didn't sound as if she understood, so I decided to change the subject, albeit subtly.

"You didn't happen to see anything last night, did you?" I asked her. "When you left the party, I mean?"

Rita started to answer, stopped. "Now that you mention it, I *do* think I saw something odd. When I left, I admittedly wasn't entirely in my right mind, what with Doris and all. She gets right under my skin and, well, I was thinking of all the things I wanted to say to her and wasn't paying attention to what was right in front of me."

I nodded, silently urging her to go on.

"When I left, I do recall thinking it strange that a light was on in Andrew's Gifts. When I'd arrived at the church earlier that night, I remember the light being off because I'd considered stopping in to see if he had wrapping paper because I'm out and thought it would be a nice touch to have a few wrapped presents under the tree. You know, get into the spirit of things, even if the boxes were empty?"

I thought back. I was pretty sure that when I'd arrived at the church, the light had been off then too. Did that mean Andrew had left and then, for some reason, returned to the shop well into the night?

"Do you think an alarm went off?" I asked. "Someone broke into the store and he went to check it out?"

"I don't rightly know," Rita said. "Though I wouldn't be surprised if they had. From what I've heard, the prices there were outrageous."

Just as Yolanda had said.

Still, this was all speculation. We knew Andrew Carver was murdered, likely in his own store, but it was possible someone had dumped his body there. If the light was on when Rita had left the church, all that really told us was that *someone* was there then, be it Andrew himself, or his killer, or both. Then again, it could have been whoever had discovered the body, meaning Andrew could have been there since he'd closed; dead *or* alive.

Could the black clad guy have come back to

continue his argument with Andrew after I'd left and it escalated to murder?

It was something to consider.

"Did you see anyone in Andrew's Gifts when you left?" I asked. "Or lurking around outside it, maybe?"

Rita shook her head. "Like I said, I wasn't really paying that much attention. I noticed the light, thought it strange, and then went on my way."

I started to press her, just in case she *had* seen something, but wasn't able to remember it offhand because she had been distracted, but stopped myself.

What was I doing? Dad was in town with Laura. The plan was to spend the week together, and then have a great Christmas, sharing gifts and laughs, before they headed back home to California where it might be months before I saw them in person again. I couldn't let myself get dragged into yet another murder investigation.

Yes, Dad would love to be involved. Murder was in his blood, at least the literary kind. And yes, he and I could poke around like a father/daughter team, as we had done before. It would be a bonding experience.

It would also be dangerous.

"I should get going," I said. "I need to pick up some candy canes for our cappuccinos before I go on my run with Cassie."

Rita looked me up and down, but kept whatever thought zipped through her head to herself. "You do that, dear." She frowned, clearly not happy that I wasn't as interested in the murder as she was, before she turned. "Lena Allison! It's so nice to have you back. You won't believe everything that's happened since you've been gone!"

Lena looked panicked as Rita headed for the counter, talking a mile a minute. I mouthed a "Sorry" to her before polishing off my peppermint cappuccino. I tossed the cup into the trash, bundled myself up nice and tight, and then headed for the door, pushing murder out of my mind as I went.

5

Phantastic Candies was both a place I loved and the bane of my existence. Just walking through the door nearly induced a chocolate and sugar overload. Instead of a bell, the sound of a large piece of candy being unwrapped met me as I stepped inside. And the smell . . .

All I can say is, "Mmmm."

"Hi, Jules, I—" I jerked to a stop when I saw what had become of my favorite candy store.

Most of the shelves looked as if rabid wolverines had gotten to them. Chocolates were tossed into bubblegum bins. Price tags were scattered, half-torn on the floor. The chutes that ran along the walls were intact, but empty of the candy that normally shot through them into the waiting, grimy hands of the kids who'd purchased them.

"Hi, Krissy," Jules said, wiping sweat from his brow. An open box sat beside him, filled with wrapped chocolate bars. "You here for the candy canes?"

I nodded mutely, still trying to come to terms with what I was seeing.

Jules cracked his back and grimaced. "You've come at a good time. I've been positively slammed today. It was a lot worse than yesterday, and I'd barely made it through that."

No one was in the store now, but that could be because the shelves were almost empty. "That's a good thing, right?" I eyed the bin of chocolate-covered caramels. Only a single wrapper lay inside.

"Good for profits. Not so good on my joints." Jules stretched his neck from side to side with a wince. "Lance has a lot on his plate today or he'd be here to help. I'm hoping to coax him into it after I've cleaned up a bit."

It looked as though he couldn't get there soon enough. "If you want me to come back later . . . ?"

"No, I could use the break. Give me one second." Jules headed for the back room, leaving me alone in the remains of the candy store.

I wandered from bin to bin, hoping to spot something to sate my sweet tooth, but decided that candy could wait. Some of the more delicate candies were crushed, likely by the greedy hands of the kids who'd looted the place. It was almost enough to bring me to tears. Is there anything sadder than an empty candy store?

I wound my way over to the counter to wait for Jules. A gift box wrapped in blue paper sat atop it. There was no tag, no indicator as to whom it was from.

"That appeared on my doorstep this morning," Jules said, returning with two stacked boxes of candy canes. Each box held another dozen smaller boxes, each packed with the candies themselves. "I thought you or Caitlin might have left it."

"I didn't," I said. "And if Caitlin did, she didn't leave one for me." Then again, I hadn't exactly looked for a present sitting outside my front door when I'd left that morning. I could have walked right by it and not noticed. "What's in it?"

"No clue." Jules set the candy boxes onto the counter with a grunt. "I brought it to work with me so I could open it up and have a look-see, but I've been so busy, I haven't gotten the chance."

As if on cue, the door opened and a gaggle of kids ranging from four to fifteen came pouring into the store. They were trailed by a pair of harried-looking adults. The kids immediately started ransacking what little was left of the place.

I picked up the candy cane boxes. "Have fun," I told Jules over the sound of a seven-year-old wailing that his favorite candy wasn't in stock.

"Send help," Jules mouthed, before bursting into a wide grin. "Children! If you find a shelf empty, fear not! I have the candies hidden away in their secret compartments in my lab. If you tell me what you're looking for, I will do everything in my power to conjure your heart's desire."

That was met was a cheer from the younger kids, and a sniffle from the seven-year-old. I slipped out before anyone noticed me.

On the way back to Death by Coffee, I found myself slowing outside of Andrew's Gifts. The store had police tape strung across the door, but I could see movement inside. There were no police cars parked at the curb, no sign that anyone was supposed to be there. With the tape across the door, it was obvious they weren't open, so who could possibly be inside?

A burglar? In the morning? Or the killer returned to clean up evidence?

No, Krissy. Whatever is happening, it's none of your business.

I gritted my teeth and drove on.

Curiosity gnawed at me as I unloaded the candy canes and carried them into Death by Coffee. I had no reason to believe that whatever was happening at Andrew's Gifts was illegal, yet I couldn't imagine the police letting anyone inside to mess up their scene. It was possible they'd finished everything up last night and what I'd seen was a very confused and soon-to-be-unemployed employee wandering the store, but I doubted it.

I set the boxes down on the counter where Jeff was waiting.

"Did I miss much while I was gone?" I asked him.

"Not really, Ms. Hancock. It's slowed enough that we've mostly caught up."

All the unoccupied tables were clean and the pastries stocked. Lena was upstairs, shelving books with Pooky Cooper, who was talking her ear off. No matter how hard you tried to keep everything organized, someone always ended up putting books in the wrong place, which meant reshelving was a near constant job. Sometimes it was accidental. Other times, not so much.

I watched Lena a long moment. She had a faraway look in her eye, but seemed to be listening to Pooky. Every so often, she would reach up and rub at her arm where she'd been bruised. Questions about Zay and their breakup surfaced, but I swallowed them back. Like with the mysterious person at Andrew's Gifts, I was determined not to pry.

Okay, maybe not pry *directly*. "How's she doing?" I asked, nodding in Lena's direction.

Jeff was silent a moment before he answered. "She seems kind of sad. I think she misses it here. Pine Hills, I mean. And I guess, Death by Coffee too. I'm not sure she wants to go back."

"Back to college?"

Jeff shrugged, scuffed his foot on the floor. He wouldn't meet my eye, but that wasn't abnormal for him. I couldn't even get him to call me by my first name, though I'd told him to do so at least a hundred times already.

"I guess." He glanced up toward Lena, and then looked away. "I get the feeling that she wants something, but doesn't know how to go about getting it."

I knew the feeling. I just hoped that whatever was bothering her, it was something fixable. "Call me if you think she needs to talk to someone," I said. "Or if her mood gets worse."

Jeff nodded, and then carried the candy canes to the back without another word. Upstairs, while Pooky was retrieving more books to shelve, Lena turned, saw me looking, and waved. She put on a smile that never quite reached her eyes.

I wondered if it was homesickness like Jeff thought, if it was trouble with Zay, or if it had more to do with the season. A lot of people found themselves fighting off depression during the holidays. The darker, colder weather got to some. The loneliness and lack of family and friends to celebrate with for others. I didn't *think* Lena was lonely, but then again, I'd only seen her a couple times since she'd been back. There was a whole life she'd been living that I didn't know about and it made me sad to think that that life hadn't been happy.

The door opened and my friend Cassie Wise entered, dressed for running. She was Black, extremely pretty, and was short enough it made *me* feel tall.

Phantom throbbing started in my legs almost immediately. They knew what was coming and were none too happy about it.

"Cass!" I said, giving her a hug. Since everyone else had been getting one lately, I figured, why not?

"Krissy." She flashed me a warm smile. "Are you ready for this?"

I stretched a few times, though I had no idea what I was doing. "I think so. It's cold out there."

"Tell me about it. I hope you brought some tissues."

I was confused at first, thinking she meant the workout might make me cry, but then I got it. Runny noses and cold weather went hand in hand.

A few moments later, we were out the door and moving at a slow jog. In warmer months, we had to dodge past pedestrians and leashed pets, around signs and the occasional skateboarder. In the winter, we pretty much had the sidewalks to ourselves.

I'd only recently started exercising with Cassie, but I'd already started to see a difference in my endurance. Sure, I still couldn't handle a full run without passing out, and my legs absolutely hated me every time I jogged with her, but I *was* getting better. We had plans to join a new gym that was supposed to come to Pine Hills a month ago, but it had yet to open. I wasn't sure why.

We went left from Death by Coffee, jogged a good distance that way, and then crossed the street near Scream for Ice Cream, which was open, despite the season. We then headed back the way we'd come, past Lawyer's Insurance where Mason's dad, Raymond, worked, and which sat across from Death by Coffee, before we moved on toward the church, where I slowed, but not from exhaustion.

Someone was still in Andrew's Gifts across the street.

I wanted to know why.

"Do you need to take a break?" Cassie asked. She sounded barely winded.

I considered pausing there, but knew if I stopped now, I wouldn't start running again. "No," I managed between gasps for air. "Let's keep going."

Cassie gave me a worried look, but didn't object. I picked up the pace and did my best to focus on the run, but I kept thinking about that movement I'd seen, about the body being carried out of the building the night before. A man was murdered, and the killer could very well be destroying evidence at that very moment.

When we reached Phantastic Candies, we crossed the street, and started on our way back toward Death by Coffee. It wasn't all that long of a loop, truth be told, but we'd learned early on in our runs that I couldn't handle much more. Not yet anyway. Maybe in a year, I might be able to stretch it out some.

Maybe.

Andrew's Gifts came into view again. That nagging feeling that I had to do *something* surged, causing my pace to falter until I'd come to a complete stop just outside the police-taped door.

"I heard about this," Cassie said, coming to a stop next to me. "Should we cross the street so we don't step all over a crime scene?" She looked down at her feet as if she expected to find blood on the sidewalk.

I shook my head, too winded to respond quite yet. I could see the person inside now. She was middle-aged, hair a mess atop her head. She was wearing a flannel shirt which sagged on her body like it didn't belong to her. Every so often, she would raise the collar to her nose, and would just stand there, staring straight ahead, doing nothing more than breathing.

No, it wasn't a thief or a killer.

It was one of Andrew's loved ones.

I was about to tell Cassie that we should move on when the woman noticed us through the window. She wiped at her eyes and then crossed the store to open the door.

"I'm sorry." Her voice was thick with tears. "We're closed. There's been—" Her words caught in her throat.

"No, it's me who should apologize," I said. "I saw someone inside and was worried that it might have been a break-in. I didn't mean to intrude."

"You aren't." She wiped at her eyes again, cleared her throat. "The police gave me permission to look around today to make sure nothing was missing. I'm Erin. Andrew's wife. Or . . . I was." She started blinking rapidly as she fought a losing battle not to cry.

"I'm sorry for your loss." It felt inadequate, but I didn't know what else to say.

"Thank you." She lifted the shirt to her nose, let it drop without smelling it. "This was Andrew's." She plucked at the hem with a sad smile. "I threw it on when I left this morning. I really don't know why. It's making me feel worse."

"We should go," Cassie said, edging away, "and let you get back to what you were doing."

Erin nodded her thanks and started to close the door.

That's when I noticed what was sitting on the counter beside the register.

"Wait!" I didn't mean to shout, but I couldn't help myself. "What is that?"

Erin turned to look at what I was pointing at. "What do you mean? The present?"

My nod was on the frantic side. "Yeah. The present."

Cassie gave me a look like she thought I'd lost my mind. Maybe I had, but that box looked awfully familiar. It was wrapped in plain blue wrapping paper, just like the one that was currently sitting on the counter at Phantastic Candies.

Except this one was open.

Erin frowned and then shook her head. "Honestly, I don't know what was in it. The box is empty now. It showed up on our doorstep early yesterday morning, but Andrew didn't get a chance to look at it until last night right before he . . . before he . . ."

Before he died.

Jules!

Without another word, and despite the throbbing agony in my legs, I spun and started running as if my life depended on it.

Because if I was right, Jules's life very well might.

6

"**D**on't open the box!"

Jules jerked back from the gift, hands flying up into the air like I'd told him to "freeze."

I was panting, hands planted on my knees, head bobbing in time with my gasps. Behind me, Cassie entered the store, barely winded.

Jules took a breath, eyes wide. "What? Why?"

I didn't answer right away. My eyes were riveted to the gift sitting on the counter. It looked exactly like the one Andrew Carver had received; the same blue paper, the same box size. Now, Andrew was dead. Had Jules been within seconds of joining him?

"Krissy?" Jules looked from me to Cassie, who shrugged. "What's going on?"

My heartbeat slowed and I was beginning to feel a little lightheaded. If there'd been a chair nearby, I would have dropped into it. Instead, I leaned on the counter, which put me a lot closer to the gift than I'd like.

"It might be nothing," I said. My breathing was controlled, slow. I wasn't going to panic. I refused. "But the man who was murdered last night had a gift just like this one show up on his doorstep." I tapped the box with a fingernail. It didn't explode or rattle or make any other alarming noises. Yet.

"I don't understand." Jules frowned. "Am I in danger?"

"I honestly don't know." I straightened and stepped back. If the box *did* blow up, I didn't want to be too close to it.

The other box didn't explode, I reminded myself. But Andrew *had* ended up dead after opening it. I didn't know if it was poisonous somehow, or had a knife rigged inside that would stab upward the moment the box was opened.

Or I could be overthinking things and it was all just a coincidence.

But right then, I'd much rather be wrong and safe than be right about it and have Jules get hurt because I didn't say anything.

Or worse, dead.

"Call the police," I said. "I don't think you should open it, not without supervision." And maybe a bomb squad. Or drug sniffing dogs.

Jules paled and nodded as he picked up his cell. "I'll go to the back. I think I need a moment away from . . ." He flapped a hand toward the gift and then hurried into the back room.

"Do I want to know what is going on?" Cassie asked when he was gone. "You kind of scared me back there, running off like that."

"I'm sorry about that. I was worried that something might happen to Jules and—"

Cassie raised a hand to cut me off. "I get it. It just caught me by surprise and I wasn't sure if I should run and follow you or call for help." She paused. "Are you okay? You look pale."

I closed my eyes briefly before nodding. "I'm fine. I might have worked myself up over nothing." Yet, I didn't think so. Gifts didn't just drop out of the sky to land on someone's doorstep. And those same people didn't just up and die without there being some sort of connection.

Jules returned from the back. His hand shook ever so slightly as he set his phone down onto the counter. "Detective Buchannan is on his way," he said. "So is Lance. I only called him to warn him in case more presents showed up at home, but he insisted on coming here."

"You should probably close the store before people start showing up again." I was glad no kids were inside when I'd come barreling in, shouting like a lunatic. "I doubt many of your customers would be happy to have the police show up and interrogate them." Especially since that police officer was going to be John Buchannan, a man not known for compassion or empathy.

Jules crossed the room and set the sign to CLOSED before leaning against the door. "This is crazy. Why would someone do something like this?"

"I could be wrong," I said. "I didn't mean to freak you out, but . . . ."

"No, I get it." Jules straightened. "I'm all right."

"I should probably get going," Cassie said, checking her watch. "Unless you think the police are going to need me for something?" She sounded about as enthused as I was at seeing Buchannan, which was not at all.

"You're probably safe to go," I said. "Detective Buchannan doesn't even need to know you were here."

Cassie smiled and rested a hand on my arm. "Thanks. I'll talk to you soon." She squeezed, and with a farewell nod to Jules, she left Phantastic Candies.

"I think we scared her off," Jules said when the door closed again. Now that the initial shock had worn off, he was acting more like himself. "What do you think is in there?" He propped his elbows on the counter, chin in his hands, far too close to the gift for my liking.

"Probably nothing." I hoped. "What did it feel like when you picked it up? Was it heavy? Did it rattle around?"

Jules's brow furrowed. "No, it's not heavy. But it's not empty either. I felt something move around a little when I picked the box up, but couldn't tell what that something might be."

A big neon sign flashed the word BOMB in all caps over and over in my head. "It's probably not a bomb," I said.

"I hope not." Jules blew out a breath, causing his lips to flap. "What a day."

The sound of sirens approached. Less than a minute later, Detective John Buchannan and Officer Becca Garrison entered Phantastic Candies. Buchannan was scowling, which if I was being honest, he always was. Garrison looked less than happy, but when she saw me, she gave me a curt nod of acknowledgment.

"Where is it?" Buchannan demanded.

Garrison rolled her eyes and walked straight over to the box, which was, you know, sitting right there. "This the one?"

"That's it," Jules confirmed. "I brought it here from home, so it's been moved from where I'd originally found it. Otherwise, it hasn't been touched."

Buchannan and Garrison both leaned toward the box as if they could discern something from the plain blue wrapping paper. Then, Buchannan reached out slowly, hand drifting ever closer, as if he planned on opening it right then and there.

"Are you sure that's a good idea?" I asked, easing away.

He paused to glare at me. I raised my hands in surrender.

Buchannan touched Jules's mysterious gift.

A loud bang echoed in the room. I jumped about a foot into the air, and Buchannan practically fell over backward trying to scramble away before he realized that the bang was followed by the sounds of candy being unwrapped.

Lance made a beeline for Jules, letting the door he'd slammed into close behind him. "Are you okay?" He looked Jules up and down, and finding no injuries, wrapped him in a hug.

"I'm fine," Jules assured him. "We're just being cautious."

Buchannan shot me an unhappy look as he righted himself. "You know anything about this?"

"Kind of, not really."

Buchannan's scowl deepened.

"I mean, I'm the one who told Jules to call you, so, yeah, I guess."

"And why would you do that?"

"Because Andrew Carver received a gift just like this one on the day he died."

The entire room went quiet. Jules leaned into Lance, whose jaw stiffened.

"This is a threat?" Lance asked.

Both Garrison and Buchannan looked at me for an answer, one I didn't have.

"I don't know."

"We should take it somewhere safe before we open it," Garrison said. "Make sure no one gets hurt."

Buchannan nodded. "You said you moved it?" he asked Jules.

"I did."

"Then it's safe to transport." Buchannan gestured for Garrison to go ahead, making sure to stay well back himself. She gave him a half-smile and an eyeroll that he missed because he was now focused on me.

"How did you learn about this supposed other gift?"

I tried not to bristle at the "supposed" part. "I talked to Erin Carver this morning." When Buchannan's eyes narrowed, I hurriedly added, "I was jogging when I saw someone inside Andrew's Gifts. Since I was right there, I peeked inside to make sure no one was ransacking the place and Erin saw me. She came out to talk. I didn't barge my way in or force her to do or say anything."

Carefully, Officer Garrison picked up the package. When nothing happened, she sighed and carried the box out the door, arms extended in front of her as far as she could get them.

Buchannan scratched the back of his neck and frowned about the room some more before he said, "Fine. We're taking the suspicious package to the station. I want *you* to find somewhere else to be." He pointed at me.

A "but" was on my lips. I didn't say it, but I thought it hard enough that Buchannan picked up on it.

"I mean it. No snooping. No following me. Just . . . go home."

"I'm going with you." Jules extracted himself from Lance's arms and stepped up beside Buchannan. "I found it on my doorstep, which means it was meant for me. Once it's open, I might be able to tell you something about who sent it."

"And whether or not it's dangerous," I added, which earned me another Buchannan glare. I swear, the guy never smiles, not unless he's about to throw me into a jail cell.

"I can come too," Lance said.

"You should stay here," Jules said. "Keep the store open while I'm gone. I don't want to disappoint the kids if this turns out to be nothing."

I would have argued, but Lance took a steadying breath and then nodded.

"All right." Buchannan motioned for Jules to follow him before leveling that finger at me again. "You stay put."

"I thought you told me to find somewhere else to be?"

Buchannan clenched his teeth so hard, I'm pretty sure I heard one of them creak.

"Okay, okay." I raised my hands in surrender. "I'm going to see my dad anyway."

"You do that." Buchannan looked as if he might have more to say to me, but instead, all he did was sigh and say, "Come on," to Jules before they both left the store.

"You're going to figure this out, right?" Lance asked me as soon as they were gone.

Denial was on the tip of my tongue, but we both knew that if I said "no," it would be a lie.

"I'm going to try."

Lance clenched his fists. "Good."

I left Phantastic Candies then, wishing I didn't have to walk all the way back to Death by Coffee for my car. But walking *did* have its advantages over driving. Like, you know, being able to stop wherever I wanted without stalling traffic.

I crossed the street and headed toward Death by Coffee, which just so happened to take me past Andrew's Gifts. And, as if I'd planned it, the door opened and Erin Carver ducked out beneath the police tape just as I got there. She had the empty gift box tucked under one arm.

"Hi, Erin. I'm sorry to bother you again." I stopped in front of her. "Are you going to take that to the police?" I asked, nodding toward the box.

She frowned down at it. "I . . . I don't know. Should I?"

"It might be evidence." And while she didn't know about Jules's gift, it still seemed strange that she was taking it with her. Or that the police hadn't taken it when they'd searched the place last night. *If* they'd searched Andrew's Gifts at all.

"Do you think so?" Quite suddenly, she didn't look like she wanted to touch it. I held out my hands, and without questioning my motives, she handed it over.

"I'll make sure it gets to the police." A vague thought that I should leave it here passed through my head. It was chased by another that was worried that if I did, the killer might come back and take it if it *was* evidence.

Erin nodded and hugged herself. "I don't get it. Why would someone hurt Andrew? And why do it so close to Christmas? It's so cruel." She sniffed. "Could they have wanted to hurt *me?*"

I eyed her, wondering vaguely if all of this was for show. I mean, don't they always say that it's usually someone close to the victim when it comes to murder? And that spouses are the most likely suspects?

But if she was faking it, she was doing a pretty darn good job of it. Her eyes were red-rimmed, and she was shaking, though that could have been from the cold.

I shuffled my own feet to keep the blood flowing. "Do you have any idea who might have wanted to hurt your husband?" I asked.

Erin shook her head. "He didn't have enemies. Not real ones anyway. Andrew could sometimes be a little off-putting and had a short fuse, but he never got into regular fights or arguments or anything. Most of the time, he'd just walk away when he got mad."

Except when he was confronting someone in his store.

"I saw Andrew get into an argument when I was in the store yesterday," I said. "Do you know anything about that? The guy wears all black, has long hair." I thought back but was coming up blank on any other description. "He said something about Andrew's prices."

Erin considered it before hugging herself even tighter. "I don't know anyone like that. But if Andrew had a confrontation in the store with someone, he wouldn't have told me."

Which made me think that if Andrew Carver *did* get into regular fights, there was a chance his wife didn't know.

"Did he talk about the store at all?"

Erin looked toward Andrew's Gifts and the police tape strung across the door before she answered. "I never really asked. This place was his thing. He worked here on his own, managed the money himself. I had nothing to do with it."

"He had no employees?"

"None. Just Andrew. He didn't trust other people to be honest around money."

I wondered if that included her, but decided not to ask. "What about something at home? Did he gamble? Have debts?"

She shook her head. "No, nothing like that." She frowned. "Could it have been a rival store? When he opened . . ." Her expression told me that she'd thought of something.

I waited her out. I knew all about jealousy when it came to rival stores. Judith Banyon from the

Banyon Tree diner swore I was trying to steal her customers at Death by Coffee, even though the only thing the places had in common was serving coffee.

But to stoop to murder over such a thing?

And how would Jules and Phantastic Candies tie into a spat between gift shops?

"There is this one place," Erin said, tapping her foot as she looked down the street in the direction I'd just come from. "They sell little hand carved trinkets and bibles and crosses and things like that. It's called Heavenly Gate."

I thought I recalled seeing it before, but since I wasn't very religious, I'd never paid it much mind.

"The owner wasn't happy about Andrew's Gifts opening?"

Erin started to nod, but then shrugged. "I honestly don't know. And it wasn't the owner, I guess, but his wife, who'd come in. She was unhappy."

"About?"

Erin considered it. "I'm not exactly sure. I was only there to bring Andrew his lunch. He often forgot it when his mind was elsewhere." She gave me a sad smile. "When I opened the door, the woman stomped off, so I didn't hear anything she said."

"And Andrew didn't tell you?"

"No. He just said they were talking and that was that." She sighed. "He was like that all the time." A pause. "Andrew could be secretive, but I know for a fact he'd never cheat on me."

Which I figured a lot of women thought just before finding out their husbands had been stepping out with the neighbor's daughter. If Andrew *had* been cheating, then it gave more than one person motive for murder.

But the gift. And Jules.

I clamped down on the inevitable next thought. There was zero chance Jules or Lance had cheated with Andrew Carver. None.

"Look, I really need to get going," Erin said. "Thank you for offering to take that to the police." She indicated the box. "I was just going to throw it out."

"It's no problem." I was losing feeling in my feet and my nose felt like a block of ice on my face, so I was happy to get moving again.

Erin headed for her car, head down. She glanced back once before climbing inside and driving off, leaving me standing in the cold, holding a box that could very well be the key to Andrew Carver's murder.

7

The long, winding driveway leading to Ted and Bettfast prepared me for the state of the old mansion. The hedge animals had been left to grow over long ago, and many of them had died from some sort of blight, leaving behind their sad stick skeletons. The bed-and-breakfast itself was stuck between falling down and being built back up. Partial siding replacement, a window that had been boarded up instead of being replaced.

It was almost enough to kill any joy I might have in seeing Dad and Laura.

I parked next to Dad's rental, which was sitting beside the only other vehicle in the lot. Lack of business lately hadn't helped with the funding of repairs for Ted and Bettfast that were necessary to draw in business and it showed.

I glanced at the box that was sitting in the passenger seat next to me. I needed to get it to the police station, but I'd wanted to talk to Dad first. I made a mental note to do it as soon as I was done here, and then climbed out of my car and headed for the front door of the bed-and-breakfast.

"Ms. Hancock!" One of the employees—the only one working, as far as I could tell—met me by the door. His once shoulder-length hair was cut to just below his chin, and he was starting to fill out the baggy clothes he often wore, but in a good way. "It's been a long time."

"Hey, Justin. How's your sister?"

"Great. We're doing great." Justin took care of his younger sister. There was some family drama in there somewhere, but I hadn't pried too deeply into exactly what that drama was. "At least we are now. I'm worried that won't last."

"Why's that?" Though, noting the peeling wallpaper on the walls and a light that flickered on and off irregularly, it was kind of obvious.

"I don't think Ted and Bett are going to be around much longer." He paused, frowned at that. "I mean, I think they're planning on moving somewhere else, not . . . you know? Dying or anything."

"Out of Pine Hills?"

"Yeah. They aren't really talking about it with the rest of us." Meaning him and the other two employees, Jo and Kari. "But we see what's happening. I overheard them talking about Florida real estate just the other day."

"Do you think they'll go?" Despite our occasional rocky relationship, I liked the Bunfords. It would be strange not to see them around town.

Justin shrugged. "Beats me. I hope they don't because I don't want to lose this job. I've been here forever." He sighed. "But I don't think I've got much choice. I'm pretty sure Ted and Bett are talking to the bank today. Or maybe it's a realtor."

"If they do sell, that doesn't mean you won't have a job," I said. "The new owners could keep you around."

"I hope so, but I can't count on it. The uncertainty is killer."

"I bet." And then, a thought. "If something *does* happen and you lose your job here, feel free to stop in at Death by Coffee. I'm sure we could find a place for you there."

"Really?" His eyes brightened. "I mean, that'd be great. And if you could find room for Jo and Kari . . ." He considered that a moment before amending it to, "For Jo, at least, that'd be awesome."

"I'll see what I can do, but we can both hope that it won't come to that."

"Yeah." Justin cleared his throat. "I should get back to cleaning up. Ted and Bett might not be here, and it's not exactly busy, but a job's a job." He flashed me a smile. "I assume you're here for your dad?"

I almost asked him how he knew their guest was my father, but caught myself. I mean, duh. "I am."

"Go on up, then. Room's the only occupied one. It's on the left."

"Thanks." I started for the stairs but paused. "I really do hope things work out for you, Justin. Don't forget to stop in if you need a job. Or if you just want to say hi."

"I'll do that. Thanks again, Ms. Hancock."

"Krissy." And then I headed up the stairs.

A multitude of emotions slammed into me as I

ascended the wooden stairs to the second floor. The carpet was well-worn, but clean. The whole house felt that way. It was old and falling apart, but was kept as clean as possible. A lot had happened in this building, both good and bad.

And the bad included murder.

Would the house feel the same way if someone were to buy it and fix it up completely? The mansion was over a hundred years old and standing in it was kind of like going back in time. A full renovation might erase that feeling. I'm not so sure that would be a good thing.

I passed by the door where the murder had taken place, gently touching the aged wood as I passed. There were no cold chills or feelings of being watched. I supposed that meant there were no ghosts hanging around, or at least none that wanted to catch my attention.

Not that I'm all that superstitious. But in old places like this, it's hard not to be, at least a little.

A DO NOT DISTURB sign hung on a doorknob on the left side of the hall. Dad's room. I considered it a moment, and then decided it didn't apply to me. I knocked and called out. "Dad? Laura? It's me."

The door opened and Dad peeked out. "Buttercup? I didn't expect you already." He stepped aside. "Come on in."

I entered, half expecting to find Laura in bed, covers pulled up to her chin and with a thermometer poking out of her mouth. Instead, she was seated in a chair by the window, sipping at something that smelled strongly of mint. Tea, I assumed.

"How are you feeling?" I asked her.

"Better. I think it was exhaustion more than anything, though I'd stick to the other side of the room if I were you, just in case."

"Here." Dad handed me a copy of his latest book. "Might as well give it to you now, before I forget."

"Thanks." The cover of *Scars of the Heart* was similar to that of *Victim of the Heart*, the first book in the series. It showed a chalk outline, though this time, it was a woman's body that was implied instead of a man's, and a knife was on the scene instead of a gun. A little yellow triangle by the body had a "2" on it instead of the first book's "1".

"I told him he should wrap it and give it to you at Christmas," Laura said.

Dad made a face. "I'm not big on treating my books as anything special. Giving one to Rita as a gift was more than enough for me."

"I'm happy either way." I opened the cover and peeked at Dad's messy signature before closing it again.

"So . . ." Dad rocked back onto his heel as he stretched out the word. "A murder, huh?"

By the window, Laura rolled her eyes before taking a sip of her tea.

"Yeah." I wasn't too sure I wanted to talk about this with Dad quite yet, so I tried to change the subject. Kind of. "Must be strange staying here after what happened to Rick all those years ago." Rick was his former agent and the victim in the previously considered murder.

Dad thought about it a moment before shrugging. "Not really. In fact, it's helped me come to peace with it. Strange, I guess, but it worked." He paused. "How well did you know the man who was killed?"

I sighed. There was no way I was going to get out of this. "I didn't know him at all. Well, I guess I had sort of met him, but we didn't talk." And then, since we were obviously going to discuss it, "Did you see anything strange when you left the party last night?"

Dad scratched his chin and looked to Laura.

"I wasn't paying attention to anything but making sure my feet went one after the other by then," she said.

"I wasn't watching either, but maybe . . ." Dad closed his eyes, tipped his head back, and thought about it. After a few moments, he shook his head. "I've got nothing."

Which, in some ways, was probably a good thing. If Dad *had* seen something, like someone going into Andrew's Gifts, then he'd need to talk to the police about it, which meant talking to John Buchannan, who would find a way to make my life miserable through my dad, just because he could.

Then again, if he *had* seen the killer, Andrew's murder would be solved, and Jules would be safe again.

"I think the murderer left a package," I said. "A gift-wrapped box."

"With the body?" Dad asked.

"No. Before. Apparently, the victim found a wrapped gift outside his house. When he opened it, he took it to his store, but didn't tell anyone what was inside. By the time anyone found it, it was already empty, so I'm guessing the killer took whatever was inside with him."

But why leave the box? That was a question I couldn't answer, at least not yet.

Dad started pacing. "Do you believe the gift had something to do with the man's death?"

"I don't know. But my neighbor and friend, Jules Phan, got a present just like it too."

Dad jerked to a stop. "From the killer?"

I hugged myself as worry started gnawing at me. "I don't know. I could be overthinking it and these gifts have nothing to do with the murder. When I learned about the one Andrew had received, I rushed over to Phantastic Candies before Jules could open his. He called the police and they took it somewhere safe to open it."

"So you don't know what's inside this new gift?"

"Not yet." And hopefully, when they look, it'll point right at the killer. If it was connected, that was. "Erin—that's Andrew's wife—gave me the other box to give to the police. I plan on doing that as soon as I leave here."

Excitement lit up Dad's face. "You still have the evidence?"

I could have slapped myself for letting that tidbit slip, but I wasn't going to lie to Dad. "It's in the car."

"Show me." Dad was out the door before I could respond.

By the window, Laura chuckled into her tea. "Good luck."

"Thanks." I heaved a sigh. "Feel better."

She held up her mug. "I'm trying."

Dad was already down the stairs by the time I'd left the room. He was waiting impatiently by the front door, Justin looking on with a perplexed expression on his face. As soon as I joined Dad, he pushed through the door and made for my Escape, muttering to himself. It wasn't until he started rubbing at his arms that I realized he hadn't put on a coat.

"Dad! You'll freeze."

"I'm fine." He rounded to the passenger's side door and peered in through the window. "This it?"

"It is." I unlocked the doors and immediately started the engine and jacked up the heat. "Get in. We can talk about it inside where it's warm."

Dad gingerly lifted the box, using the sleeve of his sweater to touch it. It was something I should have thought about when I'd gotten it from Erin, but at the same time, she'd been touching it too. I was pretty sure whatever evidence might have been left behind on the box was already long gone.

Once we were sitting inside the quickly warming car, Dad turned the box over in his hands.

"There's nothing on it."

"I don't think there was a note," I said. "Or if there was, Erin never told me about it. And Jules's gift didn't have one, as far as I know." Though I'd have to remember to ask him to be sure.

"So, it was sent completely anonymously?" Dad peered inside. "There's no residue or indentations." He tipped the box so I could look in at the smooth, brown surface. "See?"

"I see an empty box."

"Think back to all the packages you've ever received," Dad said.

I frowned, not following. "Okay?"

"If the package was sent through a mail carrier or a delivery service, it would show signs of that here." He tapped the blue wrapping paper. "But the paper isn't worn or torn except for where it was opened at the top."

"Okay?" I repeated.

"That means it was hand delivered. It's clean, so it didn't ride in the back of a delivery truck, where it would have gotten dirty. And the inside." He tipped it to show me again. "There're no indentations where a hard corner might have torn into the cardboard, or at least dented it. There's no powder or residue like you might expect to find with drugs or some kind of poison."

"So, you're saying the killer was careful?"

"Or the object inside was round and well-secured. Was there Bubble Wrap or some sort of packing lying around?"

I tried to remember if I'd seen anything like that on the counter at Andrew's Gifts, but came up blank. "I don't think so, but I could be wrong. I got the impression Andrew opened his gift at home, and then brought it to the store, so he could have thrown any protective packaging away there."

Dad set the box on the dash. "Find out if you can. You said your friend got one?" I nodded. "Ask him about the condition of the box, what was inside, and not just the main object. Even something like balled up newspaper used for packaging could help."

"If the police will tell me," I said. "They might not even tell Jules."

"Well, if they do, find out."

"I will."

Dad eyed the box and then reached for the door handle. "I should probably get back inside to Laura." He paused before opening the door. "Do you want to come back in with me?"

"No, I'd best get that to the police." I nodded

toward the box on the dash. "But if Laura's feeling up to it, what about dinner tomorrow? At Geraldo's?"

"Sounds great," Dad said. "And you should bring Paul."

A flare of both excitement and fear shot through me. Dad and Laura had met Paul many times, yet somehow, this time felt different. Maybe it had to do with how Paul had been acting as of late, as if he had something important to tell me. Every time he'd tried to talk about it, something would happen and it would get put on the back burner.

"I'll ask him," I said. "But he might be stuck at work, what with the murder and all."

"Could be, but I hope he'll be there."

"I'll let you know," I said. "And if Laura's feeling better tonight, you two could always stop by the house. Or I can come to you." Anything to get my mind off Andrew's murder and Jules's mysterious gift.

"We'll see." He popped open the door and stepped out into the cold. "I'll see you soon. Okay, Buttercup?"

"Call me if you need anything."

Dad nodded and climbed out of the car.

I watched him hurry back into Ted and Bettfast before turning my attention to the empty box that might hold the clues as to what was really going on in Pine Hills. "What was in you?" I asked it.

As expected, the box didn't reply.

8

The blue-wrapped gift box sat on my counter, next to a festively wrapped Christmas present. No, I hadn't found a mysterious package sitting outside my front door, though I'd checked to make sure there wasn't one there. I had yet to deliver Andrew's gift to the police, and my reason was . . .

Well, I wasn't really sure why I still had it. A part of me was afraid of what Detective John Buchannan would say when he found out I'd taken the box from Erin. I should have told her to take it back inside Andrew's Gifts and call the police.

But I hadn't. And now it was sitting on my counter, all but screaming at me that I'd made a dumb mistake.

On the floor next to me, Misfit's fuzzy orange backside wiggled as he prepared for launch.

"No," I told him, holding out an arm to block his path. "You can't sleep in that one."

Undeterred, he moved a foot to his right and started wiggling again.

I snatched the box up just as he leapt up onto the counter. "I said, no." The smaller wrapped gift held his interest for about three seconds before he jumped down and sauntered over to his food dishes. "You've already eaten."

I carried the box into my spare room, where I set it down. Misfit, like every other cat I've ever known, loved to sleep in cardboard boxes, whether he fit or not. There was no way I was going to risk having possible evidence turn into a cat bed. Paul, along with the rest of the Pine Hills police department, would kill me.

Once the box was secure, I stepped back out into the hall and closed the door firmly shut. Misfit sat beside the island counter, tail swishing as he watched me. As soon as I returned to the kitchen, he headed for the door. He pawed at it a few times before he started yowling in protest.

"No," I said, not that he was listening. Misfit paced back and forth a few times, complaining all the while, before he flopped over onto his side and began sticking his paw under the door.

I watched to make sure he couldn't pop the door open, and then I picked up my phone, considered the empty space where the box had sat, and dialed. It rang twice before Paul answered.

"Hey, Krissy, I was just about to call you."

"What for?" My chest tightened, immediately thinking the worst. "Did something happen to Jules?"

There was a brief pause. "No, not as far as I'm aware. Am I missing something here?"

I breathed a sigh of relief. "Jules got a gift. We think it might be from the killer."

Another pause. "Wait, back up. What gift?"

Apparently, Paul hadn't talked to Buchannan yet, which meant he wouldn't know anything about the evidence I was currently housing in my spare room. It made me wonder if the detective was keeping things from Paul because he was afraid word would get back to me and I'd start interfering. A stirring of guilt churned in my gut.

"We think the person who killed Andrew Carver left him a gift outside his house. Andrew took it to his store the night he died." Or, at least, that was *my* working theory. I had no idea what Buchannan thought. I wasn't sure I wanted to know. "Jules got one too."

"What sort of gift?"

"I don't know. Andrew's box was empty when his wife found it. And Detective Buchannan showed up and took Jules's so it could be opened at the police station where it was safe." It was my turn to hesitate. "You didn't know any of this?"

Paul sighed through what sounded like him rubbing his hand over his face. "No. But it's no wonder. I've been running all over town and haven't had a moment's break since the day started. It's been crazy. You'd think it was a full moon with how everyone is acting."

"I take it that means you won't be stopping by tonight?" As I said it, I glanced toward the door where Misfit was still camped, though he'd stopped the yowling.

"Probably not."

"What about tomorrow night? Dad and Laura

asked if you'd like to come with us to Geraldo's for dinner."

"I could make that work," Paul said. "It sounds really good, actually."

"Then it's a date." I bit my lower lip. Paul wasn't going to like what I had to say next. "I, um—"

Misfit chose that moment to resume his complaints, cutting me off.

"What is that sound?" Paul asked.

"Misfit." I turned to the cat. "I'm not opening the door."

He let out a pitiful meow and flopped back over onto his side. He shoved a paw under the door and then leaned his head back so he could look at me with the most pitiful expression I'd ever seen on a cat.

I was, however, unmoved.

"He sounds . . . unhappy."

"He is." There was nothing I could do but explain. "You know how I told you that Andrew Carver received a gift before he was killed?"

"Yeah? Did you get one too?" There was an edge of worry in Paul's voice.

"No. But I have Andrew's box. It's empty and there's no indication as to what was in it. It's why I called, actually. I was hoping you could come pick it up." I winced in anticipation of Paul's next words.

"Wait. Hold up. You have the gift box that was sent to a murdered man? Something that might very well be *evidence?*"

"Erin gave it to me! Erin is Andrew's wife. Or she was." I frowned. Now wasn't the time to start rambling. "She was carrying it out of Andrew's Gifts when I walked by. I promised her I'd give it to the police for her. She didn't realize it was important and was going to throw it away. As I said, it's why I called. I'm not trying to hide evidence or mess with the investigation or anything."

Paul took a deep breath, let it out slowly. "I see. Does John know you have it?"

"No. When I saw him at Phantastic Candies earlier, I didn't have it yet. I was on my way back to Death by Coffee when I ran into Erin, and by then, Buchannan was dealing with Jules's box. I swear, it was by pure happenstance that it came into my possession. I know I should have left it with Erin, but I wasn't thinking straight and . . ."

Paul sighed. "All right. Give me an hour to finish up here and I'll stop by to pick up the gift box." And before I could get excited, he added, "I won't be able to stay."

"I'll be here." My eyes strayed to the wrapped gift still sitting on my counter. "I'm going to stop over at Caitlin's to drop something off to her, but that should only take a few minutes."

"Okay. Yeah." A deep breath. "See you in an hour, Krissy. I've got to run."

"See you then."

We clicked off.

That could have gone a whole lot worse. I breathed a sigh of relief, and then gathered Caitlin's gift from the counter. I pulled on my heavy coat, checked to make sure Misfit hadn't found a way to open the spare room door, and then started the trek across the yard to Caitlin's house.

As I walked, I noticed there was an old, unfamiliar Buick in her driveway. Apparently, Caitlin had a guest. Family? A friend? Someone special?

A part of me thought it might be better if I turned around and went home. I had yet to meet Caitlin's family, outside her cousin once, so I was curious about them. Her brother lived out of the country, and I didn't know anything about her parents at all.

And of her friends, I only knew of Teek, a bandmate of hers. I knew nothing of boyfriends or girlfriends or just friend friends.

I approached Caitlin's front door, curiosity winning out. I could hear music coming from inside. Loud music; not the kind I'd expect her to be listening to if she had family in. A voice pitched ear-shatteringly high started singing something about there not being presents for Christmas, which was funny, considering I was delivering just that.

I knocked, and then quickly realized there was no way Caitlin could hear me over the music, so I pounded on the door as hard as I could. No answer. Thankfully, the music died down as the song ended and I took the opportunity to knock again. A moment later, the door opened and Caitlin Blevins poked her head outside.

"Uh, hi." She glanced past me, as if expecting me to have brought friends. When she saw no one, her gaze dropped to what I was carrying. "What's this?"

"A gift." I held it out to her. "For you."

Caitlin raised a single eyebrow. She was wearing all black and her makeup was of dark hues; purples and blues. "I don't really celebrate."

"That's all right." I handed her the box. "You don't have to open it on Christmas. It's nothing, really." I flashed her a smile that quickly faded. "You didn't receive another gift, did you? Blue wrapping paper? Was likely sitting outside your door?"

"Uh . . . No? Why?"

"No reason. But if you do get one, don't open it. Call the po—" I cut off as her guest stepped up behind her.

Long hair. Combat boots. Wallet chain hanging against his left hip. All black clothing.

"Sup," Black Shirt said, jerking his head back once in a backward nod. The skull earring dangling from his ear swung back and forth with force.

My mouth opened and closed like I was a fish gasping for air. This was the guy who'd been chased out of Andrew's Gifts before Andrew had been murdered. And here he was, in my next-door neighbor's house.

"Krissy, this is Jacob. Jacob; my neighbor, Krissy."

I was greeted with another, "Sup," and head tilt.

"Uh, hi." My mind was racing, coming up with reasons, realistic and otherwise, why Jacob would be at Caitlin's.

"He's in my band," Caitlin said, providing an answer for me.

"Bass," he added. "I hold everything together." He mimed playing.

Caitlin snorted. "Yeah right. You're lucky to be on beat half the time."

Jacob's hand went to his chest. "You wound me," he said, before turning to me with a grin.

"She's just jealous because she can't play my bass nearly as good as I can."

"That's because it's left-handed, dweeb." Caitlin rolled her eyes before she asked me, "Are you okay? You look a little pale."

"Yeah, I'm fine." I plastered on a giant, fake smile. "It's good to meet you, Jacob." And because I was struggling to come up with something to say that wasn't "Did you kill Andrew Carver?" I asked, "What are you listening to?"

Jacob glanced behind him, as if checking to make sure the music was still there. It was. The next song had started, but someone had turned it down so it wasn't deafening any longer. "King Diamond."

That meant absolutely nothing to me. "It's . . . interesting."

Jacob nodded, as if in agreement. "Yeah, it's cool. It's an acquired taste for some, but I thought it fit the season."

I supposed the first song *had* mentioned Christmas, though the current one was about Halloween.

"Hey, Jacob, can I talk to Caitlin alone for a minute." I turned the wattage up on my smile, hoping he didn't note my nervousness. "There's some neighborhood stuff I'd like to discuss."

"Yeah, sure." He flipped his hair back out of his face. "Nice meeting you."

Jacob turned and walked away, wallet chain smacking him in the leg with every step. Once he was gone, I sagged in relief. He hadn't appeared to recognize me, but then again, the last time I'd seen him, he'd had his hands full with Andrew.

"What's going on?" Caitlin asked the moment he was out of earshot.

"How well do you know Jacob?" I asked. Right then, I didn't know if *anything* was going on, at least when it came to Jacob.

"Well enough, I guess." Caitlin considered the gift in her hands and then set it down on a table just inside the door. "Teek was the one who recruited him and has known him the longest."

A cold gust of wind caused me to shiver, despite my heavy coat. I hugged myself for warmth. "I saw him yesterday." When Caitlin just stared at me, I added, "At Andrew's Gifts."

"And?"

"And now Andrew Carver, the owner, is dead."

Caitlin mirrored my crossed arms. "And?"

I stepped closer to her and lowered my voice. I couldn't see Jacob, but that didn't mean he wasn't listening. "He was murdered. Do you think there's a chance Jacob could be involved?"

"With murder?" Caitlin said it loud enough, I knew Jacob had to have heard her over the music.

I shrugged and gave her a "you tell me" look.

Caitlin started to answer, a denial most likely, before she caught herself and frowned. She looked back toward the kitchen, where Jacob strode into view and started slathering something onto a piece of toast.

"Caitlin?" I prodded. "Do you know something?"

She stepped forward, all but pushing me out of her doorway. She partially closed the door behind her. When she spoke, air puffed from her mouth.

"Jacob has been acting weird today," she said. This time, she kept her voice quiet. "Nervous."

"Like he's hiding something?"

"I don't know. He's a good guy, but he doesn't just drop in like he did today."

He's hiding. I don't know why I thought that, but now that it had crossed my mind, I couldn't think anything else. "Could he have killed Andrew?"

"Honestly? I'm not sure. If you'd asked me that yesterday, I'd say there was no way."

"But now?"

"But now he keeps checking the windows and acting all paranoid, like he's afraid someone might be looking for him. I thought he was avoiding Boo, but now I'm not so sure."

"Boo?"

"His girlfriend." Caitlin made a face. "Or whatever she is. I've only met her once and I can't say I'm a fan." She peeked back into the house, then lowered her voice some more. "Do the police think Jacob did it?"

I had no idea what the police thought and said as much. "But I did see him at Andrew's Gifts arguing with the owner."

"Everyone's always harassing him—Jacob, I mean—so I'm not surprised, honestly." Caitlin shivered, eyes drifting toward the sky. "People take one look at someone who looks like us and they expect the worst."

"Well, Jacob didn't do himself any favors with how he was acting." I paused, and then asked, "Who chose the song? The one playing when I got here?" The one that sounded anti-Christmas to me.

"Jacob did. Why?"

"You know when I asked you about whether a present was left for you?" She nodded. "Well, a gift was left for Andrew at his house. I think it's some-how connected to his death. And that song . . ."

"Is just a song." Yet Caitlin paled. "I can't believe Jacob would do anything like that."

I could almost see the thoughts zooming through her head. Jacob was a friend, a bandmate. She knew him, so therefore, he couldn't be a killer.

But lots of people have had those same exact thoughts over the years when their best friend, their neighbor, or perhaps their brother or sister, were arrested—and then convicted—for murder.

"Do you know where Jacob was last night?" I asked.

Caitlin shook her head. Her teeth started chat-tering as she ran her hands up and down her arms to warm them. "He didn't show up until today, and like I said, I thought he was here because of Boo. *Not* because I thought he killed someone."

"He might not have," I said. "But since he *did* fight with Andrew yesterday . . ." I shook my head. "It doesn't look good."

"What should I do? I don't want to just kick him out." Her eyes widened. "Wait. Teek called last night asking about Jacob. He said Jacob was sup-posed to meet him at his place to go over some music stuff."

"He didn't show?"

"If he did, it was late. What time did the—" she mouthed the word "murder" "—take place?"

I thought back, wishing I'd paid better attention to the time. "It was sometime after seven. Maybe eight? At least, that's around when the police showed up. I'm not sure when he was killed."

"Teek called close to nine. He was supposed to meet with Jacob at eight."

Which meant Jacob was missing around the time at which Andrew Carver was murdered.

"Oh, crap." Caitlin was starting to look panicked. "What if he . . . And if he thinks I suspect . . ."

"Calm down," I said, resting a hand on her shoulder. "He might not have anything to do with it." Though things were most definitely not looking good for good old Jacob Black-Shirt.

"But what if he does? I could have a *murderer* in my house!"

Two cars pulled into Jules's driveway, briefly drawing my attention. Both Lance and Jules climbed out of their respective vehicles and went inside.

"Paul is going to be here in less than an hour," I told Caitlin. "If you feel threatened, or if you want me to send him over to talk to Jacob, just text me. Or call. Or yell." I prayed it wouldn't come to that.

Caitlin was shivering nonstop now. She might be freezing, yet she didn't look like she wanted to go back into her house either. "I'll think about it," she said, closing her eyes and muttering, "Why me?" And then she pushed open her door.

Jacob was standing just inside.

I somehow managed not to yelp in surprise, though Caitlin jerked back from him like he'd lunged at her.

"Hey, you're out of jam. I didn't realize it was your last jar or I wouldn't have taken it all. Sorry about that." He took a bite from his strawberry jam-covered slice of toast.

"It's okay. I'll get some tomorrow." Caitlin looked at me, worry lining her face.

"Cool." Jacob looked from her to me, clearly curious. "Hey, don't I know you from somewhere?"

I looked down at my bare wrist. "Shoot, look at the time. I've got to go. You two have fun."

Caitlin shot me a dirty look for abandoning her, but what else was I going to do? Stand there in the cold and watch him until Paul showed up?

Jacob waved with his free hand before turning to Caitlin. "Hey, have you heard the Sabaton song, 'Christmas Truce' yet? Let me queue it up. It rocks."

I eased away, feeling guilty for leaving her, but at the same time, Jacob didn't *look* like a killer, nor was he acting like one.

But until I found out for sure one way or the other, I was going to treat him like one.

9

The doorbell looked like a piece of peppermint candy, which was appropriate not for just whose house I was at, but for the season as well. As soon as I pressed the bell, the sound of claws and barking came from inside, overriding the chime. A moment later and the door opened, revealing a concerned looking Lance Darby with an overexcited Maestro at his feet.

"Oh, Krissy." He breathed a sigh of relief. "Hi."

"Hi, Lance. How are you doing?"

He picked up the white Maltese before the little dog could escape. "As good as can be, I suppose." He stepped aside. "Come on in. Jules is in the kitchen."

I followed Lance through a meticulously clean house that put my own home to shame. I mean, I'm not a total slob or anything, but somehow, despite having a dog, Jules and Lance managed to keep their place pristine without a tuft of stray fur in sight. I assumed magic of some sort must be involved because if Misfit so much as walks through a room, he leaves a trail of orange fur behind.

Jules was leaning against the kitchen counter, a steaming cup of coffee in hand. His brow was furrowed, and a faint frown lined a face that was more accustomed to smiling. When he saw me, he tried to revert to his more cheerful self, but the smile never quite formed.

"Want one?" he asked, lifting his mug. "It's fresh. Mine has a splash of a pick-me-up, but I could make yours without it."

"No, thank you. I'll have some tea when I get home." I'd taken to drinking spiced chai tea during the evenings instead of coffee in an attempt to ween myself off nighttime caffeine. Yes, I know that tea has caffeine, but not as much as coffee. The smell of Jules's coffee, however, was weakening my resolve. "How did it go with Detective Buchannan?"

Jules took a sip of his spiked coffee before setting the mug aside. "All right, I guess. When I first got there, it was like something straight out of a cop show. Everyone was running around, acting like the world was about to end. And then . . ." He shrugged. "It was pretty anticlimactic, to be honest."

"The police wouldn't let him into the room while they opened the box." Lance sounded annoyed. He set Maestro down, who immediately ran over to Jules.

"They had me wait in a room with a table and

uncomfortable plastic chairs." Jules patted the Maltese on the head before straightening. The dog looked at him a moment longer before he padded over to me and flopped onto his back, exposing his belly for rubs.

I obliged as I asked, "And a dartboard and a couch?"

Jules's smile finally managed to break through. "I take it you know the place?"

"All too well." Let's just say I was a frequent visitor to the Pine Hills police station interrogation room. Or did they call it an interview room? Either way, it wasn't one of my favorite places.

"Well, they had me wait there for what felt like forever," Jules said.

"I just about closed up shop and went looking for him," Lance added. "The wait was awful."

"For the both of us." Jules and Lance shared a look before Jules went on. "Eventually, they came in and told me that nothing exploded and that there was nothing life threatening in the box. Detective Buchannan acted like I'd wasted his time."

A part of me was relieved, but at the same time, I felt bad for getting the police involved. "I'm sorry," I said, giving Maestro one last belly rub before rising from my crouch. "I didn't mean to scare you."

"Don't apologize," Jules said. "I'm glad you warned me. Just because the box didn't explode or wasn't rigged like some booby trap out of a movie, doesn't mean it wasn't dangerous."

When Jules didn't immediately continue, I looked to Lance for an explanation, but only got a frown as a response, which made me even more curious. Was the gift something intimately personal? Something that only Lance and Jules would understand? It would make sense, considering how Andrew hadn't told his wife what was in his own gift before running off to Andrew's Gifts to be murdered. It might also explain why the contents of the box were missing.

Which reminded me . . .

"Do you know if there was packaging in the box? Bubble Wrap, newspaper, anything at all?"

Jules shook his head. "I don't know. Detective Buchannan never said, and I didn't take the box back. I didn't want it."

Because he knew what was inside and it scared or embarrassed him? Or because it was threatening?

"Do you think your gift was tied to Andrew Carver's murder?" I asked.

"I don't know," he repeated, glancing at Lance. "The police aren't sure what it means."

"Do you have an idea?"

The two men stared at one another. I might not have been able to hear it, but I was positive something important passed between them.

"She should know," Lance said.

"Know what?" Slight panic crept into my voice.

Neither man answered. Jules picked up his mug and held it under his nose, eyes never leaving Lance's own.

"Jules? Lance? What should I know?"

Jules took a large gulp from his mug. Sweat immediately beaded his brow. He wiped it away with the back of his hand before answering. "I don't want to worry you."

"Too late," I said. "What was in the box?"

"A bag of coffee."

I opened my mouth to say something profound, but all I managed was a confused, "Coffee?"

Jules nodded. "And a note." A pause before, "From you."

"What do you mean 'from me?' I didn't leave you that gift."

"We know you didn't," Lance said. "But it was made to appear as if you had." Maestro barked once, and then left the room, apparently unhappy with the cessation of attention.

"You can expect a visit from Detective Buchannan sometime soon, I imagine," Jules said. "He doesn't believe you had anything to do with the package or what happened to Andrew Carver, but he thinks there's a chance you might know *why* this is happening."

"Me? Why?" There was a tone of desperation in my voice. "I didn't do anything!" I took a deep breath. Buchannan coming to talk to me wasn't the end of the world. In fact, I should have expected it. "What did the note say?"

"Not much, really," Jules said, setting aside his mug again and pushing it away as if he wanted nothing else to do with coffee ever again. "Only that I'm to try out the coffee and then meet you later tonight to talk about it."

A sinking filling caused my next words to come out as a whisper. "Meet me where?"

"At Death by Coffee. And I'm to come alone."

* * *

Misfit snoozed next to me as I stared at the TV, not really seeing it. The weather report stated it was looking good for snow sometime later in the week, but it wasn't a guarantee.

And . . .

And I remembered nothing else. I couldn't focus on anything but the fact that the mysterious blue-wrapped gift was a lure for Jules to go to Death by Coffee after closing. For what? To be murdered? Was I supposed to have received a gift as well, but it had somehow gotten delayed or stolen from my front door?

Or was I to be framed for Jules's death?

Anxiety tugged at me, made me want to jump into my car and rush to Death by Coffee to make sure no one was there. Jules had assured me that Detective Buchannan had everything under control, that he'd told him *not* to tell me about the threat. Apparently, Buchannan had a plan.

A cheery, holiday commercial starring a re-worked version of the old *Rudolph the Red-Nosed Reindeer* movie came on. I snapped the TV off just as Rudolph exclaimed how great the seasonal sale at the car dealership was going to be.

Doris Appleton would have just *loved* that commercial.

A car pulled into my driveway, lighting up the living room briefly as the headlights passed by the windows. I patted Misfit, who'd raised his head at the sound, and then went to the door. I opened it just as Paul stepped out of his car.

As always, a flare of warmth shot through me. It happened every time I saw Paul Dalton, even when things were at their most dire. Like now.

He stepped up and immediately wrapped me in a hug. "Are you all right?"

I nodded and stepped back long enough to let him in. As soon as he was through the door and had removed his hat, I snuggled up close to him.

"As good as I can be, I suppose," I said. "I've been sitting here worrying my head off."

"I talked to John before coming over." Paul put his arm around me and escorted me to the island counter. "Do you know what was in the box Jules received?"

I nodded. "I talked to Jules a little while ago."

"Well, John's setting up an operation at Death by Coffee that will hopefully catch whoever sent the gift." *And killed Andrew Carver* was implied.

"Good." I frowned. "He's not going to break the windows or anything, is he?"

Paul smiled. "No. But he and a few other cops are watching the doors. If anyone tries to get in, they'll catch them."

I wasn't reassured, not with John Buchannan in charge. "Shouldn't you be there?"

"John has everyone he needs." Paul hugged me close before releasing me. "I'm needed here."

There was that flare of warmth again. This time, it was accompanied by a toe curl.

"Do you still have the gift box?" Paul asked, glancing around the room. "The one you said came from Andrew's Gifts?"

"Yeah. One sec." I hurried to the spare room and retrieved the blue-paper wrapped box. Misfit watched me with interest as I handed it over to Paul. "I can't believe someone would target Jules like this."

"We'll hopefully know more soon," Paul said as he examined the box I'd given him. "There's not much to it, is there?"

"Andrew's wife, Erin, didn't know what was inside it. I doubt it was a bag of coffee, though."

"Probably not." I'd hoped Paul might speculate, but he simply tucked the box under his arm. "Did Mrs. Carver say anything that might be important when you talked to her?"

"Not really. She mentioned Andrew might have had a problem with another business called Heavenly Gate. I'm not sure how that would involve Jules." Or me, for that matter. "Do you think someone is targeting businesses in town? Has anyone else received a present like this?" I motioned toward the box under Paul's arm.

"Not that I'm aware," he said. "And if all goes well tonight, not one else will." His brow furrowed. "How sure are you that the gift is tied to Mr. Carver's murder?"

"It almost has to be, doesn't it? I can't imagine it *not* being connected. I didn't send it to Jules, which means someone else was trying to lure him to Death by Coffee in the middle of the night, when no one would be there."

Paul patted the air. I hadn't realized my voice was rising to a shout.

"I'm not dismissing your theory," Paul said. "We have to consider all of the possibilities or else we might miss something important. The gifts could be a joke, one done in bad taste. Mr. Carver could have walked in on a theft and the thief panicked and killed him."

"And what? The thief just so happened to steal whatever was in the box?"

"I know, it's unlikely, but it could have happened." Paul sighed, squeezed my shoulder. "I don't want to fight. I believe you. And I believe that all of this does tie together. I'm just telling you what John might be thinking, and that we're looking at all angles here. You have nothing to worry about."

I took a deep breath and closed my eyes. Paul was right. There was no reason to get angry with him. No, I didn't believe that it was all just one big coincidence, but if the gifts really *didn't* have anything to do with the murder, then a killer might go free because Buchannan was focused on the wrong thing.

"Have you had any unwanted guests recently?" Paul asked. "Seen anyone prowling around the neighborhood? Both here or at Death by Coffee?"

"I haven't seen anyone," I said. "At least, no one has come to my door. And if they did show up at some point, I've been over at Jules's and Cait—" My eyes widened. "Jacob!"

Paul frowned. "Who's Jacob?"

"Jacob . . . I don't think he ever said his last name. He's Caitlin's friend. He's next door right now."

"And?"

"And I saw him fight with Andrew Carver the day of his death. Andrew's death, not Jacob's." I took a breath to calm myself. Babbling madly wouldn't help anyone. "Andrew accused Jacob of being a thief or something like that and then kicked him out of his store."

"That doesn't mean he killed him."

"No, but when I talked to Caitlin, she mentioned that Jacob was late for a meeting with another friend of theirs; a guy named Teek."

Paul's eyebrows rose. "Teek?"

"Yeah, I know. I don't know if that's his real name or a nickname. But he was supposed to meet with Jacob last night and Jacob was late."

"Once again—"

I finished for him. "That doesn't mean he killed him; I know." Still, it was starting to look bad for Jacob. "Caitlin said that Jacob was acting strange, like he was nervous about something. She thought he'd stopped by because of Boo . . ."

"Do I want to know?"

"His girlfriend. I don't know her."

"I see." Paul shifted the box from one arm to the other, handling it gingerly. "Go on."

"That's kind of it," I said. Now that I'd said it out loud, doubts were starting to creep in. "I know being late for a meeting and acting nervous doesn't really mean much."

"No, it doesn't," Paul agreed.

"But add to that the argument with Andrew, and that Jacob is now next door . . ." I gave him a meaningful look.

Paul caught on quickly. "Where he could keep an eye on both you and Jules to see if you took the bait."

I pointed at him and nodded. "What if Jacob is angry about how everyone treats him. Caitlin said he's always getting harassed by people because of how he looks and how he dresses."

"But neither you nor Jules would treat him like that."

I paused. Paul was right. Jules and Lance treated everyone with respect. And I'd never harass someone for how they looked. I mean, I wasn't winning any fashion awards. Who was I to judge how anyone dressed?

But could someone else at Death by Coffee have said something Jacob took the wrong way? I didn't think anyone *would*, but that doesn't mean it didn't happen. And if not a worker, a customer, perhaps? That made more sense, but why would Jacob target the store for something a customer said? Could he be angry that no one stepped in to stop it?

"If Jacob was the one who'd sent the gift and is watching Jules and me, then he won't end up at Death by Coffee for Buchannan to catch."

Paul glanced toward the window facing Caitlin's house. The curtain was drawn, so there was nothing to see. "I'll look into him," he said. "But without a last name . . ."

"I know. It won't be easy."

Paul leaned forward and kissed me on the corner of the mouth. "Lock up good and tight tonight, all right? And if you hear anything at all suspicious, call me. I don't care if it's coming from inside or outside your house, don't investigate on your own, okay?"

"Okay." And then, because I couldn't resist. "If you want, you could always stay here."

Paul smiled. "I wish I could, but I've got to get this box to the station and fill John in on what you told me. It might affect his plans tonight."

I didn't like it, but I understood. "You're still coming to dinner tomorrow at Geraldo's, right?"

"I am." Paul sucked in a deep breath and let it out in a huff. "I think I'm going to need the break."

That went doubly for me.

"All right," he said, hefting the lightweight box. "I'd better get this back to the station. Be safe tonight, Krissy. If you hear *anything*—"

"I know. I'll call." I leaned in for another kiss. With how I was feeling, I needed it. "I'll see you to-morrow."

Paul placed his hat on his head, touched the brim with a crooked smile that was reminiscent of a sheriff in an old cowboy movie, and then he headed for the door.

As soon as he was gone, I made sure to lock the door and then went around to all the windows to check that they were secure. When I reached the living room window, I parted the curtain and peeked outside, toward Caitlin's house. Jacob's car was still in the driveway, and the lights were on in her house, but I couldn't see anyone.

Be careful, Caitlin.

I checked the lock on the window one last time, and then I let the curtain fall.

10

A chocolate chip cookie sat at the bottom of the Death by Coffee to-go cup. Small bubbles rose and burst as I poured in coffee, bringing with them tiny chunks of the cookie. Bleary-eyed, I took a sip, savored the flavor, and then let loose with a yawn that threatened to go on forever.

Needless to say, after the day I'd had, I didn't sleep all that well. I spent half the night at the window, watching Caitlin's house, worried that Jacob would come sneaking out of it at any moment, intent on murdering both Jules and me in our sleep. When I did attempt to lie down, I ended up tossing and turning until I was up again, peering out the window.

Which was why I'd seen Jacob leave Caitlin's house a few minutes after midnight. Instead of crossing the yard to my house, knife in hand, he instead climbed into his car and drove off with a chugging of an engine that would have woken me up if I had been asleep. He wasn't sneaking up on anyone in a car like that.

After that, I managed to get a little shut-eye, but every sound had me jerking awake, scanning the dark for any hint of movement. Misfit slept through it all.

I leaned against the counter and continued to sip at my coffee, ignoring the questioning stares coming from the dining room of Death by Coffee. Almost everyone who worked for me was there, sitting in a small huddle. Even with the heat on, I felt chilled, and it was only going to get colder.

The door opened and the last employee staggered in, looking as pooped as I felt. Then again, Eugene Dohmer always looked that way. His long, skinny legs appeared as if they belonged on a scarecrow as he crossed the room and took a seat next to Lena.

"All right, everyone is here." I stifled another yawn as I straightened. "I'm sure you've all heard about the murder that happened down the street the other night?" Nods followed. "And I'm sure rumors have gone around about how and why the man was killed."

Jeff Braun raised a hand. He waited until I acknowledged him to speak. "Was Mr. Phan attacked?"

It appeared as if rumors of what had happened at Phantastic Candies had also spread. "No, Jules is fine." Relieved sighs went around the room. "But he *did* receive a package that was similar to the one Andrew Carver found on his doorstep before his murder."

This was met with grumbling. Beth asked, "Are we in danger?"

"I don't know," I admitted. "That's why I called everyone in here so early." I took a large gulp of coffee to consider my next words. Should I bring up the note luring Jules to Death by Coffee? Or should I skip over it in the hopes that nothing would come of it now that the police were on the case?

There didn't appear to be a right answer. If I told them about the note, that might scare them. At the same time, leaving it out would leave them unprepared if the killer were to make a move.

"The police don't know for sure if the gifts are tied to the murder," I said, "but I wanted to be safe and let you all know about them. If you receive a mysterious package, here or at home, call the police immediately. If you see someone lurking around here or at your home, do the same."

Pooky Cooper's eyes were so wide, they looked as if they were about to fall out. "Any sort of package? Like from Amazon?" she asked.

"Honestly? I don't know. The one Jules received was wrapped in blue paper and had no identifying marks." I took a breath. "A note inside attempted to lure him to Death by Coffee after closing."

"Here?" Beth's brow furrowed. "Why here?" Her question was met with raised voices as the rest of the group chimed in.

I raised my hands to quiet them. "I'm not trying to scare anyone," I said. "I'm telling you just so you're prepared in case something *does* show up. The police were here last night—"

"Detective Buchannan?" Lena asked.

I nodded. "From what I was told, he set up a trap for the killer." Though I didn't know if anything had come of it. I figured I would have heard *something* if the killer had been caught, but so far, I'd been told nothing, though it was still early.

"Should we do something?" Eugene asked. "Like, check the ID of everyone who comes in?"

"I don't think that will be necessary," I said. "As I said, I just wanted you to know what happened and for you to be on the lookout for any mysterious packages. It's not a bomb. It's not poisoned or rigged with knives or anything of the sort."

Worried glances and more grumbling followed.

I knew I was only making them worry, but I didn't know what else to do. I'd rather make everyone nervous than have a box show up on one of their doorsteps with them having no idea that it might have come from a killer.

A glance at the clock told me we were nearly out of time. "I'm sorry I woke some of you for this. You can grab a coffee or a cookie on your way out." And then, because I wanted them to be reassured, "The police are on the case."

As one, they rose, though only a few took me up on my offer of coffee. Jeff headed for the door looking like he expected a killer to slither out of the tiles, or leap from the top of a nearby building, at any moment. As he exited, someone else pushed in past him, ignoring the CLOSED sign still hanging from the door.

Donnie Cooper scowled as he came to a stop, just inside the door. Pooky's brother, Donnie, had recently fallen on some tough times and had been staying with Pooky before she was forced to kick him out for taking advantage of her hospitality. I had a little something to do with that, and Donnie obviously hadn't forgiven me for it. He glared a hole through me before he turned to Pooky, who'd just finished pouring herself a coffee to go.

"Donnie? What are you doing here?"

"Claire."

I winced. Pooky hated when anyone called her by her given name. A part of me wanted to step in and help her deal with him, but at the same time, it wasn't my place to interfere, not without her permission.

Besides, it didn't appear as if she needed my help.

Pooky jammed a fist into her hip, eyes narrowing. "Excuse me?"

"Sorry," Donnie said, ducking his head. "Pooky." He made a face like just saying her nickname put a bad taste in his mouth. "I tried you at home."

"This early? You know I'd either still be asleep or here at work."

Donnie shrugged, would have looked embarrassed but for the half-sneer on his face. "I was up and decided to check in on you. Can't fault me for that."

Pooky sighed. She noted me standing nearby, obviously eavesdropping, but instead of pulling Donnie aside, she seemed to gain strength from having me there.

"Look Donnie, we're not going to do this here. I understand your predicament, and I care, I really do. But there's nothing I can do for you right now."

Donnie glanced at me out of the corner of his eye. "Yeah, I know, but—"

"No." Pooky cut him off with a slash of her hand. "I'm not doing this. Not now. Not here. If you want to come back to my place, we can sit down and talk like two grown adults."

His scowl deepened, but he nodded. "Whatever. I guess I'll see you in a little bit." He paused to shoot me one more death-glare, and then he turned and walked out.

I opened my mouth to speak, but Pooky beat me to it.

"I'm sorry about that. Donnie still thinks he can keep pressuring me and he'll eventually get his way. He's my brother and I love him, but there's no way I'm going to go through that again." The last time she had let him move in with her, he'd taken over her life. Her work had suffered and she'd been miserable.

"You'll be okay?" I asked.

Pooky's smile was reassuring. "I will. Thank you." The smile faltered and died. "But I think I might talk to him about that gift thing, just in case. If something were to happen to him . . ." She shuddered, and then followed her brother out the door.

No more early morning surprises followed. The next twenty minutes were spent solely on finishing morning setup. The plan had Eugene working upstairs with Beth handling taking orders downstairs. Lena would serve as a floater between them, jumping in wherever she was needed. That left me free to do as I pleased, which included heading out to run errands.

But even though they had everything well under control, I decided to stick around and chip in where I could. I kept expecting Detective Buchannan to show up to tell me how last night's stakeout had gone, but he never did. When we opened the doors to the morning rush, I forgot completely about Buchannan and killers because we were *slammed*.

Peppermint cappuccinos were the order of the day. Second by second, the candy canes dwindled down to almost nothing. I was worried they wouldn't last the day and made a mental note to check with Jules about getting more.

Upstairs, Eugene had his hands full with a small contingent of older women who were determined to chat him up, despite other customers looking to check out. Every so often, he'd look to me for help, but I was stuck filling coffee orders or wiping down tables.

When the rush finally slowed, and then blessedly stopped, I helped Beth clean up behind the counter before I joined Lena in the dining area to tidy up the tables and empty the near-overflowing trashcans. I, of course, had ulterior motives in joining her.

"How are you holding up?" I asked, desperately trying not to glance toward her bruised arm and failing miserably.

"Good." Lena shot me a smile and then turned quickly away. "Been keeping busy. Thanks for letting me come in to help."

"You know you're always welcome." I eyed her with a frown. Her shoulders were hunched as if she expected a blow. "Are you okay? Really?"

Lena picked up a half-eaten candy cane and tossed it into the nearest trashcan. "Yeah, sure."

That wasn't reassuring in the slightest.

"Zay—"

"We're good," she said before I could finish the thought. "It's just been a lot, you know?"

No, I didn't, but I wished I did. "If you need to talk . . ."

She turned a smile on me. "Thanks. I'm okay. Just got a lot on my mind."

The door opened and two women came in, carrying similar well-wrapped bundles. Lena used the distraction to slip away to the back, muttering something about grabbing fresh trash bags as she went.

"Trisha!" I said, turning to the new arrivals. "Shannon. It's good to see you both." I approached them, unable to keep the goofy grin off my face. "And R.J. and Shay. How are you two doing?"

There's a thing about babies that makes some people lose their minds. I'd always thought it was something that only happened to other people, yet from the moment I'd laid eyes on Robert Dunhill Jr. and Shay Pardue, I turned into one of those people.

Strange sounds burbled from my lips as I looked down at their chubby faces. Even the fact that R.J. was my ex-boyfriend's son couldn't damper my excitement at seeing the two babies, despite past tensions I'd had with their mothers due to them each having dated boyfriends of mine; Trisha with my ex, Robert, and Shannon with my current, Paul.

"Hey, Krissy," Shannon said, handing over Shay without me having to ask. The baby girl was snoozing so deeply that she didn't stir with the transfer. She was practically lost beneath the layers of blankets protecting her from the cold. "I'm going to run to the restroom real quick. Be right back."

I was too busy making faces at Shay to respond, let alone notice when she hurried off.

"These two are a handful," Trisha said, bouncing R.J., who unlike Shay, was wide awake and babbling incomprehensibly. "I wouldn't be surprised if she takes a quick nap in there."

"How's Robert handling it?" Robert Dunhill was a man I'd never imagined as a father, yet here we were.

"Surprisingly well, actually," Trisha said with a laugh. "Though I think he's starting to worry himself a little too much over making sure R.J. is taken care of. He's been looking for opportunities to increase our income."

"Like a second job?" Not that I knew if he even had a *first* job.

"Kind of." Trisha moved R.J. from one arm to the other. "He's been talking about getting a loan to buy a local business. I'm not sure how he expects to secure a loan of all things, but he's pretty adamant about it."

Robert had a tendency to act before he thought, hence his cheating on me back when we were dating. He'd also followed me all the way from California to Pine Hills, Ohio, in a vain attempt at winning me back. I was worried that he might be following a similar dead-end path with the new business and would drag both Trisha and R.J. down with him.

"What do you think about his plan?" I asked.

Trisha shrugged one shoulder. "If it works out, I'm all for it. Babies are far more expensive than I realized. Don't get me wrong, I wouldn't give him up for anything, but we've had to tighten our belts these last few weeks."

Considering Trisha had recently been twice as big as she now was due to her pregnancy she could have meant literally, but I got what she meant.

"Do you know what place he's looking to buy?" I asked, wondering if I already knew, considering my conversation with Justin about Ted and Bettfast.

"Honestly? I'm not sure. You know how excited he gets about things. He sometimes forgets to fill the rest of us in on what he's thinking until *after* he's gone through with it."

Oh, I knew all right. "Well, I hope it works out."

Shannon returned then and took Shay back. She didn't look as if she'd napped, but she *did* look refreshed, like the brief break had helped rejuvenate her. Trisha had Robert to help her keep up with the newborn. Shannon was on her own. The baby's father wasn't in the picture. I didn't even know who he was, or if he even cared that he had a daughter.

"I really should get her to her crib," Shannon said. "If I can get her to sleep for more than an hour, it'll be a miracle." She yawned. "I could use a little shut-eye myself."

"R.J. should get his nap too," Trisha said, though R.J. looked as if he was ready to spend the rest of the day wide awake. "We saw your car outside and wanted to stop in after our morning class and say hi." Both Trisha and Shannon had signed up for some sort of parent and baby bonding class. Not being a parent, I had no idea what that entailed, but it made them both happy.

"I'm glad you did. If either of you need someone to watch the little ones while you get some sleep, let me know. I'll happily babysit them for you."

"I might take you up on that," Shannon said.

"Me too."

R.J. made a high-pitched squeal I took for a third vote in my favor.

I followed Trisha and Shannon to the door, intent on walking them out. And to get a little more time with the little ones, of course. When they stepped outside, a cold blast of wind shot straight though me, causing my teeth to chatter.

"I hear it's only going to get worse," Shannon said, pulling Shay close to her chest.

"Maybe it *will* snow for Christmas," Trisha said, looking to the flake-free sky.

"We can hope," I said, although a part of me wouldn't entirely miss it if it wouldn't. I hated driving in the stuff, though it *was* pretty.

The two women said their goodbyes and hurried for Shannon's car. It took them a few moments to get the babies safely secured in the back seat, and then they were off with a honk and a wave.

I went back into the warmth of Death by Coffee to grab my coat and purse. I had a few things I wanted to get done before dinner with Paul, Dad, and Laura tonight, and I was already behind schedule, thanks to the morning rush keeping me at Death by Coffee longer than I'd planned.

Once I was bundled up, I headed for the door, but stopped dead when I saw the black-clad figure standing on the sidewalk outside.

Jacob was looking in through the window, a leather jacket covering a shirt with some sort of indecipherable scrawl across the chest and a black-robed figure in a forest beneath. He saw me looking at him, but instead of waving or coming in, he suddenly turned and started walking at a quick clip away from the store.

Well now, that was odd.

So odd that I found myself moving forward at a quick pace of my own. I stepped out into the frigid cold and turned toward where Jacob was hoofing it down the sidewalk, hands shoved deep into his pockets, with his wallet chain slapping the side of his leg.

My car was sitting right there. The smart thing to do would be to climb in and drive off so I could get my errands finished.

But when did I ever do the smart thing?

With shoulders hunched against the cold, I followed after a man who very well might be a murderer.

11

"Jacob!"

He didn't acknowledge my shout, which, admittedly, wasn't all that loud to begin with. I was torn between getting him to stop and seeing where he'd go. Had he been watching me, plotting a way to get me alone to enact his foiled murder plot? Or had Jacob merely been considering whether to stop in for a quick cup of coffee?

He was moving at a quick pace, but not at a run. If I'd really wanted to, I could have caught up to him, yet I found myself walking at the same speed as he was. My nose was running and my cheeks were starting to turn a vibrant red from the cold. Clouds had moved in, and I hoped that if they did decide to drop snow on us, they'd wait until I was someplace with a roof.

As Jacob approached Andrew's Gifts, he slowed until he was standing in front of it, hands shoved into his pockets, breath pluming from his nose and mouth. He stared at the front door for a long time, long enough that the cold started to seep in through my coat, all the way into my bones. And then, with a shrug, he turned away and started walking again.

There weren't very many people on the sidewalks of downtown Pine Hills, not in this weather. Most everyone was driving anywhere they needed to go, even if it was only a block away. That meant that if Jacob were to glance behind him, I'd have nowhere to hide, no groups to blend into.

But so far, he seemed to have a singular purpose, though I had no idea what that purpose might be.

He's probably just out for a walk. Which meant I was freezing my butt off for no reason.

I was considering calling off my tail, when Jacob came to an abrupt halt. It took me a moment to realize he was standing outside Heavenly Gate. Even from as far away as I was, I could see the calculation on his face as he scanned the front window.

"What are you up to?" I muttered, moving up next to a place called Fern's Perms. Inside, women, and one man, were getting their hair done. Two of them were watching me, curious as to why I was loitering. If Jacob were to glance my way, I could duck inside, and hey, maybe getting my hair done before dinner tonight wouldn't be such a bad idea.

But he didn't look my way. Instead, Jacob heaved a sigh, wiped a hand across his nose, and then entered Heavenly Gate.

I lingered outside Fern's as I debated on what to do. As far as I knew, Jacob's parents worked at Heavenly Gate, which would explain why a black-clad guy into loud, heavy music would go inside a place that sold religious items. On the other hand, Jacob *had* also stopped outside of Andrew's Gifts, a place where he'd gotten into a fight before the owner had been murdered. He'd been near my house on the day the gift had arrived for Jules. And now he was here, at another local business.

Coincidence?

There was only one way to find out.

I started forward, mind working overtime. If Jacob *was* related to, or friends with, the owners of Heavenly Gate, it didn't help him all that much considering what Erin had told me about Andrew's trouble with someone from the store. They could have sent Jacob to take care of Andrew like he was a hitman out of a crime movie.

Or I'm overthinking it. Not that I'd ever do that. I could almost see Paul's eyeroll.

Just as I reached the front of the religious craft shop, the door opened and Jacob came hurtling back out, arms pinwheeling as he fought to keep from falling face-first into the street.

"Stay out of here you little punk!"

A man with hairy, overly large forearms stood in the doorway, tiny glasses perched at the end of a rather round nose. His face was cherry red, though I couldn't tell if that was because he was angry, or if it was from the cold.

"I didn't do anything!" Jacob said, righting himself.

"You sort of people don't have to."

"Yeah? And what's that supposed to mean?"

"Look at you!" The man jabbed a thick finger

into Jacob's chest, knocking him back a step. "Look at *that.*"

Jacob glanced down at his shirt and the indecipherable lettering that made up what I assumed was a band name. "What about it?"

"You're promoting evil and you come into *my* store? I don't think so."

"It's not evil." Though Jacob did cross his arms over his chest, covering the band name. "It's called music. Entertainment. You know, just like horror movies and scary books?"

The man laughed. "And you think that helps your case?" He shook his head, and in doing so, noticed me standing a few feet away. He straightened his back, his condescending smile vanishing like smoke. "Just stay out of here. You're not welcome in my shop."

And with that, the big man turned and walked back into Heavenly Gate.

Jacob looked like he might march right back in after him, but he too saw me standing there and said instead, "Can you believe this sh—" He paused, cleared his throat and finished with a lame, "crap?" He shot a side-eyed look at a handmade wooden cross in the window.

"Why'd you even go in there?" I asked, genuinely curious. I mean, I wasn't one to judge anyone for their appearance, but Jacob's outfit didn't scream crosses and angels.

"My mom." He sighed and shoved his hands back into his pockets, giving him a hunched, almost aw-shucks appearance. "She's into this sort of thing. You know, religious stuff? I thought I might get her something for Christmas, but that guy . . ." He made a frustrated sound.

"This seems to happen to you a lot."

"No sh—" He cut off again and amended it to, "No kidding. I haven't done anything to any of these people, yet they treat me like I'm some sort of delinquent. Aren't we *not* supposed to judge people by their appearance? Just because I listen to this sort of music, doesn't mean I'm a criminal or out looking to burn down churches or something. I mean, I heard Tom Araya is Catholic!"

I had no idea who that was and didn't ask. "So, you came here to shop? Like you did at Andrew's Gifts the other day?"

Jacob's wind-chapped, scarlet cheeks reddened further. "Yeah." He sniffed and wiped at his nose. "I'm not trying to start anything. But I guess I do tend to goad these people a little bit when they start in on me like that." He flung a hand toward Heavenly Gate, which caused my attention to shift to what was going on inside the store.

The owner was standing near the counter, which was situated at the back of the store, talking to a woman. A woman I recognized.

Agnes, one of Doris's outraged crew, said something to the man, touched him on a hairy arm, and then walked through a door behind the counter. I caught a glimpse of wooden shapes lying next to sharp-looking tools on a long, metal table, and then the door closed, cutting her, and the equipment, from view.

Why would one of Doris's friends be here? I wondered. Could she be the wife Erin had mentioned?

"What am I supposed to do?" Jacob complained,

drawing my attention back to him. "Dress up and pretend I'm someone else just so I can shop without being harassed? It's not fair."

No, it wasn't. Despite my concern that Jacob might be the killer, I found I was sympathetic toward him. No one should be treated like an outcast because of how they looked or what kind of music they listened to.

Still, sympathetic or not, I wasn't going to let him entirely off the hook. "What does Boo think?" I asked, watching his face to see what kind of reaction I'd get.

He simply raised an eyebrow at me. "Caitlin talked to you about her?"

I didn't want to get Caitlin into trouble, but I didn't know how else to explain how I knew Boo's name. "She mentioned Boo when I asked her why you were at her house yesterday. Did you and Boo have a fight?"

Jacob scratched his cheek. "No, it's nothing like that." He looked away when he said it.

The wind picked up, causing my eyes to water. If I stayed standing out there for much longer, I'd freeze to the spot. "Do you want to head back to Death by Coffee and get a hot drink?" I asked. "We could talk about it if you want to." Not that I knew what "it" was.

Jacob glanced at me, a slight frown on his face as if he wasn't sure he should trust me. "Actually, I'd best get going."

"Meeting Boo?" When he flinched, I added, "Teek?"

"See you around. Krissy, right?" He looked me up and down and I got the distinct impression he was passing some sort of judgment on me. Good or bad? I had no idea. "Maybe I'll see you at Caitlin's." And with that, he spun on his heel and walked away.

Chilled to the bone, I decided to warm up by entering Heavenly Gate. From what I'd seen and heard, I was leaning toward Jacob's side of the story when it came to how he was being treated, but it couldn't hurt to get another perspective.

Besides, if I could learn something about Andrew and his alleged problem with the people here, it would go a long way in helping me make up my mind on whether I should be concerned for Jules or if it was an intra-shop squabble that had turned deadly.

As I entered, the shop owner snapped, "You with him?" jerking his chin toward Jacob's retreating back.

"No, I'm not, but he's a friend of my neighbor's," I said. "Did he do something to earn that tongue-lashing, Mr. . . . ?"

"Komph. Lee Komph. And, yes, he did. He disturbed the peace."

I glanced around the shop. Other than Agnes, who was still in the back, we were the only two people inside Heavenly Gate. Almost everything on the shelves looked handcrafted and had a religious bent, jibing with what I'd seen from the window.

"Did you make all of these?" I asked, hoping to bring down the hostility levels. "They are impressive."

Lee eyed me a moment before nodding. "I did. It's a lot of hard work."

I picked up a woodcarving of the nativity scene. It was surprisingly detailed with faces not just being intricately painted, but with eye sockets carved out, with tiny little mouths cut into the wood. It had to have taken a steady hand and a whole lot of patience.

"These are very good," I said, returning the carving to its place.

"Thank you." Lee's tone suggested he wasn't entirely mollified, but was getting there. "It's why I can't have people like that in here. They ruin the atmosphere bringing their hostility in with them. It breaks my concentration."

"He was shopping for his mom."

Lee snorted and shook his head. "Is that what he told you? People like that never buy anything. They lie, cheat, and steal. No exceptions."

"Andrew Carver thought the same way about Jacob."

Lee's entire body went rigid, eyes cold as the wind outside. "Andrew Carver and I had nothing in common."

"You both owned shops on the same street here in Pine Hills," I pointed out.

Lee ground his teeth briefly before turning away. "Look, I've got work to do. If you're not buying anything, then I'd appreciate it if you left."

I remained right where I was. "I heard your wife and Andrew didn't get along. Do you know anything about that?"

Lee spun back around and took two large strides toward me. He stopped directly in front of me, so close I could feel his breath on my cheek. Our noses were inches apart, eyes locked so that I could see the tiny red veins in them.

"Agnes had nothing to do with that man. He was a scourge on our town and if she spoke to him, it was to tell him so."

Every instinct screamed at me to take a step back, but I held my ground. Lee Komph appeared to be a volatile man who wanted to dominate every situation. It seemed a strange contrast to a guy who spent hours carving and painting peaceful trinkets in such beautiful detail.

"I saw her with Doris," I said, not sure where I was going with this. "Do you know Doris Appleton?"

"Of course, I do." Lee was near shouting now. "I don't see how any of this has to do with that punk who'd come in here to disrupt my work." Thankfully, he took a step back then, giving me space to breathe. "I think you should go."

Me being me, I really wanted to press him about Andrew, about Doris and Agnes and Jacob.

But what would that accomplish other than getting me bodily thrown out of Heavenly Gate like Jacob before me? Lee was angry, and I supposed it was understandable since I'd implied that he or his wife could have had something to do with Andrew Carver, and quite possibly his death.

"I'm sorry if I bothered you," I said, ducking my head in a way I hoped he took as subservient. If he *was* Andrew's killer, I didn't want him targeting me next. "I wasn't trying to start anything. With everything that's happened . . ." I let him fill in the rest on his own.

Lee's jaw worked silently before he said, "Well, if

you keep hanging around people like that—" That phrase again. It was really getting on my nerves, and I think Lee could tell because he smiled. "—you'll end up like Andrew and his ilk."

A threat? Or just Lee being a jerk because that was who he was?

"I guess I'll take my chances," I said, and then I turned and walked out of the gift shop.

The cold met me like a slap, but I barely felt it. My skin was hot with my own rage, and it was all I could do to keep from marching back inside and giving Lee Komph and his wife a piece of my mind.

Jacob might be a little strange, might like his entertainment and clothing dark, but that didn't mean he was a bad person. If he killed Andrew and had planned to do the same to Jules or me, then, well, yeah, he was. But clothing and music didn't make someone evil, no matter what Lee Komph thought.

And to look down upon me, just because Jacob and I had talked? I supposed that meant Lee was a proponent of guilty by association. Was that why he was so adamant that his wife had nothing to do with Andrew Carver? If she'd talked to him in a way that wasn't antagonistic that meant . . . what? That she was on his side? That she would help Andrew smear Lee's name because she didn't treat him like the enemy?

To Lee Komph, that very well might have been the case.

And an angry man like that might take it upon himself to do something about it.

12

"Excuse me. Sorry."

I adjusted my hold on my bags and turned so the young couple could pass. Despite wearing heavy gloves, they were holding hands and were reluctant to let go of one another. There was a murmured apology, a "Thanks," and then they were gone, walking down the freezing sidewalk, still hand in hand.

I also continued on my way, but without the hand holding. I'd gone a smidge overboard during my shopping trip, but after all the negativity swirling around Pine Hills thanks to the murder, I needed to focus on something happy. My tree at home was already crammed full of gifts underneath, so I'd have to come up with somewhere else to put my most recent purchases, including the pack of new catnip-filled toys for Misfit. If I left them anywhere his nose could find them, they wouldn't last an hour.

The tips of my ears were burning from the cold, as was my nose, so all I wanted to do was get back to my car, dump my purchases inside, and then grab a steaming hot cup of coffee from Death by Coffee before heading home to deal with my plethora of gifts.

But that plan was derailed the moment I started to walk past Andrew's Gifts and saw movement inside.

Erin Carver was standing at the counter, back to me, shoulders hunched. She was making subtle movements, but from my angle, I couldn't tell if she was working on something or if she was crying.

No one else was in the store, which was no surprise, considering. The lights were off, meaning Erin was standing in gloom.

Then, as if she'd sensed me watching, she abruptly turned. Her eyes were dry and she was holding some sort of package in her hand that reminded me of the older version of the army ration bags; MREs, I think they're called. She set the dark brown, thick plastic bag aside, smoothed down her hair, and then approached and opened the door.

"Come in before you freeze to death," she said, stepping aside.

"Thanks." I entered and set my purchases down on the floor before flexing my stiff fingers. The blood rushed back into them, making them tingle. "They should make bags more finger friendly. I swear they're designed to cut your circulation clean off."

Erin managed a wan smile before she returned to the counter. She picked up the brown bag, considered it, and then rounded the counter to place it on a shelf underneath.

"I don't know what I'm doing here," she said. "This was Andrew's haven. I don't even know what's going to happen to this place or everything in it now that he's gone. Knowing my luck, I'm going to be on the hook for it all."

"He didn't leave a will?"

"He did, but the business wasn't specified in it. And the details are . . ." She frowned. "Hazy is the best word I can come up with." She glanced down at where she'd placed the brown package. "All of this was a part of Andrew's life that I wasn't much interested in. I wish I would have paid better attention or asked him some questions, but how was I supposed to know someone was going to kill him?"

I didn't know what to say to that, so I took a moment to glance around at the items on the shelves. Everything was priced higher than what was standard, though I wasn't an expert. I had no idea how Erin was going to sell everything, or if she'd even be allowed to. I assumed that since she was Andrew's wife, it would all pass down to her and she could choose to do with it as she pleased, but I couldn't be sure.

I picked up a nearby board game, and on a whim, carried it to the counter.

"It might not help much, but if you're willing to sell it, I have someone I could give this to."

Erin took the board game and stared down at it for so long, I was worried she might reject the sale. She ran a hand over the top of it, almost lovingly. It was as if the game reminded her of Andrew somehow, and she was reliving a happy memory.

Finally, she took a shuddering breath and carried the game to the register. She rang it up and I paid without a word. Erin bagged the game—a gift for Yolanda and her board game group—and handed it over.

"Thank you for that," she said.

"It's not much."

"No, but it's more than you owe me." She sniffed and rounded the counter. She walked past me, down an aisle full of name-brand toys. She touched each item as if it held some personal significance, much like she had with the board game.

I followed her, building up the nerve to ask her questions about her husband. Erin was hurting, that much was clear. But was she upset because Andrew was dead and she was left with his store with no idea what to do with it? Or was there something more to it? Could she be suffering from something he did to her? Something she did to *him*?

There was only one way to find out.

"I talked to the Komphs," I said. "Or, at least, to Lee."

Erin's step faltered, though she didn't turn around. "I see."

"He seems very angry."

Erin laughed. There was no amusement in the sound. "That, he is."

"How well do you know him?" I asked. "Or his wife, Agnes?"

She ran a hand along a shelf before flicking a hanging price tag and turning toward me. "Okay."

I waited for more, but nothing else appeared forthcoming. "Okay?"

"I know Lee and Agnes Komph a little better

than I might have let on the last time you were here."

She thinks I know something. But what? I decided to play it carefully, letting her continue to make assumptions and hope that she let something slip. "Lee got upset when I brought up Andrew. He insisted Agnes had nothing to do with your husband. We both know that's not true."

Erin dropped her eyes and started worrying at her hands. "No, it's not."

"But they did fight?" At her questioning look, I added, "Agnes and Andrew. You told me you saw them arguing."

"Among other things." Her jaw quivered. In anger? Or sadness? I couldn't tell. "And not just here. I . . . he . . ." She took a deep breath and let it out in a soul-rattling sigh. "Agnes and I were once in a group together."

"The one run by Doris Appleton?"

Surprise flashed across Erin's face before she nodded. "It started out innocent enough, but Doris . . ." She frowned. "She grew too fervent in her faith. She chose a very strict path and if anyone in her circle strayed from that path, she rejected them. There was no room for growth, for other opinions."

That definitely sounded like the Doris I knew.

"Things got so bad that if you even ate something Doris didn't approve of, she'd call you out on it in front of everyone. She'd make it seem like you did it to spite her, to spit in the face of her faith, just because you craved an unapproved alcohol. So, I left." Erin shrugged it off like it was no big deal. "Agnes didn't like that one bit. She accused me of betraying my faith, which was ridiculous. I think Doris put the thought into her head and Agnes ran with it."

"Was Andrew a part of the group?"

Erin grunted a laugh. "Not hardly. He wasn't a man of much faith, not unless you counted money. *That,* he believed in wholeheartedly."

"I bet that didn't go over very well with Doris."

"She didn't like it, no. But her group . . ." Erin frowned, seemed at a loss as what to say. "She prefers surrounding herself with likeminded women. Men, she says, sway with the wind and can't be trusted to stick to the righteous path, even with the guidance of a good woman. I was expected to keep Andrew in line to the best of my ability, and if he strayed, did something that angered Doris, it was my fault." A pause. "My failure."

Interesting. Doris obviously didn't like how Andrew was exploiting Christmas for profit; she said as much at the church. She'd even made it sound like she didn't even *know* Andrew, which struck me as strange. Could she have been trying to distance herself from him? Make it appear as if she didn't know him so that when he died, she could claim she had nothing to do with it?

I wasn't so sure how she thought that might work considering those around her knew Erin was once a part of the group, as did Erin herself. But if they were all afraid of becoming outcasts, then perhaps she expected them to fall in line and pretend right along with her.

But if that was the case, and Andrew's murder had to do with his lifestyle, why target Jules?

Why target *me?*

"I saw Agnes with Andrew."

I blinked, thrown off by the abrupt shift. "Excuse me?"

"Together." Erin wiped at her eyes, which were blinking nearly nonstop now. "I'm not talking about that time I mentioned before where I'd seen them here in the store, but a few days before that. And it wasn't here. It was at home." She swallowed so hard, I actually heard it. "At *my* house."

"Were they . . ." I couldn't bring myself to say it, but Erin understood my meaning.

"Not when I saw them." A tear slid down her cheek, fell from her chin. "I was visiting my sister in Levington, or well, I was supposed to be. I got halfway there when she called and told me that she had to cancel because her husband broke his arm at work and they were stuck in the waiting room. Can you believe it took three hours before a doctor saw him?"

"That's awful." It made me happy that I lived in a small town like Pine Hills where it was far easier to get in to see a doctor. We might not have hospital-quality facilities, but they could set a broken arm in a timely manner.

"Since I was already out, I went ahead and stopped by the Banyon Tree for lunch. If I hadn't done that, I might have caught them doing more than talking. She must have showed up the moment I was out of the house because I wasn't gone all that long before I went home and . . ."

"And saw Andrew with Agnes."

She nodded. "They were in the living room when I got there. I could see them through the window. They were so wrapped up in whatever they were talking about, they didn't hear me pull into the driveway. They were standing close and Andrew had his hand on Agnes's shoulder. Their noses were practically touching."

"Do you have any idea what they were saying?"

Erin shook her head. "I couldn't hear them and I never asked Andrew about it. I couldn't bear to think . . ." She took a deep, shuddering breath. "If something was happening between them, I didn't want to know. I thought maybe Agnes was trying to get back at me, or that she was attempting to convince Andrew to talk me into coming back to the group." She closed her eyes. "Honestly, I don't know what I thought. I want to blame her so badly, but what if Andrew was the one who called her over?"

I was about to ask her point blank if she suspected Andrew and Agnes of sleeping together when my phone rang.

"Go ahead and answer that," Erin said. "I need a minute." She turned and walked to the back of the room, leaving me free to answer the call.

A quick look at the screen showed me a Californian number, but no name. I answered with a tentative "Hello?"

"Hey, Krissy, it's Valerie."

Confused, I replied with a simple, "Valerie?"

"Kemp. You remember me."

Oh, yeah, did I. Valerie had been an absolute terror for me growing up. To this day, I still thought of her as my personal bully despite us living so far apart. Lately, she kept popping up in my life in odd places. At a coffee convention. Outside of Death by Coffee. And now, on the phone.

I wouldn't say these recent interactions were completely unpleasant, but they weren't something I looked forward to.

"I remember," I said, trying to keep the distaste out of my voice. "What can I do for you, Valerie?"

"Oh, not much. But I do I have a quick question for you if you can take a moment from . . . whatever it is you do."

I ground my teeth together to keep from saying something snarky. Valerie knew what I did for a living. This was the pettiness I'd come to loathe.

Across the room, Erin appeared to have composed herself and was pulling on her coat as if preparing to leave.

"Look Valerie, this isn't the best time right now, so if you—"

"How much are you paying your employees?" she asked, completely ignoring my dismissal.

"What?"

"How much money are you paying them?" Spoken slowly. "I was thinking minimum wage, but isn't there some way you can pay them less than that? Like, they take tips or something and you can get away with less?"

My mouth opened and closed, yet I couldn't come up with anything to say other than, "Why?"

"Because employees need to be paid?" I could visualize the massive eyeroll.

"No, but why do you want to know?"

"It's part of my research. You remember, right?"

"I remember you taking pictures of my store."

"Right. So, I could make plans of my own. You know, improve on . . ." She didn't finish the thought, which saved her from having me hang up on her.

"I'm not going to get into the details of what Vicki and I pay our employees," I said. Erin was bundled up and motioned toward the door. I nodded and waved a finger at her: *One minute.* "I've got to go, Valerie. Perhaps—"

"Just a hint? I need a baseline here. It's not like I'm asking you for their checking accounts or anything."

I really should have hung up on her right then and there. I owed Valerie Kemp nothing, but I also didn't like being rude if I could help it. "They get more than minimum. I really do—"

"*More?*" Valerie sounded scandalized. "How could you pay them *more?* They're not doing anything but serving coffee!"

I *so* didn't want to get into this with her right then. Or ever. "They earn it," I said. "And if you want your employees to stick around, you'll need to understand that they do more for you than just serve coffee."

"But—"

It was my turn to cut her off. "I've really got to go, Valerie." And then I clicked off with only a slight pang of guilt. "Sorry," I told Erin. "Old acquaintance."

"I understand." She stepped up to the door. "I'm sorry, but I have something I need to do."

"Yeah, no problem. I don't want to keep you." I gathered my bags, including the board game I'd just purchased, and waddled to the door. Erin held it open for me, followed me out, and then locked it securely behind us.

"Take care," she said before hurrying to her car.

She climbed in and sped off like she was fleeing the scene of a crime.

Which, I supposed, she was.

Still, I watched her go with a sense of trepidation. Something about how she'd rushed off didn't sit right with me. Our conversation had been upsetting; I got that. But why flee like she was afraid I might call the cops? Was Erin worried that she'd revealed too much?

If she caught Agnes with Andrew and thought they were sleeping together, she very well could have killed him for it.

Or told Lee. An angry man like that might act before he thought about the consequences of his actions.

But even if Lee or Erin killed Andrew for sleeping with Lee's wife, how did Jules play into it? How did I? Or Jacob? I needed to talk to Jules again, see if he knew anything about the Komphs or Carvers that would make them want to hurt him.

13

Phantastic Candies looked a lot better than it had the last time I'd been there. The colorful bins were full of candy. There were no stray wrappers scattered about the floor. Even the counter was polished to a shine.

Jules, however, looked terrible.

When I entered, he had his head in his hands where he stood behind the counter. His hair, which was usually styled, looked flat atop his head, as if he'd only managed to run a quick brush through it before sprinting out the door. His clothes were basic, just jeans and a sweater, which was a stark contrast to his usual work garb of extravagant, joyous outfits meant to make the kids smile.

At the sound of me cramming my way inside the store with all my recent purchases, Jules looked up. He had huge dark circles under eyes that were red-rimmed. "Hi, Krissy. Let me help." He started to round the counter.

"No, I've got it." I dragged my bags into the middle of the room before setting them down. "How are you doing, Jules?"

He made a "so-so" gesture. "I haven't slept much, but at least there've been no new mysteries showing up on my doorstep. You?"

"Nothing," I said. "Any strange visitors?"

"Not a one." He sighed. "Are we overreacting? Lance is ready to buy me body armor and replace the windows here with bulletproof glass. I just about had to knock him out to get him to let me come in to work today."

I smiled. The image of Jules trying to fight Lance was amusing considering how buff Lance was by comparison. "He's concerned for you."

"I know. It's flattering and all, but it keeps reminding me that someone out there might want to hurt me."

"Have you come up with any suspects?"

Jules considered it a moment before shaking his head. "Not really. I haven't gotten into an argument with anyone recently, nor has Lance, as far as I'm aware. And I have no connection to the murdered man, Andrew Carver, so why someone would target me, I have no clue." He leaned onto the counter and gave me an imploring look. "What about you? Any luck cracking this thing? I know you're not just out shopping in this cold." He nodded toward my bags.

"No luck yet," I said. "With Dad in town and Vicki and Mason in California, my attention has been split in a hundred different ways. Sorry."

Jules waved off my apology. "Family is important. You *should* be spending time with them, not traipsing all over town in search of a killer." He straightened and shed some of his malaise. "Do you have any big plans coming up? Lance and I are taking it easy this year, so I'd love to live vicariously through you."

"My life is not all that exciting."

Jules gave me a flat look.

"But I guess I *am* going out to dinner at Geraldo's tonight with Dad, Laura, and Paul."

"Really? Dinner with the *whole* family." He waggled his eyebrows.

"I'm not sure what's going to happen," I admitted. "Paul's been hinting that he wants to talk to me about something big, but . . ."

Jules motioned for me to continue. "But?"

I didn't know what to say. Every time I thought Paul was about to spit it out, something would come up and it would get pushed off for another month or so. Was he scared? Excited? Or was I overanalyzing it?

So, instead of trying to explain it to Jules, I said, "Laura's been tired the last couple of days. I think she might have a cold."

"Oh no, is she going to be okay?"

"She'll be fine. But it means we haven't hung out like we'd planned. I'm kind of worried she'll call off dinner so she can get more rest."

"Well, tell her I'm thinking of her when you see her. It's terrible to be sick during the holidays. Growing up, I was stuck with a cold every Christmas and spent most of the day in bed. I felt bad for myself, of course, but also felt like I was letting everyone else down because I was feeling too icky to be social."

"I'm sure your family understood."

"They did, but it still wasn't fun." He paused a moment, eyes going distant, as if remembering those bedridden holidays, before snapping back to the here and now. "I did notice how you didn't answer my question."

I gave him my best "Who? Me?" expression before asking, "Do you know Agnes or Lee Komph?"

If he was surprised by the shift in subject, Jules didn't show it. "I know Lee by reputation and have met Agnes a time or two. Why?"

"I'm not sure." I gave him a brief rundown of what Erin had told me. "Do you think it's possible Agnes and Andrew were seeing one another in secret?"

Jules drummed his finger on the counter before snapping his fingers. "You know, Agnes was in here a few days ago. She wandered around the store like a lost puppy for about five minutes, but she didn't buy anything."

"Was she waiting for someone?" Andrew, perhaps?

"If she was, I never saw who. She just walked around, checked the bins as if inspecting them for bugs, and then she left without a word."

"That seems strange."

"Yeah, it was, though at the time, I didn't think much of it."

"No one met her outside?"

"Not within my field of view. Honestly, I didn't watch her for very long once she left. At the time, I had no reason to."

I could feel it coming on, so I echoed his earlier, "But?"

"But now that I'm thinking about it, I vaguely remember her yelling at someone as she crossed the street. I guess some jerk was speeding and almost hit her, which caused me to look outside in time to see her turn right once she reached the other side."

It didn't take a genius to figure out what he was thinking. "Right. As in, toward Andrew's Gifts."

"Could be. Or she could have gone all the way to Death by Coffee for a hot drink. It was chilly that day. I did find it strange that she was walking around in the cold. She wasn't bundled up for it, that's for sure."

Which made me wonder. Could something have happened to draw Agnes out into the cold? What if Andrew and Erin had a fight and she revealed what she knew about him and Agnes? He might have called Agnes in a panic, told her to meet him at Andrew's Gifts once Erin left. That might explain why she'd waited around Phantastic Candies: she was waiting for Andrew to be alone, but didn't want to do it at Heavenly Gate where Lee might notice her agitation.

"Do you remember what day this was?" I asked, mind racing. Could this have happened on the day Erin claims she saw Agnes and Andrew fighting?

"I don't recall," Jules said. "Sorry."

The door opened and an elderly gentleman entered wearing one of those old hunting hats with earflaps. He touched the fuzzy front brim in greeting before he began perusing the shelves.

I grabbed some chocolate covered caramels and

handed them to Jules to ring up. "I'll let you get back to work," I told him. "And if you get a chance, I could use some more candy canes at Death by Coffee. The peppermint cappuccinos are so popular, we're running out almost as fast as I can stock them."

"Of course," he said, bagging up my purchase. "Are you sure you can carry all of that?" He eyed my multitude of bags with skepticism. "I could always take a break and help you carry everything to your car."

"I'll be fine, but thanks." I took the candy and gathered my bags, which was a bit tricky, considering I was out of hands. "And don't worry yourself. We'll both be okay."

"I hope so." He wrote something down on a pad by the register. "If I get a chance later, I'll drop off the candy canes. I'll call ahead when I've got them all packed up and ready to go."

"Thank you, Jules. Tell Lance I said hi."

"Will do."

I left and began the long walk back to Death by Coffee. Thankfully, because my mind was so far away, the cold barely registered, though my body was still affected by it. The fire burning at my nose and the tips of my ears was raging to the point I was worried I'd given myself frostbite. By the time I'd reached my Escape and shoved all my packages inside, I was anxious to be inside. I all but ran through the doors of Death by Coffee to have a peppermint cappuccino and enjoy it in peace, but alas, it was not to be.

"Ah, Ms. Hancock. Just the woman I was looking for."

I jerked to a stop, suddenly wishing I'd remained out in the cold. "Detective Buchannan," I said, keeping the distaste out of my voice. "Here for a coffee?"

He was holding a Death by Coffee cup, hence the question. He scowled at it as if annoyed to have been caught partaking before answering. "It wasn't my intent when I arrived, no."

Behind the counter, Beth gave me an apologetic look, as if Buchannan being here was somehow her fault. Eugene and Lena were up in the books, lingering at a shelf, watching. When I glanced at them, Lena gave me a thumbs-up.

"Let me get a coffee and we can talk," I said, resigned. If John Buchannan was here, that meant he wanted to discuss the murder investigation, as Jules had warned me he would.

Buchannan looked like he might object before he nodded and found a table to wait for me. He made sure to sit so he could keep an eye on me, just in case I decided to make a run for it, I supposed. I swear, one day he'd learn to trust me to do the right thing.

"He got here fifteen minutes ago," Beth said when I reached the counter. "He said he'd wait for you since your car was outside. I tried to tell him that you might not come inside, but he was determined to stick around until you showed."

"That's all right. I should talk to him." Even though I'd hate every second of it. I ordered my peppermint cappuccino and leaned on the counter to wait for it. "Aside from Buchannan, has everything gone smoothly since I've been out?"

"As butter," Beth said, handing me my drink.

"You made us all a little nervous after that talk this morning, but after a while, we all settled down." She glanced up the stairs, toward where Lena and Eugene were now chatting.

"Is she doing okay?" I asked Beth, nodding in Lena's direction.

There was a slight hesitation before her response. "I think so." A frown. "Something's bothering her, though. I just don't know what it is."

I had a sneaking suspicion it involved a bruise and Zay, though I wasn't going to say it out loud. Boy, did I hope I was wrong because I liked Zay, even though I'd only met him a few times.

Behind me, Buchannan cleared his throat.

I heaved an overly dramatic sigh. "Thanks, Beth. Let me know if something changes." My eyes flickered toward Lena.

She nodded, shot Buchannan a disgustingly sweet smile, and then turned to make a fresh pot of coffee.

I carried my drink over to where Buchannan waited, taking my grand old time. Petty? Sure. But with how Buchannan has always treated me, he deserved it.

He gave me until my butt hit the chair before he started in. "What do you know about the gift Mr. Phan received?"

"It was wrapped in blue wrapping paper."

Buchannan shot me a glare.

"That's it." I crossed my arms.

"So, you're saying you have no idea why the contents pointed Mr. Phan to your store?"

"No clue." I dropped my arms, discarding the attitude. "I wish I did. I haven't gotten a gift, a threat, or had any encounters inside or outside of Death by Coffee that would make me think someone was after me."

"And Mr. Phan?"

"Him either. I can't imagine why anyone would want to hurt him." I paused, considered. "Do you think it could be a coincidence?"

"That he received a similar package as a murdered man? A package, I might add, that you took from the scene of a crime."

I winced. "Sorry about that. Erin was taking it with her and I didn't know what else to do."

Buchannan grunted, still clearly unconvinced. I was just happy he hadn't hauled me off to jail for my lapse.

Then again, there was still time for that if he was so inclined.

"Have there been any other gifts found?" I asked. "Maybe someone is simply trying to spread Christmas cheer and . . ." I trailed off at Buchannan's pointed look. "Okay, it's unlikely to be a coincidence."

"You think?" He took a sip from his coffee. I did the same as he continued. "Do you have any theories as to who might have sent these gifts?"

"Hand delivered them." When he just stared at me, I elaborated. "The boxes were hand delivered. There were no mailing labels on either box. They weren't dirty, like they'd been in the back of a truck. Someone dropped them off in person."

Buchannan considered that, and then nodded. "Go on."

"It's possible the killer could be on video if the Carvers have one of those fancy video doorbells." I knew for a fact that Jules didn't, but now, I was thinking of telling him to buy one. I planned on getting one for myself.

"I'll look into it." Said in a way that made me think he'd already thought of that. "Anything else?"

I took a long drink of my coffee before answering. "Lee and Agnes Komph could be involved."

His brow furrowed. With Buchannan's wife's connection to the church—she helped organize events there—there was a chance he knew the Komphs through her work.

I explained my theory about Agnes and Andrew's possible relationship, how Lee could have grown angry and killed Andrew because of the affair. Or Erin might have. Honestly, the more I thought about it, the less likely it seemed, considering neither Jules nor I fit into this scenario, but what else was I to think?

Buchannan appeared just as skeptical. His next question proved as much. "And how would this lead to you and Mr. Phan becoming involved?"

"I've asked myself the same thing." Before he could comment on that, I went on. "Agnes was in Phantastic Candies a couple of days before the murder. Maybe she was meeting with Andrew about Lee or Erin. Maybe the killer saw her there and is afraid Jules will somehow put two and two together?" The last came out as a question.

"Put what together?"

I raised both hands and let them drop. I had no idea. "Maybe Lee followed Agnes, saw him with Andrew, and decided to kill Andrew for it. If he was afraid that Jules saw him, he might want to kill him too."

"And you?"

"Jules is my friend and . . ." I trailed off. "Okay. I have no idea."

We sat there in silence. Buchannan looked like a man who was regretting his decision to stop in, while I was trying to come up with some way to salvage the conversation. I wanted to help, but felt like I was only muddying the waters with my wild guesses.

Well, if I was making a fool of myself, I might as well go all in.

"There is this one guy," I said, eyes on the table instead of Buchannan. I felt awful, but it needed to be done. "Jacob. I saw him have an argument with Andrew Carver the day of the murder."

Buchannan perked up at that. "Jacob? Do you have a last name?"

"No, sorry. He's my neighbor's friend. Caitlin Blevins. You remember her?"

He nodded, motioned for me to continue.

"Well, he was at Caitlin's the night Jules would have gone to Death by Coffee if he'd opened his gift. He could have been watching to see if Jules would take the bait. Caitlin also said Jacob was late for a meeting with another of her friends on the night of Andrew's murder, and that he was acting strange while he was with her."

Buchannan pulled his phone from his pocket and typed in a few notes. "When you say 'with her', you mean . . . ?"

"Not *with* her, with her. He was just hanging out. They aren't dating."

He typed that in.

"I saw him again today." Boy, I hoped Jacob was guilty of *something* because I felt like I was setting him up for a fall. "He was lurking outside of Death by Coffee and when I followed him, he went into a store called Heavenly Gate, which is owned by the Komphs. He got thrown out of it and had an argument with Lee right there on the sidewalk."

"You followed him?"

I crossed my arms, returning to my defensive posture. "I wanted to talk to him. I thought he was looking at me."

Buchannan sighed, typed something else into his phone, and then pocketed it. "Is there anything else you can tell me?"

I considered it, and then shook my head. "I think that's it."

He polished off his coffee in one big gulp and then stood. "I'll check out your information, see if anything pans out." He tossed his empty cup into the trash before leveling a finger at me. "I want you to be good and stay far away from this Jacob character. Same goes for the Komphs and Mrs. Carver."

"I'll try."

He narrowed his eyes at me. "I mean it."

"Okay, okay." I raised my hands in surrender. "If one of them tries to talk to me, I'll run in the opposite direction."

"Good." Buchannan scratched at his cheek, eyes going distant, before he snapped back into focus. "If I have further questions, I'll contact you." Meaning, don't go looking for him.

"Got ya."

Buchannan started to leave, but I stopped him. "You were here last night, right?"

His jaw firmed, eyes going hard. "I can't discuss—"

I cut him off. "Did anyone show up?" I hated the pleading sound in my voice, but couldn't help it. I didn't want anything to happen to Jules. "Please. If you saw someone, then it would put my mind at ease to know you've got a suspect."

A tense couple of seconds passed before Buchannan's eyes softened. Was that *compassion* I saw there?

"No," he said. "No one suspicious made an appearance."

And with that, he turned and walked out of Death by Coffee, leaving me not quite convinced he'd told me the truth.

14

I stood petrified in front of my closet, hand outstretched, but holding nothing. Dinner with Dad, Laura, and Paul. All of them. At the same time. What in the world was I supposed to wear?

Misfit, as usual, wasn't being any help. He lay on the bed, watching me with a bored expression on his fuzzy face. Every so often, his tail would swish and his ears twitch. I had the distinct impression he was judging me for my indecision.

"What if Paul decides to make a big announcement tonight?" I asked him, earning me another tail swish. Paul had been wanting to talk to me about something important for months now, but had yet to do so. Could this be the night he finally spits it out?

Tonight. In front of Dad and Laura. I might die.

It was almost a blessing when my phone rang and I saw my best friend's name on the screen. I snatched it up like it was a lifeline and answered with a hearty, "Hi, Vicki! How are you doing?"

There was a pregnant pause. "Krissy. You sound . . . odd. Is everything okay?"

I cleared my throat and wandered out of the bedroom and Misfit's eyeline. Maybe a few minutes away from his judgmental stare—and the closet—would give me some sort of insight. "I'm fine. Just a little stressed."

"Uh-oh. Did something happen at Death by Coffee?"

"No, it's not that." I took a deep breath and gave her a quick rundown of my dinner predicament. I decided not to bring up the murder. "What about you?" I asked when I was done. "How's it going between Raymond, Regina, and your family?"

Vicki groaned. "Mom and Dad are unbearable, as usual. And, because it's my life, they're getting along great with Raymond and Regina."

It was my turn to say, "Uh-oh. That sounds bad for you and Mason."

"Oh, it is. Every conversation is full of disapproving looks, backhanded compliments, and outright insults. Mason's been making himself scarce, complaining that he's sick one minute, or he's wrenched his back and needs to sit down the next. When we're alone, he's perfectly fine, of course." A pause. "Actually, I'm starting to wonder if he might be on to something."

"Tell him he's a wimp for me."

Vicki laughed. "I'll do that."

In the background, I heard Mason ask, "What are you two planning? And can I be a part of it?"

"Hey, I saw Valerie Kemp the other day," Vicki said, after presumably waving Mason into silence. "Did you know she is opening a coffee shop here in California?"

"Yeah, she called me earlier today. She wanted to know what we paid our employees. Didn't she talk to you when you saw her?"

"She didn't see me. I kind of avoided her and that monstrosity she's opening. It looks . . ." I could visualize the frown. "Like Valerie."

Considering her overdone, over-sprayed hair, her too-short skirts, and less than stellar attitude, I could only imagine what that looked like.

"Do you know how long it'll be until she opens?"

"I'm not sure. I'd say soon, by the looks of it. She was there with a couple of bubblegum-snapping teens I assume are her employees. They looked like mini-Valeries."

I shuddered at the thought.

My phone beeped in my ear. A glance told me it was Rita. "Hey, Vicki, Rita's beeping in and I've also got to get ready for dinner before Paul gets here, so I'd better go."

"That's all right. I need to go too. My parents are planning a dinner at their place. I might see if I can catch Mason's faux-flu and watch Netflix instead."

I laughed. "Good luck with that." My phone beeped again. "I've gotta run. I'll call you later, all right?"

"Have fun tonight."

"I'm going to try." I clicked over. "Hello, Rita. I can't really talk so—"

"Oh, my Lordy Lou! Where is your father? I need to talk to him this very instant!"

If it had been anyone else, I might have been worried that something had happened. Being that it was Rita, and knowing her penchant for over-exaggerating, I was only mildly concerned. "What's going on?" I asked. "Is everything okay?"

"Everything's fine, dear. Well, as fine as it can be under the circumstances. I just finished *Scars of the Heart* and let me tell you, that's as aptly named of a book as I've ever read. My poor heart can hardly take it! I need to talk to James, and I need to do it now."

"He's not here right now," I said. "I'm meeting him for dinner shortly. I can let him know to call you when I see him. It might not be until tomorrow before he can get back to you, though. I'm not sure how late we're going to be out."

"*Tomorrow?*" I could hear the horror in her voice. "No, that won't work at all. Can I come over and wait with you? I'll just need him for a short little while and then you can have him back and go to that dinner of yours."

"He's not coming here," I said. "We're meeting at Geraldo's. Laura and Paul are going to be there. It's a group thing. I'm sure you understand?"

"I see." Rita sounded as if I'd just told her that Dad was on his last legs and would never speak to her again.

"Like I said, I can tell him to call you. If you don't mind waiting up, I'm sure he'll be happy to call you after dinner. It could be really late, and—"

"No, that's all right, dear," Rita said, cutting me off. "I'll manage just fine. Don't you worry about me."

Alarm bells started clanging in my head. I narrowed my eyes, despite Rita not being able to see me. "Rita." One word, all warning.

"No, no, dear, I'll let you go. You enjoy your dinner, all right?"

And before I could utter another word, she disconnected.

I would have called her back and warned her against doing anything Rita-like, but a glance at the clock told me I was quickly running out of time. I returned to my bedroom where Misfit was still holding court. I took one look at my closet, and then decided that with it being Dad, I didn't need to go overboard. Not that I had much in the way of dressy clothing to begin with.

I opted for a nice blouse and clean jeans and called it good. If Paul showed up in a suit and tie, I'd reconsider my outfit, but otherwise, I should be fine.

The next fifteen minutes were spent regretting my choices, but I steadfastly refused to change. Every so often, I'd peek out the window and check the neighbors. Caitlin appeared to be home alone, as did Jules and Lance. No prowlers. No mysterious cars coasting by.

No Jacob.

Once again, I wondered if his presence next door was a coincidence. I couldn't make out the security camera in Caitlin's window from this distance, but knew it was there. It had caught a prowler—and a killer—before. Maybe it caught whoever left the gift for Jules, whether it was Jacob or someone else.

"No, it's too far," I muttered. Still, I was halfway

to the door, ready to go over and ask, when headlights lit up the front of my house. A moment later,
Paul was climbing out of his car, a dark winter coat
over a nice button-up shirt and jeans that matched
my own outfit like we'd planned it.

"Are you ready for this?" he asked when I met
him at the door. He sounded as nervous as I felt.

I checked to make sure Misfit's bowls were full,
grabbed my heavy coat, and then nodded. "As
ready as I'll ever be."

And then we were off.

Walking through the doors at Geraldo's always
made me feel like I was transitioning into some
sort of alternate dimension. From the outside, the
restaurant looked as basic as could be. Just a sign
and a brick building. Nothing special. It was easy
to overlook.

But once you walked through the doors, everything changed. Light jazz played over hidden
speakers. The walls were painted tastefully, the colored lighting was kept dim. The staff were dressed
up in black-and-white ties and dresses, but the customers weren't expected to do the same. It was the
fanciest place in all of Pine Hills by a long shot.

"There they are," I said, waving at Dad, who'd
stood as soon as we'd entered. Laura was seated
next to him, smiling. She looked a whole lot better
than she had the last time I'd seen her. Healthy.

Paul and I crossed the relatively busy restaurant
and joined them. Even with most of the tables full,
the layout of Geraldo's gave the illusion of privacy,
so I wouldn't feel the need to whisper if I had

something important to say. But if Paul were to say something, shall we say, personal, then it would feel far too intimate.

"Hey, Buttercup," Dad said, giving me a hug. "I'm sorry we haven't spent more time together."

"It's all right. I've been busy and you had Laura to take care of."

"Still . . ." He released me and turned to Paul.

We went around the table with hugs and greetings before we all took our seats. Wine had already been ordered, and while I normally didn't drink, I decided to have a small glass anyway. Chances were, I'd be nursing that tiny bit all night, wincing after every sip, but it would feel weird to not join them.

Once the niceties were out of the way, Dad did the one thing I'd hoped he wouldn't. He folded his hands on the table in front of him, looked straight at Paul, and said, "So, a murderer strikes Pine Hills once again, huh?"

"Dad!"

"No, it's all right," Paul said, reaching out and resting a hand on my wrist. "As it happens, yes one has, but it's not my case. John Buchannan is running the investigation."

"I'm sure you're working with him on it," Dad pressed. "The force here isn't a large one."

Paul shrugged, took a sip of wine. "We all do our part. There hasn't been much for me to do other than look out for your daughter here." He put his arm briefly around me and squeezed.

I, of course, blushed like a teenager.

"That's good to hear," Dad said, but he was undeterred. "How was he killed? I haven't heard."

Actually, now that I thought about it, neither had I.

Paul shifted uncomfortably in his seat. "I'm not sure I should discuss it here." He shot a look toward Laura.

"I was just thinking that if the victim was strangled, let's say, it would reduce the number of suspects considerably."

"He wasn't strangled," Paul said, before sighing. "A sharp object was used."

"A knife?"

"Uncertain, but at this point, I don't think so."

"Why's that?"

I turned to Laura and raised my voice, hoping to change the subject. "How are you feeling?"

"Great, actually. I still felt a little stuffy this morning, but that's cleared up since then. Thank you for asking."

"Any progress on where the gift boxes fit in to all of this?"

"None that I can discuss at this time." Paul's tone told me that he wasn't going to say anything further on the matter, but Dad kept pressing.

"Do you have any suspects?" he asked.

"We do. But as I'm sure you understand, I cannot discuss them here."

"Of course, of course." Dad's smile told me he'd caught on to Paul's reluctance and was willing to let him off the hook. "I can't help myself when it comes to this stuff. If Laura had been feeling better, I'd probably be at the station, peppering the whole department with questions for half the day. With my writing, firsthand experience can't be beat. I wouldn't use the exact details of the case in one of my stories, of course, but every detail could serve as an inspiration for a new book."

"I'm sure Detective Buchannan would be willing to talk to you about it after it's all over," Paul said. "He could run you through his process, give you an inside look at how we operate."

"Would he?" Dad leaned forward, eyes gleaming. "If it wouldn't be too much trouble, that would be great."

I cut in. "What do you think about spending tomorrow together, Dad? We could go out, do some shopping."

"Sounds great, Buttercup." Dad flashed me a smile before turning back to Paul. "I heard other business owners were targeted. Should Krissy be concerned?"

Paul took another sip of wine, clearly reluctant to answer.

"James." Laura took Dad's hand in her own. "Let's talk about something else, shall we? At least, before dinner. Afterward . . ." She shrugged.

Dad sighed, and then nodded. "Okay, sure. I'm sorry about that. I get carried away far too easily."

"It's quite all right," Paul said, though he sounded relieved.

"There you are!"

My knees cracked against the underside of the table at the sound of the voice coming from directly behind me.

Rita pulled up a chair and crammed it between Dad and me. "When I talked to Krissy earlier, she told me you would be here." She spoke as if she'd been a part of the conversation the entire time. "And boy, do I ever need to talk to you!" She wagged a finger at Dad. "I finished *Scars*, and oh, my . . ." She cooled herself off with a waving hand.

"Rita," I said, trying hard not to grind my teeth. "What are you doing here?"

"Why, you told me all about this dinner, remember? I know you didn't invite me directly, but you implied it." She turned to Dad. "I hope that's all right?"

"I never—"

"Of course, it's all right," he said, cutting me off with a placating smile. "We're all friends here. Was there something about that book that displeased you?"

"Displeased?" Rita's waving hand fluttered to her chest. "Not displeased, but *shocked*. I just *have* to know how the story ends! Is there any way you can give me a hint about what is going to happen in *Fear of the Heart*? That's what it's called, isn't it?"

Dad was grinning from ear to ear now. He sat back in his chair and folded his hands atop his belly. "Well, I wish I could, but . . ."

It was as if the rest of us ceased to exist. Dad and Rita started talking about the books. Rita was barely able to contain her excitement, while Dad soaked it all in and teased her with tiny tidbits that told her absolutely nothing.

Laura gave me an eyeroll from across the table, telling me that this sort of thing happened all the time, which, I, of course, knew from experience, but had forgotten about since I no longer lived with him.

I'd contented myself on letting the evening slip away when I noticed that three new guests had entered. One of them, I knew.

I waved as Lena Allison's roving eyes found me. She looked almost relieved, until she saw Paul sitting next to me. Two people I assumed were her parents were with her, and her mom leaned over to ask her a question. A moment later, and all three were on their way over, with Lena looking like a rabbit caught in a trap.

"Ms. Hancock," Lena's mom said. "Hi, I'm Janice Allison, Lena's mother." She reached out and I shook. "This is my husband, Cliff. We're sorry if we're interrupting your dinner."

"No, not at all," I said. "It's good to finally meet you."

"Likewise." Janice's smile seemed genuine. "Lena has said nothing but good things about you and your coffee shop."

"That's good to hear. I have nothing but good things to say about her."

"We won't keep you," Cliff said, putting a hand on his wife's shoulder. "Jan wanted to meet you, and well . . . we have."

Janice shot Cliff a look that could melt steel before turning back to me. "I do hope that we can talk sometime," she said. "I'd love to pick your brain about a few things."

"Would you like to join us?" Laura asked. "If it's okay with everyone else?" She glanced around the table.

"The more the merrier," Dad said. "I'd love to meet more people in my daughter's life. I'm James Hancock, by the way."

Lena paled, as introductions went around the table. Her dad, Cliff, seemed just as reluctant as she was, but Janice was determined to have her way.

A waiter was flagged down and in moments, we were all standing as another table was pulled over and chairs added. All the while, Lena looked sicker and sicker. Every few moments, her mom would lean over and whisper into her ear and Lena would shake her head.

Once we were seated, Janice turned to Paul and said, "So, I was wondering, you're a local police officer, are you not?"

Before Paul could answer, Lena shot to her feet. "Excuse me a moment." She bolted toward the restrooms.

I stood, worried. "Sorry. Me too." I gave the table at large an apologetic smile, and then followed her.

Lena was leaning with her hands on the sink, head down, inside the women's restroom when I entered. She jumped, looked ready to flee, before she realized it was me and breathed a sigh of relief. "I can't believe she did that."

"Your mom?" At her nod, I said, "She seems nice."

"Yeah. Nice and nosy." Lena took a deep breath and pushed away from the sink. "I'm sorry about all of this. I can tell you wanted to have a nice dinner with your family and we butted in."

"It's okay." When she gave me a skeptical look, I added, "Really. Rita had already crashed the party, so what's three more?" I smiled, but when she didn't return it, I let it fade. "Lena, what's going on?"

"What do you mean?" She wouldn't meet my eye.

"You've been acting strange ever since you've gotten back. Is it Zay? The bruise?"

Lena's face bunched in confusion. "Zay? I told you what happened with him."

"Are you sure that's all there is to it?"

"I'm sure." Firm, and with no hint of deception. "I mean, I didn't tell you *everything*, but it had nothing to do with why we broke up. It was hard living on our own. I told you about our money issues. And then campus security cracked down on a group of us skateboarding in the lots at night when no one was around." She rubbed at her arm.

A lightbulb went on in my head. "Is that how you got your bruise?"

"Yeah. I don't want to make them out as bad people, but one of them grabbed me pretty hard, pulled me from my board, and just about cracked my skull on the concrete when he threw me down. They threatened to call the police on me, claiming I was causing trouble when all I was doing was blowing off steam with my friends."

"Is that why you've been looking at Paul like that?" I asked. "Like you don't trust him?"

"No. I don't know. It's just . . ." She frowned, looked at the tops of her shoes. "I guess I realized that this sort of stuff happens all the time. Not just to oddballs like me, but to anyone deemed a little different. You know what I mean?"

I nodded. I hadn't experienced it myself, but I knew it happened a lot more than any of us would like.

"So, I started thinking. I was in school yet I didn't know what it was I really wanted to do. I have stuff I like, but it feels more like hobbies than anything that would be an actual career. It might be fun and all, but it won't pay the bills."

The bathroom door opened, which caused Lena to tense. The woman who entered saw us standing at the sink, hesitated, and then turned and walked right back out.

Lena waited until she was gone before dropping it on me. "I think I want to be a cop."

I blinked at her, surprised. "Like Paul?" Dumb question, but I didn't know what else to say.

"Yeah. Maybe even here in Pine Hills. You know, make sure they treat everyone with respect, no matter who it is. I know the police here probably already do, but I keep thinking that if I were there, I could make sure of it."

"And that's why you're so nervous around Paul and Buchannan." I felt like I should have figured it out on my own, but that bruise had me thinking the worst.

Lena nodded as she scuffed a shoe on the floor. "His mom is the police chief. I thought that maybe he could help get me started, put a good word in for me or something." Her shoulders sagged. "It's stupid, I know."

"No, it's not." Quite suddenly, it seemed like a perfect idea. "Talk to him. Tonight."

Her eyes widened. "I couldn't. That's what Mom wants me to do, and I just . . ." She was shaking her head nonstop. "I wouldn't know what to say. And even if he helps me out, I'd still have to go through training and I'm sure that'll cost money I don't have. And . . . and . . ."

"And I'll help," I said. "You can work at Death by Coffee for as long as you need to. We'd love to have you back. And I'm certain Paul would love to mentor you too. We all really do like you here, Lena."

"Are you sure?" She looked pained. "I feel like I'm invading your space, forcing you into it."

"I'm sure." I pulled her into a hug and then led her toward the door. "Let's go back out there and talk about it, all right? If Paul doesn't think it'll work out, he'll tell you up front. But if he does . . ."

Lena took a deep breath, and let it out in a nervous laugh. "Okay. I guess we're doing this then."

"*You* are," I said. "And I'll be right there beside you."

15

A bear strode across me, bringing me squinting awake to a frigid morning in my own bed. As soon as my eyes opened, Misfit hopped down, meowed, and then strode from the room, ready for his breakfast.

"I'm up," I muttered, extracting myself from the tangle of sheets with some difficulty. The floor swayed ever so slightly as I made my way to the shower. My head felt stuffy and the crust around my eyes worried me. I was hoping it was due to my late night out and the little bit of wine I'd consumed, and not that Laura had given me whatever ailment that had been affecting her. I couldn't afford to get sick, not with Christmas fast approaching and a potential killer on the loose.

Despite my grogginess—and worries over a possible growing cold—I felt pretty good about how the night had turned out. Talk of murder had evaporated as the group grew. Rita got to talk to Dad about the book. Lena talked to Paul nearly all night about police work and how she can best prepare for a meeting with Chief Patricia Dalton that he planned on setting up for her. Lena's parents—mostly Janice—were enraptured by Laura and her fondness for exercise.

And me? I happily sat back and enjoyed myself without being the center of attention as I feared I might be when the night had begun. A good meal, with good friends and family, what could be better?

Well, I know what could have capped the night off perfectly, but it was not to be. Paul, citing an early morning, had dropped me off with a simple goodnight kiss before heading home.

Believe me, by the time we'd finished dinner and had driven back to my place, I was ready to end on a high note. You know, cuddles with the man of my life, and waking up with his arm thrown haphazardly across me.

Instead, I was roused by fuzzy footfalls across my bladder.

I made it through my shower, slowly waking up as I did. The stuffiness clogging my head, as well as the fog swirling in my brain, receded bit by bit. By the time I was out of the shower and making a pot of coffee, I was feeling far more like myself. I wasn't up to whistling or smiling or anything that took much brainpower, but I wasn't about to fall flat on my face either.

While I waited for my coffee and toast, I went to the window and checked on my neighbors via their cars. Caitlin appeared to still be home alone, while Jules had already left for Phantastic Candies.

Lance's car was still in the driveway, but I didn't know if that meant he was home, or if he'd ridden in with Jules. Considering his worry, I was betting on the latter.

I let the curtain fall with a frown. Whoever had sent those gifts needed to be caught, murderer or not. I hated that everyone was having to walk on eggshells, that Jules didn't feel safe anymore.

My toast popped and I headed over to butter it, mind a million miles away.

Every time I thought about the murder, I couldn't help but think about Heavenly Gate. Everything seemed to tie back to the gift shop. Jacob. The Komphs and their issues with the Carvers. Agnes's relationship with Doris Appleton.

My coffee finished percolating as I polished off my toast. A cookie later (in the coffee, of course) and I was out the door. I didn't know what I planned on doing, only that I needed to talk to the Komphs.

It took all of two seconds for my steaming hot coffee to turn lukewarm in the arctic freeze that had befallen Pine Hills overnight. I gasped at the shock of it and instead of climbing into my Escape, I started the engine with my fob and rushed back inside the house to let the car warm up before even attempting to drive anywhere.

Curious about my abrupt about-face, Misfit sauntered in from the hallway, head cocked.

"Too cold," I managed through chattering teeth. I took a gulp of coffee, which barely helped now that it was no longer hot.

Misfit didn't seem impressed. Or to care. He swished his tail and headed into the kitchen to make sure I'd remembered to top off his food and water dishes. That done, he headed for the couch for his morning nap.

I gave it ten minutes before going back out into the chill. There was no snow, but the sky was an icy gray that hinted that it very well might be coming. It was cold enough for it, that was for sure.

My teeth chattered all the way downtown, and I was unable to stop myself from shaking. The inside of my vehicle *had* warmed, yet I was chilled to the bone, and I wasn't sure anything short of a scalding hot shower would warm me up again.

I parked outside Heavenly Gate and then just sat there, idling. The thought of sprinting from my car to the door, which was only a few feet away, was almost too much for me to bear. I am a wimp when it comes to the cold. And pain. And this cold *was* painful, so it was a double whammy.

But I did it. In one not-quite-fluid motion, I shut off the engine and jumped out of the Escape. I jogged to the door in a cloud of expelled breath that froze on contact with the air. I pushed inside the gift shop with a gasp as warm air blasted into me, causing my entire face to feel as if it had burst into flames.

Two pairs of eyes turned toward me.

Neither appeared happy.

Doris Appleton stood at the counter where Agnes Komph leaned. I couldn't tell if their identical frowns were because they'd been arguing before my arrival, or if they were unhappy about being interrupted.

"It's really cold out there," I said, hoping to break the ice, both figuratively and literally.

All it earned me were two continued stares, and Doris's already pressed lips thinning even further.

"I could browse, if I'm interrupting?" I made it a question.

Doris heaved a put-upon sigh. "I don't have time for this." She picked up a pair of knit mittens and pulled them onto her hands.

"For what?" I asked, all nosy innocence.

"*You.*" Doris turned to face Agnes. "Think about what I said." And then she zipped up her coat and walked past me with a haughty sniff. A blast of cold air entered as she stepped out onto the sidewalk, and then into a large Cadillac that, while old, looked well cared for.

"She's not very subtle, is she?" I asked, taking Doris's place at the counter.

Agnes didn't so much as crack a smile as she straightened and picked up her handbag. She pulled the metal strap onto her right shoulder as if fearing I might try to steal it. "Can I help you?"

"I'm curious," I said, eyes roaming the store. "How well did you know Andrew Carver?"

A beat, and then, "Not well."

"You never met with him?"

I could almost see the wheels spinning in Agnes's head as she considered how best to answer that. "We might have spoken," she admitted. "What business is it of yours?"

"None, really. But I figure you might want to know about a rumor going around . . ." I trailed off, letting the implications dangle in the hopes that Agnes would take the bait.

She blinked at me. "And?"

"It's about you and Andrew." When she still didn't

react, I added, "You were seen together. There are some people who believe that you might have been—" I leaned in close and lowered my voice, just in case he was in the back, "—stepping out on Lee."

Agnes's eyes widened and a hand went to her chest, causing the strap to slip from her shoulder. She slid it back up as she said, "You *dare!*"

I raised my hands, palms outward, in front of me. "I'm not the one saying it. But there's been talk. I thought you should know."

"Who would say such a thing?" Agnes seemed genuinely offended. Either rumors—and Erin Carver—were wrong, or Agnes Komph was a fantastic liar.

"It's not true?"

"Of course, it isn't! I would never . . . who would . . . This is preposterous! Someone is out there trying to smear my name."

As she spoke, her entire body shook. And because she was clutching her handbag, every time she raised that hand, the strap slipped from her shoulder to dangle by her right leg before she slipped it back up.

"Why would they do that?" I asked, voice calm.

"How should I know?" Agnes snapped, as if she thought *I* might be the one spreading the rumors. "There are people out there whose sole goal in life is to make others miserable."

My first instinct was to ask, "Like Doris Appleton?" but I figured that would get me nowhere with her. I nodded for her to go on, keeping my mouth firmly shut.

"I am a person of faith." Agnes punctuated each

word by jabbing the top of the counter with her index finger. "I would never cheat on my husband. *Never.* And I would most definitely not do it with a man like Andrew Carver."

"So, you never went to his house while Erin was out of town?"

Agnes's mouth opened, but no sound came out. Those wheels were spinning in her head fast enough that I imagined smoke leaking from her ears.

"Look," I said, "I'm not trying to upset you. I'm just worried. Someone murdered Andrew Carver in his own store. They lured him there by leaving a Christmas gift outside his door."

Agnes continued to stare, though her mouth did close.

"My friend Jules received a similar gift. A note inside made it appear as if *I'd* left it for him and wanted him to come to Death by Coffee that night."

"And you think that was another lure?" Agnes licked her lips, swallowed hard.

"I do. But Jules called the police and they got involved, likely spooking the killer. He's safe now, but that doesn't mean they won't try again."

"I understand your concern." Agnes had paled and was picking at her nails. Her handbag strap was now dangling against her thigh and she didn't bother to replace it. It reminded me of Jacob and his wallet chain. "What does any of this have to do with me?"

"I'm not sure," I admitted. "I want to help Jules, help find the killer before they strike again. So far, the only thing I know for sure is that businesses on this street have been targeted. Andrew's Gifts, I believe, was the first. Then Phantastic Candies and Death by Coffee followed."

"Do you think we could be next?" She glanced toward the back where I presumed Lee was hard at work.

"I don't know. Right now, I'm looking for any and all connections." I hated doing it, but I had to ask, "Do you know a guy named Jacob? He was here yesterday. Your husband kicked him out."

"I remember." Another furtive look toward the back. "Do you think he is responsible for what's happening?"

I spread my hands. "I wish I knew. But he *was* seen arguing with Andrew the day of the murder." I still couldn't place him at Phantastic Candies or Death by Coffee, but that didn't mean he'd never been there. I can't be everywhere at once.

"And then he was here, causing Lee distress." Agnes nodded slowly as she thought it through. "As if scouting his next victim."

"Jacob might not be involved," I said, feeling the need to point it out, though it wasn't looking good for him. "And the gifts could be unrelated to the murder." Doubtful, but possible. "But I'm willing to consider anything if it means catching a killer. That's why if you know anything . . ." I trailed off with raised eyebrows.

Agnes considered it for a long couple of moments. She slipped her handbag strap back onto her shoulder, physically putting herself back together. When she spoke, she started slowly, almost carefully. "There is something you should know—"

The door burst open behind her and Lee Komph stomped from the back, curls of wood clinging to his clothing. He was holding a partially completed cross in one hand, a chisel in the other. When he saw me talking to his wife, his jaw muscles bunched, and his fists tightened.

"What are you doing here?" he demanded as he rounded the counter and marched on me. I could smell the wood shavings on him. If he wasn't so darn intimidating, it might have been pleasant.

I took a step back, but he kept coming. "I'm talking to Agnes."

"About?" Before I could answer, he snarled, "I don't care what it was about. I don't want you bothering my wife."

"I wasn't bothering her." Not really. I took another step back. His intensity was making it hard to breathe.

Lee continued to loom over me, his tiny glasses perfectly perched on the end of his nose. He used his size and radiating anger to push me toward the door, step by step. He never touched me, never looked as if he might, yet I was compelled to back up all the way down the aisle until I was standing just inside the door to Heavenly Gate.

"We don't need you coming in here trying to start something," Lee said. "Neither Agnes nor I had anything to do with Andrew Carver's death. And we most definitely don't want to have anything to do with you."

I almost blurted, "How did you know we were talking about Andrew?" but held my tongue. Chances were good Lee had been eavesdropping the entire time I'd talked to Agnes.

But if that was the case, what was said that triggered this outburst? Was he afraid Agnes might have said something that would implicate him in Andrew's murder?

"I'm not trying to cause you any trouble," I said, knowing it was pointless. Lee had pegged me as a troublemaker, and nothing I did or said would change that.

He reached past me with the hand holding the chisel—the tip came within an inch of my cheek—and pulled the door open. I had to skitter out of the way or he would have bopped me in the back with it. Or stabbed me with the end of his wood chisel.

"Go," he demanded with a harsh jerk of his chin toward the exit. "Don't come back."

I glanced past him, to Agnes. She was still standing behind the counter, hand at her throat as she watched. She didn't look concerned for my well-being, which I supposed wasn't much of a surprise. She looked contemplative, as if she was wondering if *I* might be the killer.

"Now," Lee barked when I didn't move right away. His hairy bicep flexed when he did, showing me that Lee Komph was a well-built man more than capable of squishing me with his fists. Apparently, hand-carving wooden figures was good for your arms.

I scurried out into the cold like a chastised child afraid of further punishment. I turned to apologize, to try to smooth over whatever antagonistic thoughts Lee had about me, but before a puff of air could leave my lips, the door slammed closed and Lee was marching over to where Agnes stood. She said something to him before he vanished into the back with a fling of a hand. I assumed it was accompanied by an expletive targeted at me.

That went well.

I watched Agnes a moment longer, hoping she might come to the door to finish whatever thought she'd had before her husband had come bursting through the door to interrupt us.

Instead, she turned and followed her husband to the back, leaving me standing alone in the cold.

There is something you should know . . .

And whatever it was, it was something Lee Komph didn't want me to hear.

16

The short run from my Escape to the entrance of Ted and Bettfast looked miles long as I sat in the frost-covered lot. I'd just gone through this at Heavenly Gate, and here I was again, fearing stepping out into the cold. All I wanted to do was to go inside to ask Dad and Laura if they wanted to get breakfast, but I was now considering just calling them instead.

Stop being a wimp. The voice sounded a whole lot like my third-grade teacher's who'd routinely berate us whenever we didn't want to work on one of her plethora of boring projects in class.

Oddly, her phantom voice had the same effect on me now as the real one had then.

I shut off the engine and popped out of my car like it had caught on fire. Breath pluming, I waddle-jogged to the door and was just about to reach for it when it burst open and a heavily wrapped figure barreled directly into me.

"I'm sorry!" I said, staggering back a step, while simultaneously clutching at the person so I wouldn't fall over. "I didn't see—"

"Let go of me," she snapped.

I jerked my hands free.

Vanna Goff glared at me from beneath her furry hood. Strands of curly hair, artificially grayed to make her look more knowledgeable, poked out around her stern face. A Realtor by trade, she'd tried to sell my neighbor's house back before Caitlin had moved in, and had failed to do so. Another Realtor had taken over, and Vanna had blamed me for her troubles in selling, even though I'd done nothing wrong. Her less-than-pleasant personality likely had more to do with it than anything I did, but try telling her that.

"Vanna," I said through chattering teeth. "It's good to see you." It wasn't.

She didn't even try to fake a smile. Just glared. "Are you going to move out of my way or do you plan on standing there until we both freeze to death?"

I stepped aside and without another word, Vanna stomped her way to her car, gunned the engine, and sped out of the lot like I was contagious.

That pleasant encounter out of the way, I entered Ted and Bettfast to find both Ted and Bett Bunford standing to the right of the doors, talking to one of their employees, Jo, who looked stricken. When the younger woman saw me enter, she excused herself and hurried off toward a downstairs bathroom.

Uh-oh. Between Vanna and my earlier chat with

Justin, I had a feeling I knew what that conversation had been about.

"Hi, Ted. Bett." I crossed the room toward them. "It's good to see you."

Bett was leaning heavily on a cane, bony fingers wrapped tightly around it. She trembled ever so slightly, as if it was taking all her energy to remain upright. I noted Ted stayed close to her side, hand at the ready, just in case she was to fall. They both looked to have aged greatly since I'd last seen them.

"Ms. Hancock." Ted was the one to speak. "Your father is staying with us."

A statement of fact, but I answered anyway. "He is. That's why I'm here."

"To see him?"

"And his girlfriend, Laura. Are they in?" I knew they were since the rental was sitting in the lot, but it felt polite to ask.

"They are." Ted's hand drifted ever closer to Bett's elbow. She wasn't swaying, though she was getting there. "Do you know their room number?"

"I do, thank you." I paused, and then said, "I heard you were thinking of selling Ted and Bettfast. I saw Vanna Goff when I left, so I assume the rumor is accurate?"

Bett closed her eyes briefly. It was she who answered in a wavery voice that made me even more concerned about her health. "The upkeep has become too much for the both of us to handle."

Ted took his wife's arm and squeezed. "We've tried, but it's clear that we can't keep this up any longer. We decided it best to turn the manor over to someone who can return it to its former glory."

"As a bed-and-breakfast?" I asked.

"That's the hope," Ted said.

"I've insisted that the new owner continue our legacy and finish the work we started," Bett said. "But Ms. Goff isn't so sure that's a good idea."

"She says that it will limit possible buyers." Ted scowled at that.

I could see Vanna's point, but at the same time, I didn't want to see the bed-and-breakfast go away. For all the trouble I've had here over the years, I liked the place. "Have you heard about anyone wanting to buy?" Robert Dunhill, perhaps?

"There's been some interest," Ted said before glancing at his wife, who had paled. "We should let you get to your father. If you'll excuse us."

"Of course."

Ted helped Bett as they turned around and shuffled to the back office where I knew they had a pair of reading chairs sitting next to a window. Bett looked as if she might collapse before she got there, and Ted seemed acutely aware of that fact. His right arm went around her, while his left hand rested on her closest wrist. If her legs were to give out, he'd have her.

When they were gone, I headed for the stairs, heart heavy. Bett and I didn't always get along, but like her bed-and-breakfast, I liked her. Seeing her look so weak was a tough pill to swallow considering how strong she'd once been. I hoped that when they finally sold, she would get the rest she needed and would find that vitality again.

I reached Dad's room and knocked. He answered right away.

"Hey, Buttercup, come on in." Stress made the

lines around his eyes stand out. He did his best to hide it, but I could see him fighting to keep the frown off his face, to keep his brow from furrowing in concern.

I hesitated a beat before entering.

Laura was sitting across the room, in the same chair at the window that she'd been in the last time I was there. Her eyes were heavy and she yawned as she attempted a greeting. "Sorry about that," she said. "Late night got to me, I guess."

"Did you two stay up long after dinner?" I asked, hopeful that was all it was.

"A little," Dad said. "Well, Laura did, anyway. Like an old man, I passed out almost as soon as we got back."

"I think I'm still getting over that cold, or whatever it was I had." Laura stifled another yawn. "You'd think the wine would have helped me settle down, but I found myself too wound-up to sleep. And now, here I am."

"I'm sorry we didn't get to talk much at dinner," Dad said. "I feel like I abandoned you."

"It's all right. I think Rita would have exploded if she hadn't gotten a chance to talk to you about the book." And considering she'd talked nearly nonstop the entire night, she'd had quite a lot to say.

"I still feel as if I should make it up to you somehow." Dad crossed the room and rested a hand on Laura's shoulder. She covered it with her own.

"You don't need to do that. It was a good night." I glanced around the room, and seeing no evidence of food, I asked, "Would you two be interested in breakfast at Death by Coffee this morning? If you're feeling up to it?"

"I haven't eaten," Dad said. "I wouldn't mind a bite, but . . ." He looked to Laura.

"You two go," she said, patting Dad's hand before dropping her own into her lap. "I think I'm going to lie back down for a little while to try to catch up on some sleep. I don't want to be nodding off at Christmas."

Dad hesitated before withdrawing his hand. "Are you sure?"

"Yes. You two need to spend some time together." She tried a reassuring smile, but she just looked tired.

There was a moment where Laura and Dad both just stared at one another. I sensed a silent conversation was happening between them, and while it didn't appear to be an angry one, it still made me feel uncomfortable, as if I was eavesdropping on something private.

Finally, Dad nodded and grabbed his coat from the back of a nearby chair. "Do you want me to bring you back anything?" he asked Laura.

"No, I'll be okay. Have fun." She shot Dad a stern look. "Please, don't worry about me."

"I'll do my best." He kissed her forehead. "Get some rest." He joined me at the door.

"If you'd rather not come, I understand," I whispered.

"No, I want to go." He put an arm around my shoulder and, this time, I was the recipient of a forehead kiss. "But thank you."

We left Laura a few moments later and headed

downstairs. The Bunfords were still secluded in their office, but Jo was hovering near the outside door. Her eyes were a little red, telling me she'd been crying.

I gave her a reassuring wave as we passed by, and nearly stopped to check on her, but refrained when she tensed. No sense in making things worse when she clearly wasn't ready to talk.

Dad and I headed outside and briskly walked toward my car. As soon as we were inside, I cranked up the heat, but didn't drive right away. Something was bothering me, and I couldn't just ignore it.

"Is everything okay?" I asked, turning to him. "Between you and Laura, I mean?"

"Yeah. Why do you ask?"

"I don't know." I weighed my next words carefully. "She seems off. More than just being tired, I mean."

"She's been stressed lately," Dad said. "But it's nothing for you to worry yourself over, Buttercup." This time, his reassuring smile appeared legit. "Let's get that food, all right? I'm starving."

I left Ted and Bettfast not quite convinced everything was great between Dad and Laura, but there wasn't anything I could do about it. If something *was* wrong between them, I hoped they worked it out. I liked Laura. She'd never fully replace my mom—no one ever would—but she was as close as anyone could get, and she was good for Dad.

Conversation was kept light as I drove. He spent most of the time talking about Rita and her excitement over his books. He asked me a few questions about Lena and her desire to become a cop, and I answered as truthfully as I could without betraying Lena's trust. If she wanted people to know *why* she'd chosen that path, then she could tell them. It wasn't my place.

We were about to pass the church when I saw a tall, thin woman I recognized hurrying through the doors. I immediately flipped on my turn signal and pulled into the church parking lot, not quite slowing down enough to make the turn graceful. A horn blared behind me and Dad did one of those palm slaps to the dashboard to keep from being thrown around in his seat.

"Sorry," I said, pulling into a space and putting the Escape in park. "I'll be just a minute."

"I'm coming with you." Dad was already out the door, giving me no room to argue. Nor did he ask why I'd just about broken both our necks to make the turn. There was a good chance he already had an idea, and was just as anxious as I was to make progress on solving Andrew Carver's murder.

I shut off the engine and joined him just as he reached the door. He opened it and bowed to me with a flourish that was reminiscent of a butler in an old movie. "After you, m'lady."

I rolled my eyes at him and muttered, "Nerd," loud enough for him to hear. That earned me an ear-to-ear grin.

The woman I'd seen wasn't in sight, but I had a feeling I knew where I could find her. I headed up the stairs and through the room where the writers' group meetings were held—and where the party had taken place the other night. A door at the far end of the room was hanging open and movement inside told me I'd chosen correctly.

"Elsie?" I asked, approaching the small office space. "Is that you? It's Krissy Hancock."

Elsie Buchannan, John Buchannan's wife, stepped out of the office with a curious expression on her face. She'd shed her coat and hat, revealing a bob of a haircut and a conservative outfit right at home in a church. "I'm sorry, I didn't realize anyone else was here."

"We came in after you," I said. "In fact, you're the reason we stopped. I'd like to ask you a couple of questions, if that's all right?"

Elsie stared past me, at Dad, likely trying to place him. "Questions?"

Dad shrugged and gave her an "aw, shucks" smile. "I'm just along for the ride."

Elsie's gaze turned to me. "Why? What happened?" And then a frown. "It's about that murder, isn't it?"

"I'm not sure," I admitted. "It's about a member of the church; a woman named Doris Appleton."

Elsie's entire demeanor changed. She wasn't hostile toward me, but there was a hint of trepidation in her voice when she asked, "What about her?"

"She caused something of a stir on the day of Rita's party, the one for the writers' group," I said. "Both before and during the event."

Elsie nodded. I didn't know if that meant she'd heard about the fuss, or if she was just confirming that she knew about the party.

"Doris had some pretty nasty things to say about a few of the local businesses in town, and that includes the one across the street, Andrew's Gifts."

Elsie's lips thinned. "Where the murder took

place." A statement of fact, but I nodded anyway. "Doris and I don't exactly see eye to eye on church matters."

"She causes trouble for you?" I asked, glancing at Dad, who was standing with his hands folded behind his back, listening without comment.

"Not me directly." Elsie frowned, seemed to consider her next words before speaking them. "Doris and her little cult . . ." A sigh. "I suppose I shouldn't judge them so harshly, but I suppose that's how I feel about them. They have been thorns in the church's side ever since I can remember. I'm surprised it has taken this long for her to start in on the writers' group."

"Does that mean she's caused trouble for other groups?"

"Almost all of them." Elsie tapped a thumbnail against the other, making a faint click. "Doris has a very particular way of thinking and expects everyone else to fall in line with her. If your group isn't a part of her ideology, or if you say something she doesn't agree with, she'll hound you until you give in to her. Or she'll send someone to do it."

"Someone like Agnes Komph?"

"Among others," Elsie said. "It's frustrating because they truly believe they are the most pious people in town, yet they don't seem to realize that you can't just call yourself a good person and make it true. You have to look out for others in the community, strive to make the world a better place for everyone, not just yourself."

"And Doris doesn't do that?"

"Not that I've ever seen. She talks a lot about doing the right thing, but her view of what that is leans heavily toward her own personal beliefs and tastes. Even if you've done everything right, the moment you cross her by wearing the wrong shirt or by forgetting to tell her how amazing she is, you're on her hit list."

I wondered if that last bit was a figure of speech or if Elsie believed Doris could be responsible for the murder. Doris *had* talked badly about Andrew's Gifts the night Andrew was killed. She'd even been in the area when it had happened, though she'd had her crew around her. Then you add in her comments about Death by Coffee, about other businesses in town, which I assumed would extend to Phantastic Candies . . .

But murder? That didn't seem very pious, even for someone with a skewed view of what that might be.

"Do you think it's possible that—"

Before I could finish the thought, Elsie's watch dinged.

"I'm sorry," she said, glancing at it, "I can't really talk. I've got a mess to sort out, calls to make." She tapped at her smartwatch. "It's funny you stopped in about Doris since I'm here now because of her. She bullied another club into cancelling their gin rummy night so she could have the space, despite there being more than enough room for both groups."

"They were having their game night here?" I asked.

"Tonight." Elsie rubbed at the bridge of her nose. "Let's just say the group that had the room scheduled isn't happy. They're making their displeasure known, and honestly, I don't blame them. I'm afraid Doris might push them right out of the church, which we can't have."

I wanted to ask her more questions, to get a better idea of who Doris Appleton was, but I couldn't force her to stay and talk.

"I hope you smooth things over," I said. I imagined the various groups that used the church for their meetings helped with funding. Donations, fund-raising activities. If Doris pushed them all out, then the church could be in trouble, which helped no one.

"Me too." Elsie started to turn toward the door, but Dad stopped her with a question.

"What time tonight?"

Elsie paused. "For?"

"The meeting," Dad said. "What time's the meeting?"

"Seven. Doris's group will be here from seven until nine."

With that, we parted.

"What are you thinking?" I asked once we were on the way again. Dad wouldn't have asked that last question without a reason.

"I think it's one thing to bully people for their beliefs, but another thing entirely to kill them for them."

I glanced at him out of the corner of my eye. "You don't think Doris killed Andrew?"

"I don't know her well enough to have a solid opinion one way or the other," he said. "But if I were to guess, she sounds like the kind of person who's more likely to convince someone else to act on her behalf than to do it herself."

I was still considering Dad's comment as we pulled up in front of Death by Coffee. I was so distracted by it that I didn't notice what was going on inside my own bookstore café.

But Dad did.

"Uh-oh," he said. "Looks like you've got trouble."

When I looked, my heart sank.

Doris Appleton and Rita Jablonski were facing off inside, and it appeared the conversation was a heated one.

17

"**I** know it was you!" Doris jabbed a finger at Rita's face. "You think that because your little group has had the run of the place for years, you own it."

"I think no such thing," Rita said, crossing her arms. "You're the one who has a skewed sense of—"

"Don't you *dare* question me." Doris grabbed the pearls around her neck and started worrying at them. "Your attempts to soil my name will *not* work. I have a reputation in this town. People will flock to my side if you decide to make a fight of it."

Lena was standing behind the counter, watching the exchange with a growing sense of alarm. When she saw me enter, she gave me a desperate, pleading look.

"You think so, do you?" Rita shot back. "I'm not trying to make a fight of anything, but if I decided I wanted to, I think you'd find yourself feeling rather alone."

"What's going on?" I asked, breaking into the conversation before it could become any more heated. Dad had entered behind me and had taken up position at my back.

"This doesn't concern you," Doris snapped, giving me a healthy dose of her evil eye. "You're one of *hers,* anyway. "

"Mine? Ha!" Rita rolled her eyes dramatically before they landed on me. "Doris thinks I've been badmouthing her, which I most assuredly have not. I wouldn't waste my breath."

"You have." Doris tugged on her pearls. "I know you have. Who else runs her mouth like a—"

"Doris, please," I said, cutting in before she could finish the thought.

The woman harrumphed, but thankfully didn't continue. Rita was near fuming from the insinuation, however. If I didn't calm them down, I was afraid they might come to blows.

Death by Coffee was busy, but not so much that the fight was getting in the way of customers ordering. In fact, most everyone had taken a seat so they could watch the show while they had their coffees and pastries. Free entertainment.

I glanced back at Dad. He nodded once. *You're doing fine.*

"Doris," I said, turning back to the women. "What happened to make you think that Rita was saying bad things about you?"

"I never—"

I held up a finger, cutting Rita off.

Doris narrowed her eyes at me, as if she suspected a trick. I mean, she obviously didn't like

me, and yeah, Doris Appleton was far from my favorite person, but I wasn't about to pull one over
on her for Rita's sake. I truly wanted to know why
she was so angry. If someone was out wrecking her
reputation and blaming it on Rita, it could be important to what was going on elsewhere.

And hey, I could relate. I might not like her, but
no one deserved to be talked about, especially if
those words were full of lies.

"I received a call," Doris said. "From the church."

I waited a beat before asking, "About?"

"I was given a warning." She was wrenching on
her necklace so hard, I was afraid it might snap
and the pearls would end up bouncing all over the
coffee shop. A vision of the lot of us running
around, slipping and falling as we stepped on the
small white balls like something out of a cartoon
flashed through my head and I nearly laughed.

Thankfully, I kept a straight face when I pressed,
"What kind of warning?"

Doris's jaw worked a moment before she said,
"She claimed I was harassing other members of
the church. Can you believe such a thing? I've only
tried to do what's right for this town, and this is
how I'm repaid!"

I wondered if Elsie Buchannan was the "she"
who'd made the call, and how long ago, considering I'd just left her. From the way Doris was acting,
I assumed she must have gotten it while Dad and I
were on the way over.

Did that mean she'd already been in Death by
Coffee at the time? Or had she seen Rita afterward
and followed her inside?

"Have you considered that perhaps what you've been doing lately *is* harassment?" Rita asked. "The writers' group—"

"Doesn't belong in a church." Doris punctuated it with a stomp of her foot. "The content of some of your stories . . ." She blushed. "It's disgusting."

"Have you read any of Rita's stories?" I asked before Rita could retort.

Doris's eyes darted around the room. "Well, no, but I've heard tale of what they're about. And I've seen the contents of her car, so it isn't hard to guess what kind of *stories* she's coming up with."

"Oh?" Rita asked, temper showing as color in her cheeks. "And how would you know what the contents of my car might be? Been snooping, have we?"

"You don't have to snoop when you can see the eyesore coming a mile away. It's a pigsty." A cruel look came into Doris's eye then. In some way, I think she was enjoying this. "The smut you revel in shows in your demeanor, in the way you present yourself. One look at you and everyone knows how unclean you really are."

"Now you listen here." Rita took a threatening step toward Doris. So much for not wanting things to escalate.

"I don't have to listen to a thing you say," Doris said, bracing herself. "And you—" this time, I was the target of her finger jab, "—you should be ashamed of yourself for allowing this woman to frequent your place of business. Though, I suppose I shouldn't be surprised considering." She shot a look at the menu board and sniffed disdainfully.

"Now that's—"

"No. I'm done." Doris shouldered past me and

Dad and headed for the door, head held high, as if she felt she'd won the argument. She was still worrying at her pearls, so deep down, I think she was as upset as the rest of us.

Once she was gone, the entire room seemed to sag in relief. Conversation in the dining area resumed, with half the customers rising and tossing their empty cups away before leaving. Apparently, they'd only hung around to watch the show.

Rita was blinking rapidly, chest moving up and down in quick hitches. I couldn't tell if she was about to cry, or if she was going to explode in anger.

"Are you all right?" Dad asked her before I could.

"I'm fine," Rita said. "She came in here after me— *followed* me in—and started accusing me of all sorts of things, unprovoked. I never said a word to anyone about that woman, yet she swears I've been smearing her name all over town."

"She's upset," I said. "I'm not trying to validate her actions, but I imagine she was looking for someone to blame and when she saw you come in here, she figured you were the perfect target."

"She threatened to go to the church about the writers' group!" Rita almost wailed it. "She claims she has proof that we're performing evil rites or some malarky. All because she doesn't like what kind of stories I write!"

"Why target the group now?" I asked, genuinely curious. "You've been holding meetings in the church forever. Has something happened recently to set her off?"

Rita glanced past me, to where Dad stood, and then looked away. "I might have turned down an offer to come to one of her meetings. It was about the evils of modern literature and she thought I might benefit from sitting in. I just *knew* she'd disparage everything I care about, so I kindly told her I wasn't interested."

"Which she didn't like, I imagine," Dad said.

Rita closed her eyes, took a trembling breath. "She was never kind to me, but ever since that moment, Doris has made snide comments, dropped hints that I'm a horrible person, every chance she gets. She's always been difficult around Christmastime, but this year . . ." She shook her head. "I just don't understand why she can't let people celebrate in their own way. I'm not hurting anyone."

Dad stepped forward, moving as if to put an arm around Rita to comfort her, but to my shock, she slipped away.

"I'd best be going. I'm sorry." Rita sniffed, blinked her eyes a few times in rapid succession, and then hurried out the door without so much as a backward glance at Dad.

"She's really upset," he said.

"Very." I sucked in a breath and let it out in a huff before focusing on Lena. "You okay?"

"I'm fine. But I didn't know what to do. That woman came in here and started in on Rita and wouldn't stop. I tried stepping in, but she acted like I was invisible."

"I don't think there's much you could have done," I said.

Eugene poked his head out of the back room, scanned the dining area, and then sagged in relief when he saw Doris was gone. He vanished into the back once again.

"Jules called before all of this happened," Lena said. "He apologized for not calling sooner. The candy canes are ready. Beth left a few minutes ago to pick them up. She probably would have handled this better than I did."

"You were fine," I said. "Really. If you'd gotten involved, Doris would have started attacking you."

"If you say so." Lena scowled down at her hands. "I have to do better if I want to impress Chief Dalton. I should have found a way to deescalate the situation." She shook her head and plastered on a smile. "But it's over now. Did you want to order something or were you just stopping in to say hi?"

Dad and I went ahead and ordered our breakfast. Eugene emerged from the back and slunk around the counter to head up into the books with muttered apologies, likely for hiding. Honestly, I didn't blame him for seeking shelter. Every time I saw Doris Appleton, I wanted to hide too.

Once our order was up, Dad and I carried our coffees and pastries to a window seat, which was a mistake. The cold seeped right through the glass, causing me to shiver, despite the fact I was still wearing my heavy coat. I pulled my hot coffee close so the steam would warm my face.

"This Doris lady seems to be popping up quite a lot lately, doesn't she?" Dad said, stirring his cappuccino with his candy cane.

"She does." I looked out the window, expecting Doris to be glaring in at me, but the sidewalk was empty. "It makes me wonder what her meeting tonight is going to be about."

"Yeah." A beat of silence. "Why don't we go and find out?"

I stared at Dad from across the table. "Do what now?"

"Let's go to the meeting. The church is a public place, right? We can say we're interested to hear what she has to say. If she wants to kick us out, that's fine. We'll go without a fight. But if she's willing to let us listen, then perhaps we can learn something of value."

Like who killed Andrew Carver.

"I don't know," I said. Sitting in on a meeting run by Doris Appleton was not high on my list of fun things to do. "She doesn't seem to like me all that much, so I doubt she'd want me lurking while she talks down about me and my place of business."

Dad spread his hands. "Or she could think that her words have more power than they really do. Imagine how she'd feel if she thought she was swaying you away from Rita."

"Yeah, I guess." But did I really want to give her that impression. She'd surely rub it into Rita's face, which would have Rita calling me, asking me why I'd betrayed her. "What time did Elsie say they are meeting? Seven?"

"Seven," Dad agreed.

"Can I think about it?" I asked. "You and Laura could come to my place later for a Christmas movie. Maybe afterward, we can see about going to the meeting."

"Sounds like a plan," Dad said. "I think Laura does need to get out of the room more, get some fresh air."

"She's going to be okay, right?" I asked. Laura hadn't seemed like herself since she'd arrived.

Dad smiled, but it was strained at the edges. "She'll be fine. We'll talk about it later."

Before I could probe deeper, movement outside the window caught my attention. John Buchannan was climbing out of his car, which was parked behind my Escape. I half expected him to walk around to the front and slap a ticket on my windshield or stick a boot on my wheel. He instead turned toward Death by Coffee, rubbing his hands together as if anticipating a hot cup of coffee.

But he never made it to the door.

After only a single step, he jerked like he'd been shocked. He fumbled off one of his gloves and pulled his phone from his pocket. He barked something into it, listened, and then spat something that was obviously a curse, before shoving his phone back into his pocket. His glove slipped from his grip, but he didn't stop to pick it up. He leapt back into his car, backed up, and turned on his dash light as he pulled away from the curb.

I looked over at Dad. I could tell the same thought that crossed my mind had crossed his own.

Something big was happening.

Without having to say a word, both Dad and I rose and carried our coffees to the door, and outside into the cold. I picked up Buchannan's glove and took it with me into the Escape.

"Where did he—" I started to ask, but Buchannan sped right past us, heading back the other way.

"The church?" Dad asked, once again, thinking the same thing as I had.

"Elsie."

Unlike Buchannan, who'd gone to the intersection to turn around, I made my U-turn in the middle of the street, just barely missing bumping up onto the sidewalk in front of Lawyer's Insurance. Since traffic was mostly nonexistent, I was able to reorient myself and follow Buchannan, who was already out of sight, though I had a feeling I knew where he was headed.

But when we got to the Pine Hills church, his car wasn't in the lot, nor was it parked on the street out front.

I drove past, perplexed, before a new thought hit me.

If it wasn't Elsie he was concerned about, then it had to be Jules. You know, the one who'd received the gift in the first place?

My foot pressed down on the gas without conscious thought. Was I too late? Had the killer made his move on Jules while I was sipping coffee with Dad? I'd never forgive myself if that was the case, though what I could have done to stop it, I didn't know.

But when we reached Phantastic Candies, however, Buchannan's car wasn't out front. Instead, it was parked farther down, on the other side of the street, with one tire propped up against the curb. I pulled up behind him and parked. Dad was the first out of the car.

"Where?" he asked.

I didn't need to think about it. We were parked in front of Heavenly Gate. "Here."

Detective Buchannan was standing just inside
the gift shop, talking to both Lee and Agnes Komph,
who were both alive and well, though they looked
rattled. It was easy to see why.

On the counter behind them, was an unopened,
blue-wrapped gift.

Both Dad and I pushed our way inside.

At the sound of the door opening, Buchannan
glanced back. "No," he snapped, pointing past me,
to the door. "Out."

"They got one?" I asked, indicating the gift.

"Out." Buchannan marched forward, forcing
both Dad and me back out into the cold. "What
are you doing here?" he demanded, breath pluming in the air.

I held out his glove. "You dropped this."

Buchannan scowled and snatched the glove out
of my hand. "You didn't come all the way here just
to give me this."

"I was here earlier," I said. "They didn't have a
gift then."

"Or they didn't tell you about it."

Was it possible that the gift had been here the
entire time? Agnes hadn't seemed all that nervous
when I'd entered. But Lee had been angry. I'd
thought it was because I was talking to his wife, but
could it be because he'd found the gift and thought
I had something to do with it?

"Where did they find it?" I asked.

"It was discovered here."

I frowned. "In the store?"

Buchannan glared. I was asking too many questions.

"When I was here earlier, I didn't see the gift," I

said. "Agnes was talking to a woman named Doris Appleton."

"And?"

I looked to Dad, who shrugged. He hadn't been there. "And Doris has been saying bad things about the businesses in town, including Andrew's Gifts and Death by Coffee."

"You think she left the box when she departed?"

"I don't know. Maybe?" It came out as an uncertain question. "I didn't see her leave it. But she could have come back. Or waited until after I was gone before making her move."

"Her move?" Buchannan didn't look convinced. "What about this Jacob character you told me about? Was he around? Could he have left the box?"

"I didn't see him." Which meant nothing. I hadn't exactly been watching for him at the time.

"Does he have a connection to Ms. Appleton?"

I spread my hands. I didn't know.

Buchannan sighed and scratched his ear with his ungloved hand. "So, you saw Mrs. Komph talking with a friend and you didn't see her receive a gift from this friend or otherwise. You never saw this other suspect. Never saw who left the package. Do you have anything of value to provide?"

I desperately wanted to say something profound, something that would help Buchannan crack the case, but nothing came to mind. "I guess not."

He nodded as if that was exactly what he expected. "Go home, Ms. Hancock. Enjoy the day with your father."

"But—"

"I'll take care of this. If I have any questions for you, I'll let you know."

And with that, he turned and went back into Heavenly Gate. Dad and I climbed back into the warmth of my car.

"What do you want to do?" he asked.

I thought about it, and decided there wasn't much I *could* do. Not with Dad, anyway. "I'm going to take you back to Ted and Bettfast," I said, pulling back out onto the street. "You can talk to Laura and we can meet at my place later for the movie."

"And the meeting?"

I didn't answer. But at this point, I was willing to do just about anything if it meant getting to the bottom of this thing before someone else ended up dead.

18

Dad returned to his room at Ted and Bettfast, somewhat grudgingly. He promised to talk to Laura about the movie, but didn't like that we were once again missing out on spending father/ daughter time together. With everything that was going on, I wasn't too worried about it, but at the same time, I really hoped that by Christmas Eve, Laura would be feeling much better and we could all spend the next two days doing nothing but chugging eggnog and watching old movies.

Once he was inside, I sat in the lot, debating on what I wanted to do next. A part of me wanted to go back to Heavenly Gate and see if Buchannan had left yet. If he was gone, then I could go in and talk to Agnes and Lee. If they'd talk to me, that was.

Thinking back to how we'd last parted, I felt it was more likely that Lee would throw me bodily from his shop than say a word.

I pulled out of the lot and decided to take a few minutes to just drive and clear my head. Nearly all of Pine Hills was decorated for Christmas. Businesses. Homes. Even the library, which was struggling financially, had lights up and a blow-up reindeer sitting out front.

I remembered how when I was little, Dad and I would drive around our hometown to look at all the decorations. I used to carry a notebook and would take note of my favorites. By the end of the night, I'd have a winner chosen and we'd leave them a gift of Mom's cookies in the mailbox with a note telling them how much I enjoyed their setup.

Sometimes, I missed those innocent days.

I turned up the heat as I wound my way through a small residential area where each house appeared to be attempting to outdo the next. The lights weren't on this early, but it made me want to come back later that night to see them when they were. One house had used some sort of snow-maker to coat their lawn in white powder, giving it that little extra Christmas cheer that seemed to be missing due to our lack of real snow.

And then I came to a house where Santa and his elves were nowhere in sight. In their place was a yard-spanning nativity scene. Crosses hung in the windows. Unlit candles sat beneath them. It would be beautiful at night.

Doris would approve.

A wild thought crossed my mind about stopping and knocking on the door. Doris might not live here, but one of her friends might. And then what? Ask them about the murder? About Doris and how she knew the victim?

I pulled off the road, which had practically no through traffic, and coasted to a stop.

Why would Doris leave a gift at Heavenly Gate? They sold items more in line with her ideology. Agnes was her friend, a follower even. It didn't make sense.

If Agnes *had* cheated on Lee with Andrew, then sure, I could see where Doris might be upset with her. But how would that lead to Andrew receiving a gift? Or Jules for that matter?

But Jacob . . . he had a beef with Lee Komph. Had argued with Andrew Carver. And while I couldn't connect him to Jules and Phantastic Candies, that didn't mean there wasn't something there. Jules might not even know what it was he'd done to upset Jacob.

I drummed my fingers on the steering wheel before tapping the touchscreen panel on the dash. I found Caitlin's number and tapped it. She answered on the second ring.

"Hi, Caitlin," I said. "It's Krissy."

"Hi?" It came out a question, and it was no wonder. I never called her. Pop over unannounced? Sure. But never call.

"Quick question and I'll let you go."

"Okay?"

"Boo. Can I have her number? Or maybe her address? If you have them, that is. I know you said you didn't really know her that well, but I'd like to talk to her about Jacob."

There was a brief pause before, "Why?"

I considered how to phrase it. "You said you wondered if Boo was the reason Jacob was at your place the other night, right? If it was, then maybe she could tell me *why* he was hiding out with you. Or maybe she could, I don't know, tell me something about him that will help."

Another pause. "Do you think he killed that man?"

I really wanted to say no in order to reassure Caitlin that her bandmate and friend was innocent, but I couldn't. "I don't know," I admitted. "That's why I want to talk to Boo."

Caitlin heaved a sigh. "All right. Hold on a second and I'll look for her number. I think I have it written down somewhere around here. She and I aren't friends, but Jacob gave it to me in case I needed to get in contact with him about band stuff and he wasn't answering his phone."

"Thank you, Caitlin," I said.

"Yeah. One sec." There was a clunk as she set her phone down.

Seconds passed. I could hear movement in the background and imagined Caitlin sifting through drawers, looking for a number she probably never had a reason before now to think about. Knowing her history with a friend who turned out to be a stalker, I wondered how she was handling this whole Jacob situation. If he was innocent, I really hoped my suspicions didn't kill their friendship.

"Here it is." Caitlin rattled off Boo's number, slightly out of breath, as if she'd run back to the phone. "There's a good chance you'll catch her at home, though she might still be asleep. Jacob's always complaining that Boo keeps odd hours, rarely going to bed until near dawn."

"Did he say why?" I asked. The more I knew about Boo going in, the easier the conversation would be.

"She's online a lot. Games. I think she wants to be a big streamer or something." I could visualize the shrug. "I've never paid enough attention to her to know for sure, and Jacob doesn't really talk about her that much."

Which seemed strange if they were dating. "Okay, I'll call her and see if she's up."

"Better you than me," Caitlin said. "If you find something out about Jacob, something I should know . . ."

"I'll call you right away."

"Thanks. Don't take this the wrong way, but I hope I don't hear from you anytime soon."

I clicked off and, after double-checking the number, I dialed Boo.

"Wha?" came the groggy answer.

"Boo?" I asked, making my voice as friendly as I could.

"Yeah? Who's this?"

"My name is Krissy Hancock. I wanted to talk to you about your boy—" I caught myself. Caitlin talked like she wasn't entirely certain they were dating, and when I'd brought her up to Jacob, he hadn't exactly confirmed their relationship either. "About Jacob."

"What about him?" There was a shuffle of cloth, a muttered, "What time is it?"

"I'm sorry if it's early for you," I said, not quite sure how to answer the first question without coming right out and accusing him of being involved in a murder. I settled on, "Do you have a few minutes to talk?"

"Is this about how he's been acting?" Boo asked.

The words came out slowly, as if she had to focus on them to form them properly.

"It is," I said. "I own a business downtown. A bookstore café. I've seen Jacob around, seen him interact with other business owners. These interactions aren't exactly friendly."

Dead air.

"Hello?" I asked, afraid the call had been dropped, or that she'd hung up on me. "Boo?"

"I'm here."

"Would you happen to have a few minutes to talk? We could meet somewhere if you'd like? Maybe have breakfast?" I'd just eaten, but if it meant I could learn something about Jacob's activities, I wouldn't mind a second breakfast.

"Jeez." There was a clack as something metal hit the phone. It was followed by a groan I imagined was Boo rolling over and stretching to see a clock. "It's early, but I suppose I could grab a bite. How about you come here? I don't like leaving if I don't have to."

"Sure." I waited for Boo to give me an address, but all she did was make grunts while, I assumed, she got out of bed. "Where do you live?"

Boo rattled off an address, sounding half-distracted. "Just come on in. Door'll be unlocked. I'm going to get some clothes on."

"You do that." I paused as she muttered something, but apparently, she'd been talking to herself. "I'll be there in about fifteen minutes."

"Cool." She clicked off.

* * *

Boo's place turned out to be a small little house at the edge of a larger property that held a much bigger house sitting well back from the road. I pulled up in front of Boo's place and climbed out of my Escape. Halloween decorations hung in the windows and foam gravestones dotted the tiny portion of the yard out front that I supposed qualified as Boo's own.

Well, that fits with what I know of Jacob. I suspected the decorations were kept out yearly, and not just for the end-of-year season.

I approached the door, raised my hand to knock, and then remembering what Boo had said, I tried the knob instead. The door opened with a loud squeal of rusty hinges.

"Hello? Boo? It's Krissy."

There was a brief pause before, "Be out in a sec. Take a seat anywhere."

I felt that was awfully trusting since I was a stranger, but hey, it wasn't my house. I closed the door behind me, and then squinted into the gloom. Heavy purple curtains covered the windows, cutting out much of the light. The kitchen was tiny, as was the dining area, so I turned to the living room. There was a couch and chair, but instead of a TV, a trio of computer monitors sat on a massive desk with a fancy-looking chair in front of them. Pulsating lights came from behind the monitors, providing the only illumination in the room.

"Sorry." A door down the hall opened and a stocky woman wearing black pajama bottoms and a blue and pink shirt with some sort of cartoon bunny head on it entered the room. Her hair was dyed black and she was as pale as a ghost. In the darkened room, I couldn't tell if her lack of color was because she never got any sun or if it was from being coated in a heavy dose of white makeup.

She crossed the room and went into the kitchen. She pressed a button on a Keurig and just before the stream of coffee started, she shoved a mug under it. "Coffee?"

"No, thank you," I said, choosing the couch to sit.

"Man, it's early." She yawned and scratched at her cheek. She waited for the coffee to finish, head down. She didn't add sugar or creamer, just took it black as she entered the living room. She chose the computer chair to sit in. "So . . . Jacob, huh?" Her eyes flickered past me, to the room she'd recently exited. I assumed it was her bedroom.

"How well do you know him?" I asked.

"Well . . ." She frowned. "It's like . . . You know how there's guys you like and those you don't and then some that you kind of like, but aren't sure what to do with?"

"Uh, sure." I had no idea.

"Jacob's like that. He can be cool and all, but sometimes, he can annoy the crap out of me." She raised her voice at the last, and then lowered it again. "But he understands me. I don't like people. I don't leave the house if I can help it because I don't want to have to kill someone for looking at me like I'm some sort of freak."

I couldn't help it; I jumped when she mentioned killing someone.

Boo saw it, but instead of getting offended, she just laughed. "Not that I'd actually *do* it, mind you. I'm not like that."

"Is Jacob?"

"Is he what?" As she sipped her coffee, I noted her fingernails were painted the same pink and blue as her shirt.

"Like *that*. If someone were to verbally abuse him, would he hurt them?"

Boo considered the question long enough that I thought I might be on the right track. "It's like this," she said. "Jacob can let his temper get the better of him, like a lot of us, I suppose, but he tends to not let it go. He'll act out, say some stupid stuff, and maybe shove a guy who is getting into his face a bit too much. Tried it with me once. I gave him the good ole knee in the tenders, if you know what I mean?" She grinned.

Oh, I knew, all right. I'd done the same thing when my ex, Robert Dunhill, got a little too handsy, back before Trisha was in the picture.

"Jacob is on the bad end of a lot of abuse," Boo went on. "My parents are top of the list when it comes to getting on him about his looks. They've tried to pull that crap with me too, but realized they can't tell me what to do." She chuckled, and then muttered, "Jerks."

"Your parents?"

"Yeah. Noah and Sandra Holmes." Her gaze shot to the window, toward the house farther on the property. "They own this dump and are letting me live here until I can get my stream up on its feet." She tapped the desk behind her with a pink nail. "It's been slow going since I'm not willing to strip half naked while I'm playing, but I'm gaining some traction because I do have some mouse skills."

I wasn't sure what that last meant, so I focused on what I understood. "Your parents don't like Jacob?"

She shrugged. "He's a friend of mine, so nope. They call him a bad influence on me, like he's the one who made me what I am." She rolled her eyes. "They don't quite grasp that it's the other way around. I mean, Jacob was different, don't get me wrong, but before me, he was too scared to really let it show." She once again raised her voice at the last, as if hoping her parents might hear her.

"How does that make you feel?" As soon as the words were out of my mouth, I winced. It made me sound like I was trying to be her therapist.

Boo merely grinned. "They can say and think whatever they want. They don't control my life. No one does." Another near shout. I was beginning to wonder if that was how she talked all the time.

I was beginning to see why Caitlin wasn't a fan. Boo wanted to be in control of not just her life, but it sounded like the lives of others. Did that mean she was that way with Jacob?

And if so, could she be the reason he was now a suspect in Andrew Carver's murder?

"I heard Jacob was supposed to meet with Teek a few nights ago," I said. "He ended up showing up late. Do you know anything about that?"

Boo's eyes narrowed as she took a sip of her coffee. This time when she answered, she did so carefully. "I remember that night. It was the same night that dude died."

I nodded, tension growing. She'd made the connection pretty darn quickly.

"Jacob was here. We got into it a little bit. He stuck around until we made up and then he left for Teek's. End of story."

"He was here?"

"That's what I said."

"And you fought?"

"Is there an echo?" The hostility had ramped up significantly. Boo set her mug aside, cracked her knuckles.

"Do you mind if I ask what you fought about?"

"Do I mind?" She chewed on that a moment before shrugging. "No, I guess I don't. He interrupted my stream and might have cost me some money. I wasn't happy about it and told him as much. He said he was having a rough week and I told him boo-hoo, cry me a river. He didn't like that, got into my face. I showed him that wasn't a good idea. By the time I was done with him, he knew not to mess with me. He made sure to show me that he understood afterward." A waggle of thin eyebrows followed.

"Was he angry when he left?"

Another shrug, this one dismissive. "Could have been, but he wasn't showing it by then. I just know he didn't have time to kill that guy. He knows people wonder about him, about what he might be capable of. But he was here, with me, so he couldn't have done it."

I moved on from therapist to police officer with my next question. "Can you prove that he was here? You said you were on stream when he interrupted you? Do you have that saved?"

"Sure do. 6Boo9." She spelled it out for me, emphasizing that they were the actual numbers in the name, and not spelled out. "That's where you can find me online. Sub if you wanna help me out."

I glanced past her, to her PC, hoping she'd get the hint and would show me what she had, rather than make me go looking for it on my own.

Instead, Boo stood and stretched. "I've really got to get some sleep," she said. "You know the way out." And with that, she turned and walked over to her bedroom door. She opened the door just wide enough for her to slip inside, and then closed it behind her.

I sat there a moment, half shocked by the abruptness of her departure. Boo was . . . odd. There was no other word I could think of to describe her. I could also understand why Caitlin didn't like her.

When I left, I went ahead and locked the front door before stepping outside. She might be okay with leaving it unlocked and letting strangers come and go as they pleased, but I wasn't. I climbed back into my car, jacked up the heat, and then backed out.

I took one last look toward Boo's house and saw the bedroom curtains were parted and someone was watching me go.

But it wasn't Boo's face peering out at me.

It was Jacob's.

19

After leaving Boo's, I made straight for home, and within minutes, I was sitting at my table, hunched over my laptop, vainly trying to make sense of what I was seeing.

A heavily armored man darted out of a room. A sudden movement, a scope being raised for a split-second, and then he was down. His guns and boxes of what I assumed were ammo spilled out onto the floor. His killer bobbed up and down as she reloaded and sorted through his belongings so fast, I couldn't make heads or tails of them.

Superimposed over the game, in a window in the bottom right corner of the screen, Boo was in her chair, talking nearly non-stop. Her face was made-up to be almost ghostlike, and she kept talking about fragging out like it was something I should understand. Another person slid into view, and another lightning-fast aim and shot put him down.

"I swear, people don't anticipate quick scopes often enough," Boo said. "They just blunder into the room and boom!" She chuckled. "Hey, thanks for the sub Killztheclown. Appreciate it."

I'd been watching Boo's stream for twenty minutes and had yet to see or hear Jacob. I also didn't have a timestamp to go by, just that the stream had taken place on the same evening in which Andrew Carver was killed. Since Boo kept her house shrouded in darkness, I couldn't tell if it was morning or night, though there did appear to be a faint glow to her curtains, telling me there was some sort of light outside.

"Look at that newb," Boo said with a laugh. "Thinks no one can see him." This time, she took the time to aim before downing her opponent who was crouched at the side of a building. "Look behind you next time, loser."

I shifted in my seat. Listening to Boo on her stream had me siding with Caitlin; I wasn't a fan. There was a cockiness to her that I didn't like. I had no idea if the people she was playing against could hear her, or if it was all for the benefit of her audience, but she seemed awfully unsportsmanlike.

"What?" Boo glanced to the side, off camera. I couldn't hear anyone else, but apparently, someone—Jacob, most likely—was speaking. "No. I'm busy."

I turned up the volume and leaned forward. A faint voice could be heard, but not clearly. Whatever was said caused Boo to frown.

"I don't know what you did with it. Jeez." She

turned back to her game. "Ignore him, chat. He doesn't even know what *Warzone* is."

A hand flashed into the screen, blocking Boo's face—and her vision.

"Jacob! Come off it." She leaned to the side, craning her neck so she could see the screen. "The circle's coming. I've gotta get to safety. There's only nine of us left."

"I need to find my—"

"Find it yourself!" she shouted, cutting Jacob off and jabbing him with a violent elbow. "Sorry chat. My jerk-wad of a friend doesn't understand how important this is."

"Friend? Is that what you—" Jacob finally appeared on screen. He was facing Boo, back to the camera, and appeared to be intentionally getting in her way.

Another violent elbow sent him sideways, out of the picture. "Get out of the way!"

A shot rang out. Boo's screen went red around the edges. She cursed loudly, bobbed and weaved into a room, before ducking behind a desk. She then used some sort of item which caused the red edges to vanish.

Jacob reappeared, smacked the headset off Boo's head. She jumped to her feet, said something unintelligible, and then dropped back into her chair just as more shots rang out. On-screen, she jumped through a window, ran a few more feet, and then exploded as everything she was carrying spilled to the ground.

Boo shouted a very unladylike word while flinging her mouse out of sight. She then spun and started screaming obscenities at Jacob, who was screaming them right back.

And this is supposed to clear him of murder?

The yelling went on for a good five minutes before Boo threw herself back down into her chair. Her normally pale face was red with anger. "Sorry chat, I've gotta go. I'll catch you tomorrow, same time, same place. We'll scare up a few wins then." And then the screen went black.

I blinked and checked the next saved video. It was from the following day. And yes, it was the same game. I couldn't tell if it was taking place at the same time of day, only that Jacob was nowhere in sight.

That's because he was hiding out at Caitlin's.

I closed my laptop with a frown. Boo and Jacob *did* fight, just as she'd said, but I had no idea what the argument was about or if he'd left right after she'd signed off. Boo claimed they'd made up, so the assumption was that he'd hung around for a little while longer, but I had no evidence of that. As far as I knew, he'd left as soon as she'd turned everything off.

And I still didn't know what time any of this had happened.

I'm sure there was a computer expert out there somewhere who could determine what time the stream took place. But even then, what I really needed to know was what happened *afterward.* Had they made up like Boo had said? Or had Jacob left, angry with the world?

Either way, I was skeptical of their story. Yes, they'd fought, but much of the encounter was incomprehensible. And with Jacob hiding in Boo's bedroom while I'd talked to her, I was finding it hard to believe anything she'd told me.

The cynical part of me wondered if they'd concocted the story together before my arrival. It would explain why Boo had decided to talk to me when she had no reason to otherwise.

A knock at my door brought me to my feet. I answered, half expecting it to be Buchannan come to grill me about my trip to Heavenly Gate. Or perhaps Jacob to warn me off about looking too deeply into his whereabouts the night of the murder.

Turns out, it was neither.

"Hi, Krissy, I hope we're not bothering you," Jules said as soon as the door was open. Behind him, Lance was holding a steaming cakepan. He was still wearing oven mitts.

"No, of course not." I stepped aside. "Come on in out of the cold."

Jules and Lance entered.

"We won't keep you," Jules went on. "But we wanted to drop off a lava cake for you. Call it a thank you for warning me about that gift. If you hadn't told me, I don't know what would have happened."

"You didn't have to do that," I said, mouth already watering. The smell of chocolate filled the room as Lance set the cake down on the island counter.

"Of course, we did," he said, pulling off his oven mitts. "You saved Jules's life."

"I wouldn't go that far." I paused, noting the

time and the fact that both of them were here. "Who's at Phantastic Candies?"

Jules glanced at Lance before answering. "We decided to close early today. I need to do some serious inventory anyway. And with everything that's happened lately, my mind hasn't been on work."

"We figured it would be best to close before something else happened," Lance added.

I wanted to reassure them, but what could I say that would help? I couldn't guarantee that the killer wasn't still out to get him or that the police were close to finding the culprit. It made me wonder if perhaps I should close Death by Coffee, give the employees more time off before Christmas, to be safe. Paid, of course.

"I don't want to think about that," Jules said, shaking his head. "Besides . . . Cake!"

I licked my lips, and after about point-zero-one seconds of thinking about it, I grabbed three plates from the cupboard. "Have some with me."

Lance looked like he might object, but Jules smiled and sat down at the counter. "Only a tiny piece. I wouldn't want to spoil my dinner."

I cut into the lava cake and placed what I thought were small slices on each plate, though both Lance and Jules looked appalled, as if I'd cut the thing into thirds.

"You should be stocked up on candy canes," Jules said, taking a bite. Chocolate oozed from his fork. "Beth came by to pick them up. I went ahead and added a few extra boxes as another thank you. No charge."

"You don't have to do that." I took a bite of my

own cake and just about melted into my seat. It was pure bliss. "I'll happily pay for them."

"No, I do." He sighed. "I'm trying hard to put all of this behind me, but I keep thinking about it. Why would someone target me?" He reached for Lance, who clasped his hand. "It got so bad, I kept thinking that every time someone came through the door at Phantastic Candies, they'd be wielding a knife."

Lance muttered something under his breath before he chomped down hard on his cake-filled fork.

"Lance has been acting as my watchdog," Jules said with a smile. "I can't go five feet without him checking to make sure there are no killers waiting for me."

"That's sweet of you," I said. "Hopefully, this won't go on much longer."

"That would be nice," Jules said. "Has there been *any* progress on who might have left the gift?"

I considered it before speaking. "Well, the police are involved now, so I'm sure they've figured something out. And with the Komphs receiving a gift at Heavenly Gate, there's even more evidence for them to consider."

Jules's eyes widened. "There was another gift?"

"There was." Another bite. I chewed and swallowed before continuing. "It was strange because I was there earlier and they didn't appear worried. Angry, yeah, but not like they'd found a threat outside their home."

"You think it was dropped off there?" Lance asked.

I shrugged. "I don't know what to think, honestly. I suppose it's possible they'd found it and had yet to decide what to do with it when I showed up." Perhaps that was why Doris was there. Agnes could have called her to talk about it before informing the police.

Jules tapped his fork on the edge of his plate. "Do you know what was inside their box? Maybe it will tell us something about who sent it."

"Beats me. Buchannan got there before me and he wasn't about to tell me anything."

We fell silent then, focusing on our cake and own thoughts. I was torn. On one hand, I was almost positive Jacob had something to do with the murders and Boo was covering for him. They might have fought during her stream, but that didn't mean she didn't care about him. Not every relationship consists solely of flowers and hugs.

Yet, on the other hand, I couldn't shake the feeling that Doris Appleton had to be involved. She'd complained about the local businesses, and despite what was going on, she was *still* harping on us. She was at Heavenly Gate before I'd shown and could have left the gift when she'd departed.

But why Jules? Whether it was Jacob or Doris or someone else, I just couldn't make all the pieces fit.

A car pulled into my driveway just as I finished the last bite of my cake. I checked the clock and was surprised to find it later than expected. I stood. "Keep eating," I told Jules and Lance, who both looked as if they might rise with me. I went to the door and opened it just as Laura and Dad reached it.

"Hey, Buttercup," Dad said, giving me a kiss on the cheek.

"Krissy." Laura's smile was a little tired, but seemed genuine enough. "Thank you for having us tonight."

"No problem." I stepped aside, letting them in. "Jules and Lance brought cake."

"Cake?" Dad's eyes lit up. "I smell chocolate."

"We should probably go," Jules said, rising. "We don't want to intrude."

"Nonsense." Laura waved him back down. "We're going to watch a movie. You should join us." She paused. "If it's okay with James and Krissy?"

"Of course," Dad said. "We'd love to have you." He leaned over the lava cake and breathed in deep. "Do you mind?"

"No, go ahead." I turned to Jules as Dad dug in. "Please, stay. You can help Laura choose the movie."

Jules and Lance shared a look. "Are you sure?" Jules asked.

"Positive." I led him and Lance into the living room. Laura followed. "Choose anything you'd like." I handed Lance the remote. "Something Christmasy."

"That might have been a mistake," Jules said with a grin. "Never let Lance control the TV if you can help it."

"I'll be good," Lance promised. "Unless . . ." He raised his eyebrows at Laura, who grinned mischievously.

"Let's see what we can find," she said.

I left them to it, somewhat nervous. Dad had already inhaled most of his cake, and was holding an unpopped bag of popcorn. I nodded for him to toss it into the microwave.

He waited until it was going—and everyone else was busy with the TV—before he spoke.

"Have you thought about what we discussed earlier?"

"About Doris's meeting?" I asked. "A little."

"And?"

I looked over to where Jules, Lance, and Laura were laughing over something they'd found. Since they were standing in front of the TV, I couldn't see what it was.

"I'm not sure we can, not with everyone here."

"Are you sure? I think it gives us a better opportunity." Dad moved closer and we turned our backs to the others. "With Jules and Lance here, they could keep Laura company. I'd hesitate to bring her with us to the church, just in case . . . well, you know?"

In case Doris is a murderer. I got it. "We'd have to tell them where we're going. We couldn't just up and leave them."

"I know. And it's not like we'd have to *tell* them, tell them."

"Tell us what?"

Dad and I both jumped. Jules had snuck up behind us. Laura and Lance were seated on the couch, having seemingly settled on the movie.

"It's nothing," I said.

Jules put a hand on his hip and gave me a flat look. "That didn't sound like nothing."

I looked to Dad for help.

And, like Dad, he went for honest. "There's a meeting tonight. It's at the church."

At Jules's questioning look, I added, "Doris Appleton is running it."

"And you want to go to it," Jules said.

"It could give us some insights into her thought process," Dad said. "And there's a chance she could let something important slip."

"Something important, like she's involved in what's happening around town?" Jules asked.

I nodded. "And if she's not, then perhaps someone else there is." Someone like Agnes Komph.

The microwave dinged. I removed the popcorn, and then put in a second bag before filling a large bowl with the first.

"If you're going, I want to go too," Jules said once the microwave was humming again.

"We haven't decided yet," I said.

"It starts at seven." Dad moved closer to Jules, lowered his voice further. "We have time for the movie, and then we'd have to head that way. Do you think Lance would be okay with you going? I'm still not sure what Laura's going to say."

Jules considered the question before shrugging. "Honestly? He won't be thrilled, but I can't keep sitting around, waiting for something bad to happen."

"Doris and her group might not be connected to the murder at all," I said, feeling as if this whole thing was spiraling out of my control. I mean, taking Dad was one thing. Adding Jules, especially if it was against Lance's wishes, was another.

"This could be our best opportunity to find out if she is," Dad said.

Both Dad and Jules turned to face me. It appeared the final decision was up to me. By their expressions, I was pretty sure I didn't really have much choice.

"All right," I said, relenting. "After the movie."
The microwave dinged again and I filled a second
bowl with popcorn. "But if Laura and Lance say
no, then we don't go."

"Deal," Dad said.

Jules nodded before scooping up one of the
bowls of popcorn. "Shall we?" he asked.

I carried the other bowl into the room and
handed it to Laura before grabbing a dining room
chair for myself. As I sat, I noted what movie they'd
chosen.

"*Bad Santa?*" I asked. I'd expected something a
little more, well, wholesome.

"I think we all need a laugh," Lance said, drap-
ing an arm across Jules's shoulder. "And something a little raunchy."

"A little?" Laura laughed.

I could only imagine what Doris would think if
she knew we were watching something this vulgar
so close to Christmas.

20

I don't know how they did it, but as soon as the movie was over, Dad and Jules took Laura and Lance aside, and spoke to them separately. The next thing I knew, I had my heavy coat on and was sitting in my Escape with Dad and Jules, while Laura and Lance remained behind to watch another movie. They were all smiles as we left.

A part of me wanted to ask Dad what he'd told Laura, but decided I probably didn't want to know. The same went for Jules with Lance. I didn't think they'd lied to them, but I couldn't imagine that whatever they'd said was the full truth. I mean, we *were* hunting for a killer, after all.

The night had turned downright frigid, so I had the heat on full blast, yet it wasn't making much of a dent in the frost-covered windshield—or my chattering teeth. I could see the road, so it wasn't like I was driving blind, but it did make everything appear blurry around the edges, which in turn, made me even more nervous about the trip.

While I focused on the road, Dad and Jules were deep in conversation, mostly about the gift Jules had received and any suspicions he might have about who had left it. I listened with half an ear, but thus far, Jules had come up with no new suspects.

When I pulled into the church parking lot, both men fell silent. I parked beside Doris's old Cadillac, but left the engine running.

"Do we really want to do this?" I asked, peering through the circular clear spot on my windshield where the heat had finally started to eat through the worst of the frost. The church looked like it always had, yet the thought of walking in there filled me with the sort of dread normally reserved for walking into a dentist's office.

"We're here, so we might as well." Jules sounded as nervous as I felt.

"We won't stay long if we're not wanted," Dad said. "But I feel like we have to at least poke our heads inside long enough to see who's here. Maybe someone will stand out."

Like us.

I shut off the engine. The silence that fell made me shiver. This was going to be awful.

We piled out of the car as if headed for a funeral. Our footfalls sounded especially loud in the crisp air, and peering up into the sky, I noted the clouds were gone and the stars were shining bright enough to leave an afterimage in my vision when I looked away.

Dad led the way to the door and held it open for Jules and me. As soon as I was inside, I could hear Doris's voice echo down the stairs. She wasn't yelling per se. She sounded more like a preacher talking to a room full of ardent believers. I could imagine her standing at front of the room, arms spread as she lectured, while the other women sat with their hands clasped, as if clutching at her every word.

Up the stairs we went, and into the room where the writers' group meetings were held. Doris wasn't standing, but was seated in front of a semi-circle of chairs, each occupied by women, all of whom I recognized as the same group who always followed Doris around. There were no surprises there.

"We must make an examp—" Doris's mouth snapped shut with a click when she saw the three of us enter.

"Sorry to interrupt," I said, hands held up in preemptive surrender. "We're not here to cause trouble. We just want to listen."

Murmurs rippled through the small gathering, and then all eyes turned toward Doris to see what she would say.

Doris, for her part, didn't immediately start shrieking that we were unclean and unwanted. She weighed us one by one, starting with a narrow-eyed look at me, and then moving on to Jules, who received a similar glare, and then on to Dad. She stared at him for twice as long, likely trying to place him, before she heaved a sigh.

"Fine. You can take the empty chairs in the back."

Sure enough, a pair of seats near the back of the group were empty. I took another quick head-count and realized that Agnes Komph was missing. I didn't know the group well enough to know if the last seat was always a spare or if someone else was a no-show.

A brief argument followed where Dad and Jules insisted I sit and I steadfastly refused. Everyone watched us with disapproval, and after a few moments, I won out and the two men sat.

"Don't mind us," I said once that was settled. "Go ahead."

Doris scowled at me, and for a moment, I thought she might change her mind and give us the boot. Another sigh followed, this one dramatic enough that I knew it was for my benefit, and then she began to speak.

"Now, where was I?" She plucked a thin white thread from her shirt and dropped it onto the floor. "Ah, yes. I was talking about our beloved town and the travesty that has infected it." A pause long enough for me to wonder if she might be talking about the murder, before, "Commercialism of the worst kind. It's disgusting!"

Nods and murmurs followed. I expected someone to shout "Amen!" but so far, none were forthcoming.

Doris leaned forward in her seat. "It's a shame that it's come to this. Greed was Andrew Carver's downfall. I fear that others will follow suit if nothing changes."

Both Dad and Jules looked over at me. I could read the question in each of their eyes: *Was that an admission of guilt?*

"I don't condone what happened to Andrew," Doris went on. "It has crushed a former member of ours, a woman who was once a great friend, Erin Carver. We should reach out and see what we can do to bring her back into the fold. She needs us, needs our support."

More nods, more grumbles of agreement. But I did note there was one head that moved less vigorously than the others, someone whose lips barely parted while others were voicing their agreement and support.

"And now, another member of our community has been targeted."

This was met by gasps and a good amount of head shaking.

"As many of you have noted, our dear friend, Agnes, is not here with us tonight. She and her husband, Lee, received a gift, much like Andrew and Erin before them. A threat meant to scare them. They do not deserve this, as they are the only business in town that hasn't attempted to exploit Christmas, and yet . . ." She closed her eyes, bit her lower lip as if moments from tears.

"What can we do?" This from a woman whose name I didn't know.

"We can pray, of course," Doris said, clasping her hands together, as if she planned on praying for Agnes and Lee right then and there. "And we can push for change. Go out, pressure these other businesses in town. Get them to change their ways. It is because of them that the rest of us suffer."

Next to me, Jules shifted uncomfortably. Around the room, heads turned, revealing thin-lipped, disapproving stares.

"This might have been a bad idea," Jules muttered, though he remained seated.

Doris spent the rest of the meeting calling for action against those of us who marred the holidays by trying to profit off it. She also turned her attention to the various groups that met in the church, mentioning both the gin rummy group she'd forced out that very night, as well as the writers' group. Apparently, it was their presence that caused a perceived dip in the church's attendance numbers.

It was all I could do to not to speak out. At one point, Jules grabbed my hand, causing me to realize I was halfway to my feet, ready to give Doris a piece of my mind. It was hard to listen to her words and not get angry, especially since it appeared as if she was making it a point to target people and groups close to me.

By the time she was done, I was in a foul mood, but was determined to make something of the night. I'd come here, not because I believed in what Doris preached, but because I wanted to find Andrew's killer before someone else was hurt. To do that, I needed to mingle, see what I could learn.

Coffee and snacks were set up on a nearby table. As soon as Doris finished speaking, the congregation rose and headed over that way, breaking off into small groups to talk. Some went to stand off to the side on their own, including one woman I was very interested in talking to.

"What do we do now?" Dad asked.

"I'm going to talk to her." I nodded to the solitary woman. "If you want to join me, you can."

"Actually, I'm going to step outside for a few

minutes," Jules said. There was actual anger in his eyes, something I wasn't accustomed to seeing. "This was . . . something."

"It was," Dad said, before turning to me. "If it's all right with you, I think I'll go with him. I need some fresh air."

I'd hoped Dad would back me up like he had been recently but understood. "I'll see you two shortly." I rested a hand on Jules's arm. "Don't take what Doris said to heart. She doesn't know what she's talking about."

"Oh, I know," he said. "But thank you."

As Dad and Jules headed for the door, I turned toward the woman I'd noticed earlier. She was standing alone with a Styrofoam cup of black coffee in her hand. She looked almost as unhappy as Jules about being there, and I hoped that meant she would be willing to voice her concerns about Doris—if she had any. I plastered on a smile as I approached her.

"Hi! Cleo, right?" I held out a hand. "I'm Krissy."

Cleo shot a look toward Doris before briefly touching my hand. She pulled back like she was afraid that too much contact with me would infect her. "I'm Cleo, yes."

"I noticed you didn't seem to agree with everything Doris said." When Cleo didn't answer, I pressed. "Do you think she's pushing you, as a group, too hard? I mean, a man was murdered, someone whose wife used to join you here for these meetings."

Cleo held her cup close under her nose, eyes darting around the room like she was a trapped animal. "I, um . . ." Her gaze once more landed on Doris, who was staring right at us. Cleo wilted under that stare. "I'm sorry. I should go."

Before I could object, she set her mostly full coffee on the table and then scurried for the door, shoulders hunched as if against a blow. She snatched a coat from the rack near the door, dropped it, and then grabbed it as she left, not bothering to put it on until she was out of sight.

Well, that was interesting. Cleo was clearly afraid of Doris. Was that because she feared for her life? Or was she scared that Doris might kick her out of the group for talking to me?

I hoped Dad and Jules would stop her outside, and that Cleo would be more willing to speak to them than she was me.

"What did you say to her?"

I jumped at the harsh voice that had come from over my right shoulder.

I turned to find the woman who'd badmouthed Death by Coffee the first time I'd met Doris and her group standing so close, I could have kissed her. "You're Annie."

Her smile was tight-lipped. "I am. And you're the owner of that bookstore café." It came out as an accusation. "Cleo is a delicate soul. You should leave her alone."

"I didn't mean to upset her," I said. "Truly. I only asked her what she thought about the meeting."

Annie continued to give me that condescending smile, though her eyes had hardened. "Why *are* you here, exactly?"

Some rather unkind thoughts passed through

my head then, but I kept them to myself. Who was this woman to question my motives? Okay, yeah, I wasn't there because I agreed with Doris's views, but that didn't mean I meant any ill will toward them.

"I was curious," I said, going for diplomatic instead of confrontational. "I thought that maybe I could learn something by sitting in on one of your meetings."

"Did you?"

I blanked. "Did I what?"

"Learn something?" Her self-satisfied sneer made me want to slap her. "Considering you were here with . . ." Her gaze darted toward the door where Dad and Jules had gone. "Well, I'm not one to throw insults around, but you know what I mean."

I did, and the urge to tell her off was so strong, I had to clench my fists to keep from snapping at her.

"Doris had a lot to say," I said. It wasn't much of an answer to the question, but it was better than, "That you're a bunch of hypocritical, unkind, overly opinionated women who wouldn't know the Christmas spirit even if it slapped you upside the head."

"Doris has her finger on the pulse of this town," Annie said. "If everyone would learn to follow Doris's lead, all these murders would stop."

Because Doris would quit killing people? The question was on the tip of my tongue. I bit it back and merely smiled and nodded for Annie to go on.

She was more than willing to keep talking.

"There are bad people in this town, doing horrible things on a daily basis." She looked me up and down, implying I was one of those people. "The only way to get them to stop is to put the fear of a higher power into them."

"It sounds like you approve of Andrew Carver's murder."

Annie's smug grin faltered ever so slightly. "Murder isn't okay, no," she said. "But there's no reason why we can't use Andrew's death to our advantage. Perhaps others can be saved thanks to his sacrifice."

Andrew hadn't sacrificed himself willingly, and I almost said so. "Do you have any thoughts on who killed him?" I asked instead.

Annie's gaze shot past me, to where Doris stood with a trio of other women. "Well, I can't right say. We are not here to judge."

The heck you're not. Another thought I decided best to keep to myself.

Doris saw us looking and started messing with the gigantic ring on her finger. It brought another question to mind.

I turned my attention back to Annie. "Is Doris married?"

"What?" She seemed genuinely perplexed by the question.

"She's wearing a ring on her ring finger. I was wondering if that meant she was married."

"Oh." Annie frowned. "No, she's not married anymore."

"Divorced?"

Annie hesitated before answering. "Her husband, Dave, died. Some say it was under suspicious circumstances."

I stepped up closer to her, lowered my voice. "Are you saying he was murdered?"

Annie cleared her throat and suddenly looked a lot like Cleo when I'd tried talking to her. "It happened about the time Erin Carver began drifting away from us. There were . . . tensions between Doris and Andrew, if you know what I mean?" She gave me a pointed look, one that said as clearly as words, *Which was why Andrew killed her husband.*

"When was Dave killed?" I asked. Had I somehow missed a murder happening in Pine Hills?

"It's been a few years now." Annie went stiff, almost panicked. "I should let you go." She spun and walked briskly away.

I didn't need to look to know that Doris was approaching. I could *feel* the hostility following her like a dark cloud. When I turned to face her, she was smiling, but there was no kindness in it.

"I'm surprised to see you here," she said, voice chilly. "Especially with those two men."

"We heard about your meeting and wanted to come." Which was all true. So what if I left out *why* we'd decided to sit in?

"I have nothing against you personally," Doris said. "But you really should reconsider who you call a friend. Others see you with these people and, well, your reputation takes a hit."

My reputation? Boy, did Doris miss the mark on that one if she thought I cared about my reputation. "I like my friends. They haven't hurt anyone."

"Not physically, no," Doris said. "But when you associate with bad people, it impacts your very soul. If you continue to spend time with them, to let them infect you, you will eventually be beyond saving."

"Saved from what?" I asked, my anger finally bubbling over into my tone. "From receiving a threatening gift like Andrew and Jules? Like Agnes? From your insults?"

Doris's lips thinned. "What are you implying?"

That you killed Andrew in retaliation for your husband's death? But if she had, what did Jules have to do with it?

Since I had no other answer, I motioned toward her finger instead. "I like your ring."

"Do you now?" Doris covered the ring with her other hand, as if afraid I might steal it.

A tense moment followed where neither of us spoke. It was broken when Jules and Dad returned, looking half-frozen.

"It's getting colder out there," Dad said, tone light. "Hello. I'm Krissy's father, James Hancock." He held out a hand to Doris, who stared at it like he'd just wiped his nose with it.

"I think it's time you should go," she said, backing away. "There's nothing for you here. None of you." She shot a glare at Jules before turning away.

"I don't think she likes me," he said. I got the impression the feeling was mutual.

One look around the room told me that no one else would be willing to talk to us. Doris was right: It was time for us to go.

"Hey, Jules?" I asked once we were back in the Escape. "Did you know Doris's late husband, Dave?"

"No. Why?"

Why indeed? "I'm not sure. Just trying to put everything together." Like why any of these people would target Jules and Phantastic Candies. They might not like his Christmas candy sales, but that didn't seem like a very good reason for murder.

21

"This is a terrible idea," I muttered as I peered out of the plate glass windows of Death by Coffee into the gray morning. "I'm going to die. This is it; the end."

"What was that, Ms. Hancock?"

I turned away from the window to find Jeff giving me a worried look from near the stairs.

"Nothing," I said. "I'm just talking to myself."

"I do that sometimes." He ducked his head and then slunk upstairs into the books like I'd scolded him.

I'd come in and helped open the store, but that wasn't the main reason as to why I was at Death by Coffee in the frigid early morning. No, I was here to meet my friend Cassie Wise for what I was quickly realizing was going to be a death-run.

The morning rush had already come and gone, leaving only a handful of die-hard coffee drinkers sitting as far away from the plate glass windows as they could get. My own coffee was steaming hot, and yet, no matter how much I drank, I just couldn't seem to get warm.

Pooky and Eugene were busy restocking and re-supplying behind the counter, while Jeff was handling the shelving of books upstairs. I had a feeling that it was going to be a slow day because no one in their right mind would want to be out with it being as cold as it was.

And it's supposed to only get colder.

I sat and held my coffee close as I watched out the window for Cassie's arrival. After last night's festivities, I wasn't in much of a mood for a run, but I'd promised her I'd be here. If I canceled on her, then she wouldn't go, and then I'd feel bad for ruining her exercise.

So, I was going to do it. Though I did have an ulterior motive for going out. No, make that two of them. Erin Carver and Agnes Komph.

If anyone would know more about Doris's late husband Dave's death, it would be Erin. And if Andrew's murder was retaliation for Dave's murder—not that I was positive it *had* been murder, but it was a decent assumption after what I'd been told—I was curious as to how Agnes fit in. What better way to "happen" upon the two women than to do so while on a morning jog with a friend?

There were still the same holes in my theory as there were with my other theories. If Andrew's death was tied to Dave's, then why target Jules? A distraction? A mistake? When I'd asked Jules if he knew Dave, he'd said no, and I believed him.

Five more minutes passed before Cassie appeared, walking briskly down the sidewalk. She saw me in the window, grinned and waved, before she entered, bundled from head to toe.

"I'm going to grab a quick coffee and warm up before we head out," she said.

"Take your time." I might want to talk to Agnes and Erin, but I had no problem putting it off for a few more minutes if it meant I could stay inside a little while longer.

Cassie went to the counter, ordered, and then carried her coffee over to me. She sat without taking her heavy coat off.

"The cold will be good for us," she said. "Fresh, crisp air. It's good for the lungs."

My lungs were already burning from my short sprint to and from my vehicle. "Are we doing the usual loop today?" I asked.

Cassie sipped her coffee, nodded. "Unless you want to add to it?"

"Maybe a little." Our normal route didn't take us past Heavenly Gate. I didn't know if Agnes or Erin would be in the shops, but I was holding out hope that at least one of them would be. "I'll see how I feel once we get going."

"Don't force it for my sake," Cassie said. "I know there's a lot going on for you right now, so if you want to call it off . . ." She trailed off, leaving me an opening I desperately wanted to take.

"No, I'll be okay," I said, knowing I was going to be anything but. "I was wondering . . ." It was my turn to leave the thought hanging. I was curious about something, yet I wasn't sure Cassie would want me prying.

"About?" She drained her coffee and stood so she could start her pre-run stretching routine.

"On our last run, when we went to Phantastic Candies, you left before Detective Buchannan arrived." I considered getting up and joining her for stretches, but decided to huddle closer to my quickly cooling coffee instead. "Was there a reason you didn't want to see him?"

Cassie spread her legs, placing her feet at shoulder width, and then bent sideways at the waist, stretching her arm over her head. She considered the question for a five count before she straightened and shrugged.

"Not really. I like going on runs with you and I'm excited for when the gym finally opens, but I have no interest in getting involved in murders and police business. I know it's your thing, and I'm totally okay with you wanting to help a friend. It's just . . ." She spread her hands. "I like my life simple. Talking to the police is anything but."

I couldn't fault her for that.

I finished off my coffee, and then attempted a few stretches myself, which mostly consisted of me bending my knees a few times. No grabbing my foot and standing on one leg or bending myself in half. Once that was done, I bundled up tight, said a silent prayer that I wouldn't freeze to death, and then followed Cassie out the door.

The cold air was like a shot of adrenaline. My first instinct was to use it to run right back inside, but I gritted my teeth and kept pace with Cassie as we started our normal route, taking a left from Death by Coffee, which put us heading in the wrong way from the other two shops. My vision was obscured by the white plumes caused by my breathing, but not so much that I didn't notice the car that pulled away from the curb the moment we started moving. A subtle glance back told me the car was indeed following us.

I couldn't make out the driver without turning and staring. I kept hoping the car would pick up speed and pass us, but it never did. It crept along, pumping out a thick exhaust that blew past us every time the wind picked up.

"Cass?" I said, keeping up the pace, all while fighting the urge to stop and confront our tail. "Did you see that car? It's still behind us."

"I see it." There was the slightest twinge of nervousness in her voice. "Should we cross?"

With a car coasting slowly behind us? A car that might hold a killer, nervous about my nosing into his or her business? I didn't think so and said as much—leaving out the whole nervous killer bit, as not to scare Cassie more than she already was.

But we couldn't keep running in a straight line forever. Turning might spook our tail, but it *would* make them have to act. Speed away, stop and confront me. Either would be better than having them behind us.

"Let's go back to Death by Coffee," I said. "Turn around as one?"

Cassie nodded, her pretty face showing her stress in pressed lips and a pinched brow.

"Now!"

We spun in unison. The car turned out to be a small blue Mazda that looked like it might have been old and rickety twenty years ago. A woman sat behind the wheel. She was wearing a heavy fur-lined coat with the hood pulled up and cinched under her chin. She was leaning forward to peer at us over the steering wheel, eyes wide and scared.

Cleo?

The car jerked to a stop as she slammed on the brakes, causing more exhaust to bloom. It was enough to cause me to cough and to have to wave it away. Both Cassie and I slowed until we were standing right beside the car. Cleo rolled down the window.

"Krissy Hancock?" she asked, voice trembling. She sounded unsure.

"Cleo." I stepped up to her car. "Are you following me?"

"I . . ." She frowned, then nodded. "I suppose I was. It's just . . ." Her eyes flickered to Cassie, who was keeping warm by jogging in place. "I think I need to talk to you."

"About?"

Cleo hesitated and looked into her rearview mirror as if she expected to have a tail of her own. When she spoke, she kept her voice low. It was nearly drowned out by the rumble of her car. "It's about Doris."

That was all I needed to hear.

"We're heading back to Death by Coffee now. Meet me there?"

Indecision was plastered all over Cleo's face as she thought about it. It made me wonder how long she'd been sitting outside of Death by Coffee, waiting for me to leave.

"All right." It was followed by a sigh that was filled with an odd sort of relief. "This needs to be done. I'll see you there." And then, to herself as she rolled up her window, she said, "Doris isn't going to like this one bit."

"I didn't want to do this where Doris might over-hear, you understand? She is taking things too far."

We were seated in Death by Coffee, as far away from the counter as we could get and still be in the dining room, which was blessedly empty. Cassie had opted to stick around, mostly on my insistence since I still wanted to finish our run—and to talk to Agnes or Erin if either were inside their husband's respective shops. She sat with her arms crossed, look-ing like she wanted to be anywhere else. Cleo didn't look much better.

"How so?" I asked.

"She's pushing everyone hard this year, forcing us to act on her impulses, even if we don't want to." Cleo shook her head. "It's not right. Some of what she's telling us to do flies in the face of what many of us believe in."

My tongue wanted to blurt out, "Like murder?" but my brain told me that might cause Cleo to change her mind about talking with me. She was perched at the edge of her chair, a finger snap away from bolting for the door. Every couple of seconds, she'd glance toward the window, as if she expected Doris to be peering in at her like a stalker in a horror movie.

"Is it about the local businesses?" I asked in-stead. "What does she call it? That we're 'exploit-ing the season'?"

Cleo nodded. "In some cases, I suppose I agree with her. There are stores that push unnecessary junk onto their customers, all for profit, and in the name of the holidays. It's a disturbing trend that seems to only get worse as time goes on." She paused. "But here? Selling a coffee drink or a Christmas book? How is that so bad?"

I agreed wholeheartedly, but didn't say so. No sense in pushing the issue when she was willing to talk.

"And I'm not so sure that trying to get other groups thrown out of the church is such a good idea either. Everyone is entitled to the space, not just us. It's gotten so bad lately, a few of the ladies have started to question Doris's ways."

I couldn't help myself. "Like Erin Carver did?"

Cleo hesitated before answering. "That was a rough time for many of us. At first, I didn't understand why Erin decided to leave. None of us did. But now, after seeing what Doris is capable of, I truly do wonder if Erin didn't have the right idea. Her and Agnes."

"Agnes?" I asked, sitting forward. "Was Agnes thinking of leaving the group as well?"

When Cleo spoke, she did so while staring out the window, voice barely above a whisper. "This was a few months back. Erin was already long gone, and while Agnes was dead set against her leaving at the time, something changed. She started becoming more and more reserved at group, wouldn't immediately agree with whatever Doris said."

Because what Doris was saying ran contrary to what Agnes was doing? I wondered. If she *was* cheating on Lee with Andrew and Doris found out . . .

I nodded for Cleo to go on.

"Eventually, Agnes started missing meetings. Doris

couldn't have that, not when she wanted to present herself as being strong and in control. So, she sent her a reminder of her faith."

The phrasing caught me as odd, so I asked, "A reminder of her faith?"

Cleo nodded. "It's a collection of items meant to remind—" She frowned. "Well, I suppose they're meant to *guilt* those with flagging faith back into the fold. I think we've all received one from Doris at one time or another. There's always something in the reminder that makes you feel like you have no choice but to come back, that if you don't, your life will be over."

I wondered if that meant *over* over, as in dead, but didn't ask. "Do you know what was in Agnes's reminder?"

Cleo shook her head, looked almost offended I'd even ask. "They are often very personal." She got a far off look in her eye, as if remembering what was in her own. "Doris takes care to put them in these thick, brown plastic bags so no one else can see inside."

Like the bag I'd seen Erin holding.

These reminders of faith sounded a lot like the blue-wrapped gifts that had started appearing around town. Could Doris have changed tactics and moved on from trying to work on her own flock, and instead, decided to go after those she felt were leading them astray?

It was something to think about.

"Annie told me Doris was once married," I said. "And that her husband died under suspicious circumstances."

Cleo paled, making me think I'd gone too far,

but she didn't flee like the last time I'd tried to talk to her. "Dave was a nice man," she said. "Doris cared for him deeply, though she didn't always show it."

"They fought?"

"Don't all couples?" Cleo started fidgeting. I was losing her. "I don't know the details on what happened to him, and I don't want to."

"Could Andrew's and Dave's deaths be connected?" I asked.

Cleo swallowed hard, gaze drifting to Cassie, who had yet to speak a word. It was as if Cleo was begging her to speak up, to say something that would allow her to avoid answering the question.

Cassie, for her part, stared right back.

"Doris has a way about her." Cleo spoke slowly, carefully. "She speaks and those who are willing to listen act on her words as if they are scripture." She abruptly stood. "That's all I have to say. I'm sorry if I wasted your time."

And with that, Cleo pulled her hood up, and cinched it so tight I wondered how she could breathe, before she scuttled out the door.

"That." Cassie said, pointing at Cleo's vacated chair. "That's what I was talking about. I can't even imagine the stress that woman is dealing with, all because of this Doris lady. It's upsetting."

"I'm sorry," I said, and before I could ask her to finish our run, my phone rang. I checked the screen and was surprised to see it was from Shannon.

"I should take this." When Cassie nodded for me to go on, I answered. "Hello? Shannon?"

"Krissy!" She practically shouted my name. "I

really hate to do this, but can I borrow you for a little while?" In the background, a baby wailed. "I don't know who else to call."

"Is Shay all right?" Panic filled my voice. It didn't sound like a pained wail, but what did I know about baby sounds?

"She's fine," Shannon said. "But I have an emergency to deal with. It's . . . personal."

I caught on quickly. "You need a babysitter."

"Please, if you would? I know it's short notice and if you can't, just say so. I tried Trisha, but she and Robert are meeting with the bank and she can't get away and—"

I cut her off. "It's all right. I'll be right there."

"Really?" The relief in her voice was palpable. "Thank you so much. I didn't know who else to call."

"Give me fifteen minutes," I said. "There's no need to thank me. It'll be my pleasure."

After another unnecessary "thank you" and "I'm sorry" we clicked off. I turned to Cassie, ready to apologize myself, but she waved it off before I could speak.

"Go. I overheard. It's too cold to run anyway."

"Are you sure?" I asked. I hated disappointing her, especially after making her sit through Cleo's confessional.

"I'm sure." She smiled to prove it. "Let's try this again another day."

"It's a date." I grabbed my coat and threw it on. "Thanks, Cass. I'll make it up to you."

"No need. Although . . ." A gleam came into her eye. "I think I'll hold you to that route extension. It's time we started pressing ourselves."

My heart dropped and my knees weakened, but I put on a brave face. "I can't wait." I only hoped that when we did decide to push harder, it happened sometime *after* the New Year when both the cold *and* Andrew Carver's murder were long behind me.

22

Shannon Pardue lived in a rental that looked as if it could use one of those house makeover shows. The siding was aging and dirty, the roof had missing and flapping tiles. I knew from experience that it wasn't as bad inside. Shannon did what she could while living solely on a waitress's salary, but when the landlord didn't care about maintenance, it's hard to keep up on your own.

A car I didn't recognize sat in her driveway. The exhaust was working overtime, pumping out smoke like there was a fire inside the engine. I could make out the silhouette of someone sitting in the driver's side. Longish hair, a thin frame bulked by a stiff coat I thought might be a leather jacket. Man or woman? I couldn't tell.

There was just enough room for me to pull up beside the car's passenger side to park. I climbed out and tried to sneak a peek at the driver, but they were looking out the driver's side window, so

all I could see was his or her hair and a somewhat
pointy chin.

It's none of your business, Krissy. As I made for the
front door, I fought the urge to glance back toward the mysterious car. I was curious to know if
the person inside was Shay's father. Or an aunt. Or
one of Shannon's disapproving relatives. The car
itself was pieced together without the usual identi-
fiers that would tell me what make and model it
was. A Frankenstein's car.

The door opened as soon as I reached it. A fraz-
zled looking Shannon was holding a crying Shay.
Both looked to be at the ends of their respective
ropes.

"Thank you for coming on such short notice,"
Shannon said, bouncing Shay a few times. "Come
on in."

I entered. The house looked much the same as
it had the last time I was there, though admittedly,
back then, I hadn't paid it much mind considering
the circumstances. There was one of those col-
lapsible playpens in the middle of the living room.
A stuffed bear lay forgotten inside it. Baby blankets and other random toys and baby supplies
were strewn about the room.

"Are you sure you're okay with her for a little
while?" Shannon asked. "She's been an absolute
bear today."

Shay's face was bunched as she wailed, little
hands balled into fists. Terror gripped my gut, but
I stood fast.

"I'll be fine." I hoped. "You go ahead and take
care of whatever you need to."

Shannon looked torn, but then a honk from

outside steeled her resolve. "She's been fed. If you can calm her down, she should be good for a nap. Let me show you where I keep the diapers."

I followed Shannon and the crying Shay around the house. Once I was given the baby-tour, Shannon handed Shay over, who looked at me once, and then redoubled her wails.

"If you have any trouble at all, just call. I won't be too far away and can come right back."

Another honk. This one caused a frown to crease Shannon's brow.

"I'll be fine," I assured her. "Go."

With a peck atop Shay's head, Shannon grabbed a long winter coat that went down to midcalf and headed out the door before throwing it on. She just about sprinted to the car, climbed inside, and then they were off in a cloud of black smoke.

"Looks like it's just the two of us now," I said.

Shay responded by crying even louder.

It took all of five minutes for me to realize that babies were *so* not my thing. I mean, they're cute and all, and when they weren't screaming their heads off, they made me feel all soft and gooey inside.

But Shay's tantrum . . . just, no. I gently bounced her like I saw Shannon do, to no avail. I tried to play peek-a-boo with the teddy bear in the hopes it would cause Shay to smile. Instead, I think I traumatized her further.

Nothing I did helped. At fifteen minutes in, I considered throwing in the towel and calling Shannon to come rescue me. I was in over my head and wasn't afraid to admit it.

But then Shay's wails lessened. She was in her

playpen, lying on her back. I removed the bear like Shannon had requested, leaving the space empty of all but the baby. Her cries died down to sniffles, and then, blessedly, Shay closed her eyes, little hands still closed into fists.

She was asleep.

I sagged down onto the couch feeling more exhausted than when I'd spent an entire day working at Death by Coffee. I knew babies were work, but this was nuts. How Shannon was managing it while living and working on her own, I'll never know.

If Paul and I ever get married, I don't think children will be in our future.

And speaking of Paul . . .

Carefully, as not to wake Shay up, I rose from the couch and tip-toed into the kitchen. There, I pulled out my phone, put it on vibrate just in case I were to receive a call, and then placed one myself.

"Hey, Krissy." It came out as a sigh.

"Hi, Paul. Did I catch you at a bad time?"

There was a brief pause. "Why are you whispering?"

"I'm at Shannon's, babysitting. Shay is asleep and I don't want to wake her."

"Ah." Another pause. "You babysit for Shannon?"

"First time. Shay has a future as a heavy metal singer ahead of her. She's got some serious lungs on her."

Paul laughed. "That bad, huh?"

"Let's just say I've had my fill of babies to keep me content for the next couple of months. Maybe years." I peeked into the living room. Shay was still out, and I hoped she'd stay that way until Shannon returned.

Paul chuckled before he asked, "Was there a reason for your call? I'm still at work, though at this point, I could use a break."

Oh, how I wished I could give him that break. Maybe pancakes and hot chocolate in front of a fire. Or curling up on the couch, blanket thrown across our laps, while we watch a calm, quiet movie on TV.

Unfortunately, no matter how good it sounded, it wasn't to be.

"It can wait," I said. "I guess wanted to hear your voice after all of the screaming." I paused, almost stopped there, but added, "I've talked to some people who've had some rather interesting things to say."

"You're not poking around where you shouldn't be, are you?"

"No." Not really. "In fact, the woman, Cleo, sought *me* out, not the other way around."

"Uh-huh." The disbelief was obvious.

"I swear! I'm not sure if what she had to say is important to the case or not, but I thought you ought to know."

"It's Detective Buchannan's case."

"I know, but . . ." But John Buchannan didn't like me all that much and he would give me that narrow-eyed look that made me want to smack him. It's hard to talk to someone like that.

"I get it," Paul said. "How about you come down to the station once you're done with Shay? I can't promise I'll be here, but someone will be."

"Okay." Though I'd much rather talk to Paul. Over dinner. Or, better yet, *after* dinner.

I was about to ask him when he might be free when there was an eruption of voices in the background on his side of the line. The sound was muffled briefly, and then Paul said, "I'm sorry, but I've got to go. This day . . ."

"That's all right. I'll talk to you later?"

"Of course."

Before I could say another word, he'd clicked off. Something had happened, and I wondered if it had anything to do with Andrew Carver's murder. The urge to call around town was strong, but I decided it could wait until after Shannon was back. I returned to the living room and planted myself on the couch to watch over Shay like a good babysitter.

The minutes crept by. Every time Shay so much as twitched, I tensed, expecting her to wake and resume her wailing. I dreaded the possibility of having to change a diaper, and prayed Shannon returned before it came to that.

But Shay remained asleep, just as Shannon remained out, taking care of whatever emergency that had dragged her away.

With little else to do, I pulled out my phone, not quite sure what I was looking for. Over the years of sticking my nose in the middle of police investigations, I'd taken to using social media as an investigative tool. But as time progressed, more and more people started leaving their profiles private, making nosing around in their business much more difficult.

I started by looking into individual people—Agnes, Doris, and even Jacob—but to no avail. The women didn't have Facebook pages as far as I could tell, and Jacob's was full of nothing but music videos he liked. No personal info, no little posts like, "Going out to kill a mean shop owner tonight." Nothing.

Next, I tried searching for Andrew's Gifts. There *was* a Facebook page for the shop, but there wasn't much to it. There was mention of the Christmas sale, a few posts about new stock, and that was it. Judging by the lack of followers, it wasn't a popular online shop. There weren't even comments on the posts, which in this age of online trolls, was a shock.

Frustration had me wanting to scream. Heavenly Gate didn't have a Facebook page, but did have an online website that served as a shop. With no place for comments, it was a dead end as well.

I rose, double-checked to make sure Shay was still okay, and then headed into the kitchen to pace.

I had all sorts of motives for all kinds of people, but nothing concrete. Jacob could have killed Andrew in retaliation for throwing him out of his store. I'm not sure why Jules or I might be a target, but Lee Komph? Yet another person who'd tossed him out. Jacob's alibi was also weak, and Boo's video didn't do him any favors.

And then there was Agnes and her possible relationship with Andrew. If it had gone south, she could have killed him for it. Or maybe it was Doris, who might have retaliated for Andrew killing her husband, Dave. Or maybe it was Erin, who discovered Andrew was cheating on her and decided to do something about it. Or Lee. Or . . . or . . .

Snap decision.

I checked online, found a number, and dialed.

"Hello?"

"Hi, Erin? It's Krissy Hancock. I'm the one who—"

She cut me off. "I remember. Why are you calling?"

Why indeed. "I'm not sure it's important, but I was thinking about something I saw when we talked a few days ago."

"Okay? If this is going to take long, I really can't talk."

"It won't. You were holding a brown bag made out of a thick plastic. You put it behind the counter when I came in."

Silence.

"I was talking to a woman, Cleo. Do you know her?"

"I do." Emotionless.

"She told me that Doris gives those to people. They're called . . ." I acted as if I was floundering for the right words, just to see what Erin would say. "What did she call them?"

"Reminders of faith."

"That's it. Was that what I saw you holding when I came in?"

A long pause before, "It was."

"When did you receive it?"

"I don't see how that matters."

"It might not," I admitted. "But I'm curious. Humor me."

Erin sighed heavily into the phone. "I suppose it can't hurt to tell you. Doris left it for me back when I first left her group. I found it on my doorstep and knew immediately what it was. I didn't let it sway me."

"What was in it."

"That's personal." Another sigh, this one resigned. "But I can say that when you told me about how that gift Andrew received might be connected to his murder, I immediately thought of the reminder, started to wonder if it was related. It felt so . . . so Doris, you know?"

"It does seem like something she'd do," I said.

"I keep wondering if maybe she's behind all of this. She's never approved of me and Andrew, and she most assuredly didn't approve of his store. I just don't understand why she had to kill him if . . . if . . ." Her next breath trembled, as if she was on the verge of tears. "Do you think she could have done it? Could Doris have killed my husband?"

"I wish I knew," I said. I also wished I knew if I could believe her. Erin *had* nearly disposed of a piece of evidence. Sure, she might not have considered the gift box as such at the time, but that's what it was. And yeah, she'd given it to me, seemingly willingly, but she could have panicked, not known what else to do, when I'd brought it up. I mean, what was she supposed to say? No? That she'd rather throw away evidence in her husband's murder?

And, hey, the box was empty either way. Her fingerprints were on it, but she could say that was because she'd handled it *after* Andrew's death. What harm would giving it to me do? It would make her appear as if she was trying to help, though why she hadn't saved it for the police still bothered me.

"I've really got to go," Erin said, cutting into my thoughts.

Always so busy. I wondered if that was because she *was* a busy woman, of if she was simply trying to get rid of me. "Thank you for talking to me. I really do appreciate it."

Erin didn't respond to that, other than to hang up.

A whimper from the other room had me tensing, thinking Shay was about to wake, but whatever it was that had bothered her—discomfort or a bad dream—it wasn't enough to wake her fully.

I returned to the living room to keep an eye on her, just in case, while my mind churned over what little I'd learned. And what had I? Not a whole lot, to be honest. My suspect list was the same size as it always had been, and I felt no closer to an answer as to who killed Andrew Carver.

The sound of a car door slamming startled me. Shay whimpered again, but remained asleep. I rose just as the door opened and Shannon entered, looking as if she'd just run a marathon.

"Are you all right?" I asked her as she bent over the playpen to check on Shay.

"Yeah. Just pooped." Satisfied her daughter was fine, she collapsed onto the couch. "Family issues are draining." She started to rise before she could get comfortable. "Let me get some money to pay you for your time."

I waved her back down. "There's no need for that. I'm helping out a friend. It was my pleasure."

Shannon hesitated a moment, before falling

back onto the couch. "I'll pay you back somehow. Thanks."

"Don't mention it." I paused, and then asked, "Was that . . . ?" I trailed off and jerked a thumb toward the door, while glancing at Shay. I didn't know what to call Shay's father since he wasn't in the picture.

Shannon caught my meaning without me having to explain. "No. Slick is a friend of Jack's."

Slick? I didn't ask. "Jack your ex?"

Shannon nodded, closed her eyes, and rubbed at them. "Though we weren't really dating, so I'm not sure you could call him my ex. He took advantage of my bad decisions and then fled like a coward when Shay came along."

"I'm sorry," I said, not sure what else to say.

"Don't be. He's not worth it. Even if he hadn't bailed on me, I wouldn't want him in Shay's life. He's not dad material, if you know what I mean?"

"Yeah, sure."

"The jerk showed up at my parents' place and was making a scene, which is why Slick showed up here. He's not a bad guy, really, and he thought I should know what was going on. It's taken care of now, but I expect to get a call from Mom before long. *That's* going to be a conversation I could do without."

"Is there anything I can do?"

She shook her head, and then, as if she had some sort of baby-radar, she rose and stepped up to the playpen just as Shay opened her eyes. There was a second where I thought the crying would resume, but Shannon plucked her up, patted her bottom gently to check to see if it was full, and then she carried her to the couch.

"It's snack time," Shannon said with a tired smile. "You can stay, but . . ."

"No," I said. I liked Shannon and all, but I wasn't so sure I wanted to be there while she breastfed her baby. "I need to get some things done today anyway."

"About the murder, right?" She started unbuttoning, which had me stepping toward the door.

"Yeah. I need to talk to Paul."

"Good luck with that." Shannon fell silent, eyes going briefly distant. I wondered if she was remembering her time dating Paul, and how her life would be different if I hadn't broken up with my boyfriend at the time, Will Foster. She came back to herself with a smile. "Tell him I said hi."

"Will do."

And before she could finish unbuttoning, I hurried out into the cold, knowing that if I ever ended up in Shannon's situation, Paul Dalton would do the right thing and stick by my side.

23

"**M**erry Christmas."

The cop looked at me like I'd just told him to jump off a bridge before he smiled. "Thanks," he said, and then pushed the rest of the way out the door to the Pine Hills police station. I noted he had a skip in his step that wasn't there before I'd spoken as he made his way to his cruiser.

Despite recent frustrations, I was feeling pretty good. Maybe the Christmas spirit was finally taking over and overriding my worries about the murder and strange gifts. I tapped the wreath hanging from the door before I entered, humming an off-key Christmas tune.

Only a single officer lounged in the main room. He was seated at a desk, feet propped on a nearby chair, eyes closed, earbuds in his ears. His soft snores told me he was asleep, and not just relaxing while waiting for a call.

Paul's car wasn't in the lot, so it wasn't a surprise

not to see him inside the station. Chief Dalton's door was closed, though I could see a pair of moving shadows through the partially closed blinds on the window that told me she was inside with someone.

I was about to wake the sleeping officer when the door opened behind me and Officer Becca Garrison entered, not in uniform, but carrying an overstuffed laundry bag. She jerked to a stop when she saw me.

"Krissy? What are you doing here?"

"Hello, Officer. I have something I want to report."

Garrison's face bunched up. "Don't do that."

"Do what?"

"Call me 'Officer.' It sounds weird coming from you." She started walking toward the interrogation room. "Call me Becca. Follow me."

"All right, Becca." I grinned as I followed her.

The interrogation room looked pretty much the same as it had the last time I was there. The same old table sat in the middle of the room with the same old uncomfortable plastic chairs. The dartboard hung above the couch and the coffeepot held the same black sludge I couldn't imagine anyone could drink.

But now, there were added touches that told me that Becca Garrison was still using it as a temporary apartment. A box of oatmeal sat next to the coffeepot, along with a small microwave. The couch had a blanket and pillow. A tattered paperback rested atop them.

Garrison tossed her bag into the corner and then removed her freshly washed uniform from it.

She folded her clothing over one arm and then turned to me. "This has been an adventure," she said with a sigh. "Had to have a friend do my laundry, just so I'd have clean clothes. It feels oddly invasive, even though I'd asked her to do it."

"Are you holding up okay?" I asked her. She looked good, if not a little rumpled around the edges. Sleeping on a police station couch could do that to a person.

"I'm fine. It's not so bad, really. I think I'm getting used to it."

Garrison had been scammed on her place by the guy who'd sold it to her. Apparently, he'd managed to do his scheme legally, so nothing could be done about it. It put Garrison in a financial situation she had yet to climb out of. She'd taken the department up on the offer to let her sleep on the couch here, but she steadfastly refused to accept help from anyone else, and that included her friends.

"If you want to sleep in a bed, my spare room is still available."

She shook her head. "No, thank you. I think it's going to work out. I expect to be out of here in less than a month. I can tough it out until then."

"You've gotten your money back?"

She snorted. "Not hardly." Her bicep flexed as she squeezed her fist. It was the only sign that she was still angry about what had happened to her. "What was it you wanted to report? I need to get changed before Chief Dalton sees me out of uniform, but can take a minute if needed."

"Go ahead," I said. "I can wait. It's not time sensitive or anything."

Garrison hesitated before she said, "Give me a minute. You can hang out in here." She smiled. "Wouldn't want someone to think you're in trouble again."

She strode from the room and entered a bathroom down the hall, leaving me in what was really beginning to feel like a bedroom. I'd been inside the room countless times over the years, yet this was the first time I really felt like I was invading someone else's space.

I turned my back on the couch and Garrison's personal belongings, but declined to sit in the plastic chairs. This wasn't going to be an interrogation. I was there to talk, and hopefully, help the police find a killer before the killer made a move on Jules.

Garrison returned within five minutes. She was in her uniform now and had touched up her makeup, so she looked refreshed. She walked over to the coffeepot, grabbed a mug, and then glanced at me. "Want a cup?"

One look at the way the sludge oozed within the pot and I shook my head. "I'll pass."

"Good choice." She poured herself a cup anyway. "So, what's up?"

I hesitated. Becca Garrison *was* a police officer, but it was John Buchannan's case. As much as I didn't like talking to him, this was something he should hear. "Is Detective Buchannan around?"

"He's out at the moment and I'm not sure when he'll be back." She took a sip, grimaced, and then leaned against the table. "I take it this is about the murder."

"Kind of." And then, because someone needed

to know, I told her what I'd learned from Annie about Doris's husband, Dave, along with my theory that his death might be tied to Andrew's own.

Garrison was shaking her head before I was finished.

"Don't let Doris Appleton's tall tales distract you," she said.

"Tall tales? Dave didn't die?"

"Oh, he did, but he wasn't murdered."

My heart sank. "So, Andrew's death wasn't retaliatory."

"It still could be," Garrison said. "But not for Dave's death. No, he died of a heart attack compounded by a stroke. Some of the people I talked to said it was because Doris never stopped hounding him. Doris was the one who started the rumor that he was murdered, likely in response to the talk about her being the reason he'd died."

Which did sound like the Doris Appleton I knew. "Andrew was stabbed, right?"

Garrison nodded. "He was."

I bit my lip and considered. "I had a chat with Lee Komph the other day. He was holding a wood chisel."

I didn't have to say what I was thinking. Garrison caught on right away.

"It's always possible," she said. "You didn't happen to see blood on it, did you?"

I closed my eyes and thought back. I remembered seeing the chisel in Lee's hand, remembered him opening the door, putting the pointy end inches from my face. I could recall the smell of the wood he'd been working on, the anger on his face.

But of blood, I had no recollection. I told Garrison as much.

"Figured that'd be too easy." She sighed, considered her mug and then set it aside. "Besides, Detective Buchannan thinks he knows who did it."

"What?" I took a step back in my shock. "What do you mean he thinks he knows?"

Garrison checked her watch and then motioned for me to follow her out of the room. I did, trailing behind with my mouth hanging open.

He knew? Then why was I there throwing around unsubstantiated rumor? I mean, it's not like he was under any obligation to tell me anything, but still. The least he could have done was to tell me that I no longer had to worry about someone killing Jules in my bookstore café.

Nothing had changed in the station since we'd been in the interrogation room. No Buchannan. No Paul. Chief Dalton was still locked inside her office and the other officer was still asleep at his desk. Yet it all felt different somehow, like the calm before a storm.

"Is that where Paul's gone?" I asked, thinking back to the commotion I'd heard over the phone. "To catch the killer with Buchannan?"

"Paul?" Garrison looked confused before she shook her head. "No, he had something to do at home."

I blinked at her. "At home?" When a killer was about to be apprehended? It didn't make sense that he'd miss that. "Why's Paul at home?"

Instead of answering, Garrison nodded toward the door. "Here he is."

I thought she meant Paul, but when I turned, it

was Detective Buchannan who was headed for the station doors.

And he wasn't alone.

With wallet chain beating at his left thigh, head down so his hair covered his face, and his hands cuffed behind him, Jacob shuffled his way toward the doors, looking as defeated as a man could get.

As they entered, Garrison and I stepped aside. Jacob didn't look up, just allowed himself to be led past us, to the interrogation room. Buchannan, however, narrowed his eyes at me, like I was there to mess up his arrest, before nodding once to Garrison, and leading Jacob away.

"*Jacob* is the killer?" I asked. I was shocked, despite my own suspicions about him. "Buchannan's got proof?"

"Remember that night when Mr. Phan was being lured to Death by Coffee?"

"By that gift he'd received. The one you carried out of Phantastic Candies."

Garrison was smiling as she nodded. "That's the one. I was there that night and I saw someone matching Mr. Callahan's description lurking down the street."

It took me a moment to realize she was talking about Jacob since I hadn't heard his last name until then. "Jacob was there? Buchannan told me no one suspicious showed up!"

"He must not have wanted to give too much away until he was certain it meant something," Garrison said. "You know how John can be."

Oh boy, did I. "What time did you see him there?" I asked.

Garrison rubbed the back of her neck as she considered it. "It was at about ten that night. I only remember because I'd glanced at my phone to check the time, and when I looked up, the person was gone."

Ten. Hours before Jacob's car had left Caitlin's. "Are you sure it was Jacob?" I asked.

Garrison's smile faded. "Pretty sure. I only got a glimpse. Why?"

"He was at my neighbor's house that night," I said, thinking it through. "I kept peeking out the window because I knew he was there and I was nervous. He didn't leave until a little after midnight."

"It *was* dark," Garrison admitted. She sounded worried. "The person I saw was dressed in all black and was keeping to the shadows, so I didn't get a look at their face. The only distinguishing feature was a reflection off a metal object around thigh-high." She held her hand down next to her right thigh to emphasize.

Like Jacob's wallet chain. And while Jacob was of average height and weight, like a lot of people, not everyone in town dressed in all black.

Garrison was silent a long moment before she spoke again, "Are you certain about the time? Could Mr. Callahan have left and come back."

I considered it. I supposed it was possible that Jacob had snuck out, driven off, and then gotten back before I noticed his car was gone, but I didn't think so. I'd checked the windows almost religiously.

"I didn't *see* Jacob after I talked to Caitlin," I said. "But his car never left, not until after midnight. Caitlin's either. And I'm pretty sure no one showed up to pick him up. I would have seen the lights or would have heard them pulling up."

Garrison looked toward the interrogation room, a frown forming. "John needs to know about this," she said. "I'm going to go talk to him."

"If you want me to stay, I can."

"No, you go ahead. I have a feeling he's not going to be very happy and you probably don't want to be here for it."

I could only imagine Buchannan's rage once he found out I was poking holes in his theory, especially since I was the one who'd told him about Jacob in the first place.

As Garrison headed back to the interrogation room to tell Buchannan the bad news, I slipped out the door, questioning myself the entire way back to my Escape.

Was I positive I'd checked regularly enough to have seen Jacob's car during the window in which he'd had to have left in order to get to Death by Coffee at ten? I *had* attempted to sleep, so it was possible I'd dozed just long enough to miss him.

And what if it wasn't Jacob's car I should be worried about, but Boo's? She could have picked him up, parked down the street as not to alert Jules or me. If Caitlin had fallen asleep, all Jacob would have needed to do was sneak out, meet Boo, and then head to Death by Coffee. Once he saw the police there, he could have had her drive him back, and then climbed into his own car to leave, which is what I'd heard at midnight.

Someone needs to tell Caitlin.

And yet, I couldn't bring myself to do it, not

without knowing for sure whether Jacob was innocent or guilty.

I found myself headed to Paul's instead. I needed to see him, to talk to him and get his opinion before I did anything. Jacob's possible guilt was hitting me harder than expected. It made me wonder if he'd considered walking across the yard and killing me before heading to Death by Coffee. Had I come *that* close to a killer?

Paul's car was sitting in his driveway, which was a relief. I'd been half afraid I'd end up missing him and would have to decide what to do on my own.

I climbed out of my Escape and hurried to the front door, anxious to see him. I knocked. The door opened almost immediately, but it wasn't Paul who met me.

The girl had to be no more than twenty. Her hair was a tangled mess atop her head, as if she'd recently been rolling around on it. Her face was flushed and she was wearing a shirt that was too big for her tiny frame.

A shirt I recognized.

"That's Paul's," I said. It came out as a whisper with no force behind it.

The girl winced when she tried to brush hair out of her pretty face, which was coated in a fine bead of sweat. "It is. Do you want me to get him? He's here."

Thankfully, I didn't need to reply. I wasn't positive I'd have been able to speak if I'd tried.

"They should be okay for a few hours, at least until—" Paul, who'd just emerged from a back room, cut off when he saw me. "Krissy? What are you doing here?"

My mouth opened, but nothing came out. Paul was here. With another woman. She was wearing his shirt.

He came to the door and put a hand on my shoulder. "What's going on? You look upset."

Paul was in his uniform. He didn't look rumpled or out of breath or anything of the sort. Just the woman. The *girl*. It made me think of Constance, a waitress at the Banyon Tree who'd taken a liking to Paul. A lot of young women were infatuated with him. I mean, come on; a good-looking man in uniform? Who wouldn't be smitten?

"I can always take myself," the girl said. She groaned as she leaned against the wall.

"No, Susie, I'll take you."

The name rang a bell. "Susie?" I asked, failing to place it.

"My dogsitter," Paul said. "Ziggy tripped her and Susie hit her head."

"I think I'm all right," Susie said. "And don't blame Ziggy for me being clumsy. I should have been watching where I was going."

Paul's two huskies often forgot how big they were.

"She fell," I said, sense finally seeping in through my thick skull. "She was watching the dogs."

Paul gave me a funny look. "Yeah. Why else do you think she'd be here?" And then it dawned on him. He could have gotten angry, could have turned defensive.

Instead, he laughed.

"You thought I was . . . ?" He chuckled as he looked back at a confused—and pained—Susie. "My shirt. You had to think . . ." He laughed harder.

I felt like an idiot. "I've got a lot on my mind and wasn't thinking straight."

Paul's laughter ebbed. "Sorry about that. I really needed a laugh." He wiped a tear out of his eye. "Susie was watching the dogs when Ziggy took her out. She managed to rip her shirt on the way down, hence she's wearing mine. She hit her head pretty hard and might have a concussion."

"I'm fine," Susie said, though she looked anything but.

"Grab your coat and we'll go," Paul said. "You need to see a doctor."

"Will the dogs be all right?" I asked. "I could stay and watch them if you need me to."

"No, they'll be fine. I took them out, got them some food. They can handle being alone for a few hours."

Susie was pulling on her coat with a lot of grunts and winces. I stepped in past Paul and helped her pull it on. It was the least I could do after thinking she was sleeping with Paul behind my back.

"Thank you," she said. "I wrenched my shoulder pretty good, too." With her good arm, she reached up and rubbed at her jaw. "Feels like someone socked me in the chin." She turned to Paul. "If you want to stay here with her, I can drive myself." To me, "I live down the street, so it's not a long walk to my car."

"I'll drive." Firm, before he turned back to me. "Did you need something? You could always ride with us if—"

"I was just visiting," I said. "I stopped by the station like you told me to and was told you came home, so I thought I'd stop by and check on you."

"You sure?"

"Positive," I said. "I think I'm going to call Dad and Laura in a bit and see what they're up to. They're only here for a few more days and I haven't seen them nearly as much as I'd like."

Paul gently placed a hand on Susie's back and led her out of the house, into the cold. As the door closed, I heard a single bark, and then the house fell silent.

"Once this is taken care of, I can stop by if you want?" Paul said. "Or later tonight?"

"What about tomorrow?" I asked. "It's Christmas Eve and it would be nice to have a get-together at my place. Dinner maybe? You don't work, do you?"

"I can make the time," Paul assured me. "I'd better get her to the doctor."

Susie was already climbing into Paul's car with grunts and groans. She was trying to play it tough, but I could tell she was hurting.

"You do that," I said. "I'll text you the time after I talk to Dad and Laura. Maybe we can all get together again. Christmas dinner a day early!"

Paul leaned forward and kissed me on the cheek. "Sounds great. I'll talk to you later, Krissy." He climbed into his car to drive Susie to the doctor.

With nothing else to do but feel like a fool, I got into my own car and headed to Death by Coffee. Right then, a hot peppermint cappuccino sounded like the best thing in the world.

24

"Krissy? It's your turn."

"Huh? Oh. Sorry." I drew a tile from the pile, looked at it, and then found a spot where I thought it fit. Nearly the entire coffee table was already full of tiles creating cities of varying sizes, roads that went nowhere, and in one corner, a dragon just waiting for the right tile to be drawn so it could move.

Yolanda, Avery, and a woman I'd just met, Tyra, sat around the table with me. When I'd arrived at Death by Coffee for my peppermint cappuccino, Yolanda had asked if I'd join them for a game of Carcassonne. I'd agreed, not realizing how massive the game was, especially with the expansion boxes Yolanda had added.

I picked up a little red man and considered. "I'm not sure where to put the thingy."

"The meeple," Tyra corrected for about the tenth time since we'd started.

"The meeple." I'd already claimed the city I'd just added to, but there was a small road piece leading from the tile I'd placed which, for now, wasn't worth much. "It's my last one."

"You can always save it," Yolanda said. "That city is going to take a while to finish. And over here . . ." She motioned toward where most of my little guys were located. I'd apparently made a mistake. and now, most of them were trapped until I found just the right piece from a rapidly dwindling supply.

"Maybe I should." I eyed the road, and then placed the meeple anyway. "But I won't."

The door jangled open, drawing my attention from Tyra's turn. Donnie Cooper entered and made straight for the counter where his sister, Pooky, was busy cleaning up after her shift.

"Excuse me a moment," I said, rising from the couch with a popping of knees. A quick glance at the clock told me hours had passed and it was indeed time for Pooky to go. The time stated on the side of the Carcassonne box had said it would take less than an hour to play, yet two hours had passed, and we still had a lot of tiles left to draw.

"Do you need me to carry anything?" Donnie asked Pooky as I approached. "Or what about your coat? Are you sure it's warm enough? Here." He started to shrug out of his own massive coat, which would have buried Pooky beneath its bulk if he'd tried to put it on her.

"I'm fine, Donnie," she said. "My car is right outside."

"I know, but I don't want you to get cold. And I thought if I could help . . ."

"That I'd let you move back in?" She sighed. "Look, Donnie, we tried it. It didn't work."

"I've changed. I swear, Cla—Pooky." He grimaced at the use of her preferred nickname. "I just need a few months to get things set to rights."

"That's what you said the last time."

"Yeah, but it's Christmas."

I could see his words strike her like a slap. I stepped in.

"Hi, Donnie," I said. "I didn't expect to see you today."

He stiffened, but kept his smile. "Hello. I'm just here to help Claire." He held up a hand as his sister sucked in a breath. "Sorry. Pooky."

"That's nice of you," I said. "Do you need help?" I asked her.

"I'm all right." And from her tone, I caught her double meaning.

"Great. I'll see you after Christmas?"

"I'll be here." Pooky flashed me a smile, pulled her coat on over her shoulders, and with her things in hand, made for the door.

"Ah, come on. Let me help!" Donnie followed her outside, voice pitched in a whine.

I took a deep breath and let it out slowly. Tomorrow was Christmas Eve and Death by Coffee would be closed until after Christmas. That meant I wouldn't know for days if Pooky caved to her brother's pleas. Turning a family member down was hard enough. Doing it during the holidays was near impossible.

Upstairs, the three women had stood and were stretching and talking amongst themselves. I hurried back up to join them.

"Sorry," I said. "Is it my turn?"

"I think we're going to call it," Yolanda said. "You're closing early today, right?"

I nodded. "In an hour, but I'm not working."

"I know. The game's just taking a while and I'm not sure if we'll be done by then."

"I've got to get back home," Tyra said. "Dinner will be expected."

"Are you sure?" I felt bad, like my slow play and constant distraction was the reason they were quitting.

"We're sure," Yolanda said, while Avery nodded. "We can still score everything now and see who won." She turned to the mass of tiles. "Let's start with Krissy. This city here is worth . . ."

The next thirty minutes were spent calculating the value of every meeple controlled point. Avery won by a landslide, with Yolanda and Tyra coming in with near identical scores next. Me? Let's just say I don't think Carcassonne is my type of game.

Once the game was packed away and the three women were gone, all that was left was me, a single older man sipping a black coffee by the window, and Eugene and Jeff, who were lounging behind the counter, waiting out the last fifteen minutes.

Alone upstairs, I decided to make a call.

"Hey, Buttercup," Dad said by way of answer. I could hear voices in the background. "What's up?"

"I'm just checking in," I said. "Sounds like you've managed to get Laura out of the room?"

"Yeah, we saw there was going to be a Christmas play tonight and decided to go. You can join us if you'd like? We're out shopping right now."

My mind flashed on another shopper, one in black clothing and with a wallet chain. Any Christmas spirit I might have had faded.

"No, that's all right," I said. "You two have fun. I'm going to make a Christmas Eve dinner tomorrow. Paul's coming. We'd love it if the two of you would join us?"

"You're *cooking?*" Dad sounded incredulous.

"Ha-ha. Funny. Yes, I'm cooking."

He chuckled. "Of course, we'll be there. Wouldn't miss it."

"Great. I'll let you go. Tell Laura hi for me."

"Will do. I'll see you tomorrow, then?"

"I'll let you know what time. Have fun!"

I clicked off and tapped my phone against my chin. The old man in the dining area rose and left the store. Eugene quickly turned the sign to CLOSED and went to wipe down the vacated table. We were officially done until after Christmas.

I helped finish closing everything down, but my mind wasn't on the work. I kept thinking of Jacob and the night Death by Coffee was targeted. Jacob was at Caitlin's. He was seen outside the bookstore café that night. His car never moved. I could have missed Boo picking him up.

It just wasn't lining up. Why Jules, when he never targeted Jacob like Andrew and Lee had? How could Jacob slip out unnoticed? What about Andrew and Agnes's relationship? Lee was too big to be mistaken for Jacob, but he did carry around a sharp object that fit as the murder weapon.

"See you, Ms. Hancock." Jeff waved as he exited, with Eugene close behind.

"Merry Christmas!" I called after them.

The door closed, and silence fell inside Death by Coffee. I closed my eyes and attempted to settle my mind.

Jacob could be guilty. If he was, that meant Jules was safe.

In my mind's eye, I saw a shadowy figure lurking on the sidewalk. Light reflected off metal at the figure's hip. Jacob.

But something was wrong.

I tried to force my brain to pick up on whatever my subconscious was trying to tell me, but it steadfastly refused to resolve itself. I was missing something, something important. I didn't know if it would prove Jacob's guilt, or if it would instead prove him innocent.

But standing around an empty Death by Coffee wouldn't prove anything one way or the other.

I double-checked to make sure all the machines and lights were turned off, and then left, locking up behind me. A damp, cold wind blew in, causing me to shiver. I climbed into my vehicle, considered going home, and then found myself driving slowly down the street, toward the two locations I'd started the day wanting to visit.

No one was inside Andrew's Gifts. The store was closed up tight, the lights off, like they'd been the night Andrew had been murdered. It was already getting dark outside, which meant most of the store was cast in shadow.

I drove by, almost relieved no one was there. The church across the street was busy, and I noted Doris's car in the lot. I wondered if she was having another meeting, or if the church was having holiday services. It was definitely the time of year for them.

I was worried I'd find Heavenly Gate closed when I drove past Phantastic Candies and saw that Jules had also closed early. But when I pulled up, a light was on inside. Agnes Komph had her coat on, that tiny handbag of hers thrown over her right shoulder. She was standing at the counter, and at first, I thought she was waiting for Lee. After a few moments, she heaved a sigh, and turned off the lights.

I met her just outside the door.

"What do you want?" she demanded, scowling into the wind.

"Just to talk," I said.

"I'm not standing in the cold talking to you." She started for her car, but I stepped in front of her.

"It won't take long," I said. "Please. Jacob Callahan was taken into custody today."

The chain of Agnes's handbag slipped from her shoulder and dangled at her hip as she jerked to a stop. She had a firm hold on the handbag itself, or else it would have fallen.

"You don't say?" she said. "That's good news, indeed."

"You think he killed Andrew?"

"It seems obvious, doesn't it? That man was a nuisance."

I wasn't sure if she meant Andrew or Jacob, and realized she likely was referring to both.

"The police believe Jacob was outside Death by Coffee the night someone tried to lure Jules from

Phantastic Candies to there." I didn't know where I was going with that, but it was still bothering me. Why Jules?

Agnes nodded slowly. "I do recall seeing him that night."

I blinked. "Jacob? You saw him?"

"I did." Agnes pulled the chain back up onto her shoulder. "He was hanging around outside Heavenly Gate that night, watching us. Lee made sure he didn't try anything. I imagine that's why he moved on to easier targets."

That didn't make sense. "What time did you see him?" I asked. Why would Jacob come to Heavenly Gate when the lure was meant for Jules and Death by Coffee?

"Seven, perhaps?" Agnes shrugged. "Maybe eight. I wasn't watching the time. It might have been earlier. Maybe a little later. Lee was working on one of his projects, so we stayed here rather late."

Seven? That couldn't be right. Even eight wouldn't work. He was at Caitlin's by then.

"Are you sure it was Jacob you saw?" I asked.

"As sure as I can be," Agnes said. "It'd be hard to mistake him for someone else with how he looks." The wind picked up, causing Agnes to shiver. "I'm sorry, I have somewhere to be."

She walked around me. I didn't try to stop her. I was lost in my own head, trying in vain to make the timeline work. Either Agnes was lying to me or someone was out there pretending to be Jacob Callahan.

But who?

My mind went back to the gifts. Andrew, Jules, and Lee had all received one. These gifts were very

much like the reminders of faith Doris gave people who were straying from her flock. None of the
men would have received one of those.

But the women?

Erin.

I returned to my Escape, trying to fit the odd
Jacob-shaped piece into the puzzle of Doris's crew
and just couldn't do it. I pulled out my phone,
looked up the Carvers' address, and then I was on
the way, hoping I wasn't about to bother a widow
for nothing.

A single light was on in the house Erin had once
shared with Andrew. The curtains were parted,
showing me the living room. Erin was sitting on
the couch, a tablet sitting forgotten in her lap. She
looked lonely, sad even. She might have thought
her husband was cheating on her with someone
who'd once been her friend, but that didn't mean
she'd celebrate his death.

She looked toward the window when I pulled
into the driveway and parked. She rose and met
me at the front door.

"I'm sorry to bother you," I said. "I have one
quick question and then I'll let you go."

She crossed her arms over her chest and nodded. The makeup around her eyes was matted,
telling me she'd been crying.

"You said you received the reminder of faith
from Doris, that you were looking at it because of
how the gift Andrew received made you think of it?"

"It did," she said. "I already told you this."

"You also said you saw Andrew with Agnes.
Here." I nodded toward the living room behind
her. "And they were close, almost as if it was a ro-

mantic encounter. But then they were arguing at Andrew's Gifts later."

She nodded. "Is there a point to this?"

"Agnes and Lee received a gift, one like Andrew's. Did you know that?"

Erin paled. "No, I didn't."

"Do you truly think they are connected?" I asked. "The gifts and Doris's reminders?"

"I don't know," she said. "They could be." Her brow furrowed. "But . . ."

I waited her out.

"Doris talks a lot. She knows how to hurt you with her words, how to cut you the deepest." She met my eye. "I can see her leaving these gifts, especially if what's inside would hurt those receiving them. But killing someone?" Erin shook her head. "As much as I don't like her, I just don't see it."

I thanked Erin and returned to my Escape. Dad had said nearly the same thing; Doris didn't seem like the type to kill. Badger and insult and threaten? Sure. But that was all talk. Stabbing someone was vastly different, more personal. You couldn't just walk away from that.

Through the window, I saw Erin return to her seat. She collapsed there, as if her strings had been cut.

My eyes moved from her to the front door.

I tried to imagine Jacob walking up to that very door in his black clothing, his wallet chain smacking his left leg. He wouldn't have walked all the way here to deliver the gift. He'd have driven. His car sounded like a jet engine. Someone would have noticed his arrival.

My phone rang, causing me to jump. I tapped the screen on my dash to answer, pleased to note the name that appeared.

"Hi, Paul," I said, hoping I didn't sound guilty for talking to suspects in the murder investigation. "I was just thinking about you." A lie, but a good one.

"Really?" There was a hint of playfulness in his voice. "I was thinking about you too. Susie is all patched up and I'm done with work for the day."

Oh? "And what do you think you might want to do with your newfound freedom?" I asked, already imagining it.

"Well, that's up to you. Are you home?"

"I can be," I said. "Do you have plans?"

"I can't talk about them over the phone," he said. "How about I show you?"

I squeaked something that might have been "Okay." My brain was too busy supplying all the possibilities in agonizingly slow motion.

"See you at your place in ten?"

"Oh, I'll be there."

And in record time, I was.

25

Misfit glared at me from the corner of my living room, tail swishing, ears pinned back. He was wearing a red and green sweater, which was the cause of his consternation. Every so often, he would use his back foot to try to push the sweater off, but it was nice and safely snug.

"It's just for today," I told him. "Try to have some fun."

Christmas music played from my TV, which showed a crackling fireplace. I didn't have one of my own, so I'd improvised. Too bad I couldn't feel the heat from it. Or smell it. The cinnamon-scented candles I had lit weren't cutting it.

I hummed along to the music as I set out the pies I'd purchased. My guests were due to arrive anytime now, and I wanted everything to be perfect. Paul had left me snoring soundly in bed late last night so he could take care of his dogs, but promised to be back for my little Christmas Eve dinner.

My phone rang and I snatched it up. "Hi, Rita! Merry Christmas Eve!"

"Well, hello there, dear. You sound jovial today."

"I guess I am." And I swear Paul's visit last night had nothing to do with it. I noted Rita sounded far better than she had as of late, and said, "You sound happy."

"Oh, I am. You won't believe what arrived on my doorstep late last evening."

My mind instantly flashed on blue-wrapped gifts. "Please tell me it wasn't a present."

"It was!" Rita didn't squeal, but I could hear the joy in her voice. "It's from Johan."

I sagged against the counter. "That's great."

There was a pause. "Now, I know you didn't like him all that much, and I know he left on rather bad terms, but you don't have to sound so upset."

"I'm not upset," I told her. "I'm relieved. I was worried the gift was from . . . you know?"

A beat, and then, "You thought it was from the killer? Lordy Lou, I didn't even think of that. No, this was from Johan, sent through the mail, but there's no return address." A pause. "I heard they caught the killer?"

"They arrested someone," I said. "But I'm not sure they got the right guy."

"Oh? And why do you say that?"

I considered it a moment before speaking. "I keep thinking about Doris and how she's been hounding everyone, including people involved with Andrew. And then there's Lee and Agnes Komph and their issues with the Carvers." Romantic and otherwise.

"Doris is all talk," Rita said. I could imagine her waving a hand in front of her face, as if dismissing my concerns about the stern older woman. "She will nag your ear off, but when push comes to shove, she simply isn't capable of murder."

That's three—Dad, Erin, and now Rita—who'd said the same thing. "You don't think so?"

"I don't. That tongue of hers *is* sharp enough to kill, but she usually just uses it to lash her flock into shape. She could talk just about anyone off a cliff, though often it's because you just want to get away from her."

And while I'd love for Doris and her bad attitude to be the culprit, I tended to agree with Rita's assessment. "Maybe Jacob really is the guy," I said, not sure I believed it.

"I suppose we'll see, now, won't we? Oh! I've got to run, dear. I just wanted to let you know about Johan's gift. He's still out there." I could hear the smile in her voice. "I'll talk to you soon. Have a wonderful Christmas."

And she was gone.

I went back to working in the kitchen, forcing my mind back to happy holidays instead of deadly killers. Today was going to be about my family. About Paul. About Dad and Laura. I'd been tempted to invite everyone at Death by Coffee, as well as all my friends, but realized that sometimes smaller is better. I wanted today to be cozy and relaxing. Add too many people and I'd be tearing my hair out trying to please everyone.

I was soon back to humming as I checked the

dinner I'd planned. I'm an admittedly bad cook, yet everything appeared as if it was going to turn out okay. Nothing had burned.

Yet.

A knock at the door had me awkwardly pirouetting around my island counter to answer. I expected it to be one of my guests—Dad, Laura, or Paul—but instead, I found Caitlin Blevins on my doorstep.

"Caitlin?" I asked, stepping aside. "Come in. It's freezing."

"I don't want to keep you," she said, though she entered anyway. "I just . . ." She frowned, and then thrust out a hand. "Here."

I took a small, wrapped package from her. "What's this?" I couldn't keep the pleasure out of my voice.

"Not much. But since you got me something, I guess I thought I should do the same."

"You really didn't have to do that."

She shrugged, face turning red. "You've been kind to me. I should be the same to you."

"Caitlin, you've saved me from a killer." At the cost of her old guitar. "You don't have to buy me anything."

Another shrug. "I know. But still . . ."

I clutched the package to my chest. "I'll open it on Christmas. Thank you."

She smiled, looking embarrassed. "You're welcome." Her entire demeanor changed. "And I guess I had another reason for coming over."

It wasn't hard to figure out. "It's about Jacob, isn't it?"

"Yeah." She scuffed a boot on the floor. "I don't

get it. Boo called *me* of all people. She said the police picked him up at her place and that they think he killed that man." She ran her fingers through her hair before letting her arm drop. "It doesn't make sense."

No, it didn't. "What time did Jacob leave your house that night. Do you remember?"

"Yeah. Let me think." She paced over to the counter. "Smells good in here."

"Thank you."

In the living room, Misfit backed deeper into the corner, head ducked, like he thought he might be able to back his way out of his sweater. With a huff, he gave up and flopped over onto his side.

"I think it was around midnight," Caitlin said, pacing back over to me.

"Not before?"

She shook her head.

"You're positive?" I asked. "Think hard. You didn't fall asleep or leave him unattended for an hour or two or anything like that, right?"

"I'm sure. We listened to music for a while and then started fooling around with some of our own stuff, making improvements and alterations, looking for the right sound. I was nervous after your visit, but Jacob was still acting like Jacob, so I eventually got over worrying about him."

"Boo never stopped by?"

"No. Why would she?"

It was my turn to start pacing. "The police think Jacob was lurking outside Death by Coffee that night."

"After he left my house?"

"Before. And someone else placed him downtown earlier that night. At like seven or eight."

"That can't be right," Caitlin said. "He was with me."

Headlights lit up the front of my house. Caitlin took in the decorations, the TV fireplace, the cooking food, the music.

"You're having guests," she said, putting it together. She backed toward the door. "I'm sorry. I'll go."

The thought of her going back to her empty house didn't sit right with me. Everyone should have a happy holiday. "You don't have to go. You can stay if you'd like. It's just Paul and my dad and his girlfriend. They'd love to have you."

"No, that's okay. But thank you."

I walked Caitlin to the door and opened it just as Dad and Laura approached. Dad was wearing a ridiculous heavily padded Santa outfit, while Laura was dressed as Mrs. Claus.

"What in the world are you two wearing?" I asked through a laugh.

"It's a Christmas party, isn't it?" Dad asked, giving me a kiss on the cheek. His fake beard tickled. "Are you joining us?" he asked Caitlin.

"No." She was smiling as she said it. "You guys have fun."

"If you change your mind, you can always come over," I said. "None of us would mind."

"I'll think about it. Promise." And then Caitlin hurried across the yard, to her house.

"It looks like it might snow," Laura said as I stepped aside to let her and Dad in.

"It definitely feels it." The cold blast of air that followed them inside had my teeth chattering. "You do know that it's just us and Paul, right? No one else is dressing up."

"Oh, I know," Dad said. He spotted Misfit and walked over to scratch him behind the ears. Misfit leaned into it, and then turned as if asking Dad to remove the sweater. When he didn't, Misfit huffed and sauntered over to Laura. "But we wanted to get into the spirit of the season."

He then let loose a hearty "Ho, ho, ho!" that had Misfit shooting him a kitty-glare before he beat it to the safety of the bedroom.

My phone rang. A look at the screen and my heart sank. *Paul.* I answered with a tentative, "Hey."

"Hi, Krissy." Paul sounded unhappy, which, in turn, made me unhappy. "I thought I'd be able to get there on time, but Susie's running late. The pain meds they gave her knocked her flat and she fell asleep. She's going to be here soon, and then I'll head on over."

"There's no rush," I said, relieved. As a cop, Paul often got called away, causing us to miss dates or quiet evenings alone together. An hour or so late was nothing. "We'll be here."

"I'm really sorry about this," he said. "If you need to eat before I get there, go ahead. I can warm mine up. And I'll make it up to you." A pause. "Susie's keeping the dogs overnight, so . . ."

Heat washed across my face. I turned my back on Dad before he could see it. "I'm going to hold you to that." After Mr. and Mrs. Claus left, of course.

"Paul's not coming?" Laura asked when I hung up.

"He is. He's just going to be late. Dogsitter problems." I explained about Susie and her recent fall.

"Ah. I thought there might be a break in the case," Dad said. "I heard someone was arrested?"

Laura rolled her eyes, but her smile was good-natured. "I'm going to find Misfit. I have something for him." She pulled a bag of treats from her purse, and then went in search of the orange fluff-ball.

Dad waited until she was gone before turning back to me with a "Well?" expression on his face.

"Someone was picked up, but I think they might have the wrong guy." Before Dad could pepper me with questions about the murder, I pivoted, "How's Laura doing? She seems okay now."

"She's good," Dad said, glancing toward the hallway where she'd gone. "Everything's great now."

"It wasn't before?"

Dad scratched his chin beneath his fake beard. "She was stressed and it really got to her. She was worried you wouldn't understand."

"Wait. *I* wouldn't understand? Understand what?"

Dad took me by the elbow and led me into the kitchen, which because of my open floorplan, wasn't private, but it put us out of line of sight of the doorways down the hall.

"We're moving in together." When I just stared at him, he said. "Permanently."

More staring. When he didn't add to it, I asked, "So? I thought you two have been living together for a while now."

"Yeah. But this will be more . . . official?" The last word came out as a question.

And then it hit me. "You're getting married?" It was all I could do to keep from screaming it. I was bombarded by emotions and had to brace against the counter to keep from falling. I mean, this was great. And I was pretty sure Mom would approve. I couldn't understand how Laura would think that I might not be thrilled by the news.

"No," Dad said, bursting my joy bubble. "Not married."

My brow furrowed. "I thought you said you were going to make it official."

Dad pulled his beard from his face. "Is it hot in here, or what?" He let it snap back.

"Dad," I said. "What's going on?"

He sighed. "We're going to live as a couple," he said. "But not get married."

"Why not? Is it me? If you're worried I might not approve—"

"No, it's not you." He pulled me into a brief hug. "Never you. But Laura and I discussed it and we both realized that we don't want to go through the hassle again. We're not young. We're perfectly happy as we are. Why change things?"

I had no answer for that. "I'm happy for you." And I meant it with all my heart.

"I know you are, Buttercup. Laura was just worried. She wants you to approve so badly, but didn't know how to tell you."

"She needn't have worried," I said. "I like her. A lot. She's good for you."

Dad started blinking rapidly.

Oh no, please don't cry. If he lost it, I was going to lose it too and then we'd both be blubbering.

Thankfully, Laura returned then. "Kitty's happy," she announced. She set the remaining treats on the counter. "What did I miss?"

For an answer, I hugged her. "You're family, no matter what you decide to do."

The next ten minutes was spent with hugs and laughs and reassurances. Everything was going to be okay, and I was over the moon that Dad and Laura were going to stick together until the end.

Laura strode over to her purse to grab a tissue. She picked it up, causing the strap to hang down around her waist as she searched for one. My breath caught as images flashed through my mind.

Of Jacob, standing there, wallet chain dangling against his left leg. Of a shadowy shape, standing in the dark, a glimmer on their leg.

But my brain put it on their *right* leg.

Garrison had demonstrated what she'd seen that night outside of Death by Coffee by placing her hand around her right leg. Jacob's chain always hung on the left. Was I overanalyzing it? Or was it an important detail?

Another flash. This one of someone of similar size, but completely different in personality and just about everything else. Of a metal strap hanging as they clutched at a handbag.

"I've got to go." Without thinking I grabbed my coat and keys. "Tell Paul I'll be back." I needed to confirm what I thought I knew.

"You're leaving?" Laura asked at the same time Dad said, "I'm coming with you."

I didn't know how to explain, nor did I think I had time to. It seems silly, but I kept thinking that if I didn't do something *right this instant,* then Jacob would miss spending Christmas with his family. I couldn't allow that to happen, not when I thought I knew what happened.

"Okay," I said to Dad, before turning to Laura. "Could you wait for Paul? I know it's a lot to ask—"

She must have seen something in my face because she cut me off. "It's no problem. Go. I'll keep an eye on the food."

"Thank you." I gave her a quick hug, and then I pulled on my coat and was out the door with Santa Claus right behind me.

26

"This is about the murder, isn't it?"

I hunched my shoulders as I leaned forward to peer out the windshield. Laura had been right about the snow. A solid sheet of it was falling from the sky. The road was a faint outline already, and would soon be gone completely. I wanted to step on the gas, but feared it would send me careening into a parked car or a mailbox.

"Paul was going to be at your place soon, right?" Dad pressed, moving the ball of his Santa cap out of his face. "You could have talked to him when he got there."

"It's complicated." How could I explain that yes, Paul would have taken me seriously, would have looked into my epiphany, but he might not have gotten to it until after Christmas? I also wasn't positive I was right. The only way to be sure was to talk to the one person who'd been there that night.

"Some reindeer would be nice right about now,"

Dad said. "Though I doubt even Rudolph's red nose would cut through this."

My headlights reflected off the snow, creating a blinding wall I was determined to drive through. "I know the way by heart," I said, more for myself than for Dad. "We'll get there."

And by some miracle, we did.

I pulled into the Pine Hills police station lot, which held just a handful of cars. Lights on inside told me that at least some of the officers weren't taking Christmas Eve off like I half feared they might. It was a ludicrous thought considering that crime didn't take holidays off, but this *was* a small town. Anything was possible.

"You should wait—"

Dad was out of the car before I could finish the sentence. It looked like we were doing this. Together.

Christmas music was playing over a small cylindrical speaker sitting on the front desk. Plates of cookies surrounded it, and a pair of two-liter bottles of Coke sat next to them.

And standing around that, was a skeleton crew of festively dressed cops.

"Krissy?" Chief Patricia Dalton asked when we entered. "I thought Paul was going to be at your place tonight?"

"He is," I said. "Can I speak to Officer Garrison a moment?"

Becca Garrison was wearing an ugly green sweater that put the rest of the outfits to shame. It contrasted horribly with her duty belt. A cookie paused halfway to her mouth at her name.

"Is this about police business?" Chief Dalton

asked, taking a bite out of her own cookie. She spoke around it. "Because if it is, you might just want to just spit it out."

I glanced back at Dad, who shrugged. "It's about what Officer Garrison saw that night at Death by Coffee. The person." Boy, I hoped she wouldn't get in trouble for telling me about them. "I had a thought."

Chief Dalton smiled. "Did you, now?" Her eyes flickered past me, to Dad, and the smile turned into a grin. "And here I thought you might have brought us a little extra entertainment to spice up the night."

The gears in my head clicked and stuck as an image of Dad standing over the speaker, twirling his Santa hat in the air above his head while gyrating his hips, flashed through my mind.

"It's all right," Garrison said, stepping forward. "I have a few minutes to talk. What do you need to know?"

It took me a moment to use mental eye-bleach and get back on track. "That night," I said. "You saw someone that matched Jacob Callahan's description lurking in the shadows, right?"

"I did," Garrison said. "Like I said before, it was dark, so I didn't get a good look."

"But you saw the glint of metal, thought it was Jacob's wallet chain?"

Garrison nodded, a frown forming. "That's correct."

"What side was it on?"

Chief Dalton was still standing there, listening with a perplexed expression on her face. I noted how her eyes kept drifting toward Dad. It made me wonder if she had a little something extra in her Coke.

"The right," Garrison said, drawing my attention back to her.

Both dread and excitement zipped through me then. "The glint came from the right leg, not the left?"

A slow nod. "That's right."

"It wasn't Jacob."

"How do you figure that?" Chief Dalton asked.

Excitement made my words come out in a rush. "He was at my next-door neighbor's house that night. He never left. I saw his car and it never moved."

"But if he was seen—" she started, but I cut her off.

"That's just it! He wasn't seen because he wasn't there!"

Dad leaned forward and whispered into my ear. "You should probably explain."

I took a breath, slowed my racing mind. "Jacob is left-handed. When he was talking about his bass guitar with Caitlin, she mentioned it was a left-handed instrument. And every time I've seen him, he's had his wallet in his back left pocket, likely so he could reach it with his dominant hand, which means his chain . . ."

"Hangs on the left side," Garrison finished for me.

I pointed at her and nodded.

"Okay," Chief Dalton said. "Assuming that he didn't just stick it into his right pocket that night, then who was it my officer saw?"

I considered it before answering. "It was Laura's purse that made me think of it," I said. "Her strap hung down close to her waist while she was rooting around in it."

Dad scratched his chin through his beard. "I don't get it."

I looked around the room. No one else seemed to get it either. It shouldn't have been a surprise considering I had yet to fully explain, but still . . .

"Agnes Komph!"

Chief Dalton just stared at me.

"She has a small purse. A handbag. It has a metal strap that always slips off her shoulder."

"She wears it on her right shoulder, doesn't she?" Garrison asked, eyes widening. "*She* was the one who was there that night!"

I very nearly clapped. "Andrew was stabbed by something sharp. Lee Komph has those wood chisels. He very nearly poked my eye out with one."

"Wait, wait, wait," Chief Dalton said, holding up her hands. "Are you telling me Agnes Komph killed Andrew Carver?"

"It could have been Lee," I said. "He's got the size and temperament for it."

"And Agnes?"

"She could, I don't know, have been his lookout. Or maybe she knew what he planned on doing and showed up that night to stop him."

"To stop him from killing Jules Phan at your coffee shop?" Chief Dalton asked. She sounded skeptical. "Now why would he do that?"

I wished I had an answer, but came up blank. "I don't know why he'd want to hurt Jules. Maybe it's tied to his wife's relationship with Andrew Carver. Maybe Jules saw something, or Lee *thought* he did . . ."

I trailed off as Chief Dalton patted the air.

"Okay," she said. "I'll have Detective Buchannan look into it." I waited for her to go for the phone and call him since he wasn't one of the cops scarfing down cookies in the station, but she just stood there. "Go home, Krissy," she said when I didn't move. "Spend the evening with your family. With Paul."

A "but" was on the tip of my tongue. Dad took me by the arm and gently tugged me toward the door.

"You all have a Merry Christmas," he said as we stepped outside into the falling snow.

"But . . ." It finally came out.

"You told them," Dad said, leading me to my Escape. "Now let them do their jobs."

Shivering in the front seat, I tried to come up with a good argument as to why I needed to go back inside, to force them to do something *now*.

But what did I really have? A glint that might prove Jacob innocent of what? Being near Death by Coffee on one night? Agnes's presence—if it was indeed her—could have been a coincidence. Jacob could have been watching Jules from Caitlin's place, and this whole metal wallet chain versus purse strap was moot. I mean, even if he *had* shown up at Death by Coffee that night, it didn't mean anything when it came to the night Andrew was killed.

And Agnes and Lee received a gift box. How could they be guilty if they'd received a box too?

I pulled out of the lot with some reluctance, but Dad was right; the police would do their jobs. It might take a few days, which meant Jacob might spend Christmas behind bars, but there was nothing I could do about that. And that was assuming he was even locked up to begin with. They took him in for questioning, sure, but arrested? I didn't know.

Dad remained silent as I started driving. He was rubbing at his chin beneath his fake white beard, lost in his own thoughts.

It was probably why he didn't notice we weren't heading for home until we were passing both the church and Andrew's Gifts. He didn't comment. He sat up straighter, got a look on his face that made me wonder if he'd known I was going to do this the moment he'd led me from the station.

Heavenly Gate came into view a moment later. I couldn't see much through the snow, but I *could* tell a light was on inside. It was Christmas Eve, and yet someone was there. Lee or Agnes? I didn't know.

I was going to find out.

I parked out front, behind a snow-covered vehicle I thought might be Agnes's. I shut off the engine, met Dad's eye, and then we both climbed out of the car and headed for the door.

A CLOSED sign hung in the window. Agnes was at the counter, writing something into a ledger. Lee wasn't in view, but the light coming from the open door of the back room told me that he might be there.

I almost knocked, but Dad stepped forward and tried the door. Surprisingly, it wasn't locked. We stepped inside, bringing Agnes's head up.

"We're clo—" She cut off when she saw us. She frowned at me, but when she saw Dad in his Santa getup, her scowl could have peeled paint.

"Hi, Agnes," I said, stepping forward. "Is Lee here?"

Agnes didn't answer. She looked from Dad to me and back again, her expression growing angrier by the second. Her jaw worked and her fist closed on her pen with enough force to make her knuckles go white.

Lee stepped from the shadows of the back room, arms crossed, and with a wood chisel in his hand.

I swallowed, steadied myself. Agnes's handbag was sitting on the counter. The metal chain dangled over the edge, catching the light much like it might have done that night outside Death by Coffee.

"Interesting purse you have there," I said.

Agnes rested a hand on it as if she thought I might grab it and run. "Please, leave," she said. "I'm not interested in talking with you." Her gaze slid back to Dad. "Either of you."

I decided to leap right in and see what happened. I mean, I was there to get answers, so pussyfooting around it would get me nowhere. "The police saw you outside Death by Coffee a few nights ago."

Agnes tensed, telling me everything I needed to know. It *had* been her; not Jacob.

Lee stepped forward, closer to his wife. When he spoke, it was a deep rumble. "Go." One word. All command.

Dad placed a hand on my shoulder and squeezed.

Steady. "You were seen with Andrew Carver before his death," I said, keeping my eyes on Agnes because if I looked at Lee, I was pretty sure my legs would turn to jelly. "Erin saw you at her house with him."

Agnes opened her mouth, likely to deny it, but Lee beat her to it.

"Get out," he said. "Agnes has done nothing wrong."

I risked a glance at Lee. While my knees did weaken, Dad's steadying hand kept me from falling. "Did you kill him? Did you find out about Andrew and Agnes's relationship and you killed him for it?" I dropped my eyes to his hand, and the chisel he held.

Carefully, Lee set the chisel down beside Agnes's handbag. "I didn't kill anyone."

"But she was sleeping with him, wasn't she?" I asked. "She was in Phantastic Candies waiting for something to happen. I don't know what, but when she left, she headed for Andrew's Gifts. What happened that day?" I turned my attention to Agnes. "Did you try to break it off with Andrew? Did he get angry?" Back to Lee. "Is that why Jules was targeted? You feared he knew more than he did, so you sent him a gift to lure him to Death by Coffee, just like you lured Andrew to his own store?"

Lee shook his head. "You don't know what you're talking about. We received a gift too."

I desperately wanted to retort, to find a flaw with his reasoning, but I had nothing. He was right; they *had* received a gift. It didn't make sense.

"You found it here," Dad said from behind me. "Everyone else received their packages at their homes, but you . . . it was here."

Lee's brow furrowed. He removed his glasses, rubbed at the bridge of his nose. Beside him, Agnes licked her lips. She was eyeing the chisel, as if she was worried that her husband might reach past her and grab it.

Does she suspect him?

And then it hit me.

"You planted it," I said to Lee. "You realized the police were getting close to finding out who was sending people those gifts, which meant they'd soon realize you killed Andrew, so you left yourself a gift as a distraction."

"No." He shook his head. "Agnes found it. It was a threat, just like the others."

Agnes found it?

I thought it through. Agnes cheats with Andrew. Lee finds out, sees her waiting at Phantastic Candies, watches her go to Andrew's Gifts. Maybe Andrew and Agnes break it off. Maybe they don't. Angry, Lee decides to go ahead and do something about it anyway and he lures and kills Andrew. Fearing Jules saw something, Lee then attempts to lure him to Death by Coffee, likely to get rid of me too since I'm known to be nosy. Then, the police become involved, start asking questions. He panics, plants a red herring to throw them off.

It made sense.

Almost.

"Why were you at Death by Coffee that night?" I asked Agnes. "If Lee was going to kill Jules, were you there to stop him? To *help* him?"

"Agnes didn't—"

Before Lee could finish the thought, Agnes snatched the chisel from the counter. Tears were in her eyes. At first, I thought they were tears of sadness, of fear.

When she turned those eyes on Dad, however, I could see the fanatical rage in them.

"You *dare* come in here dressed like that?" she snarled. "You accuse *me* of wrongdoing while you strut around town spreading such . . . such . . . *ignorance?* No. I won't have it!"

"Agnes." Lee reached for her hand, but she jerked it away. "No, Lee. Don't you see what they're doing? They want to ruin us. To ruin *Christmas.* They want to destroy everything we care about, everything we've worked so hard for!"

My mind did a quick rewind. Agnes and Andrew together. Something happens and they break it off, but not because of Lee or Erin finding out about them.

She left him because of Doris.

"You got a reminder of your faith," I said. "A new one."

"Doris understands." Agnes was trembling now. She stepped slowly around the counter. "She helped me see the error of my ways. I knew I needed to do something, to make things right. Simple words wouldn't do, not when so much is going wrong with the world. I needed to fix it, to remove the disease."

"So, you decided to kill Andrew Carver?" I asked. "How does that make things right?"

"He tempted me. He was exploiting Christmas. He wouldn't stop, even when I told him to."

The fight Erin witnessed. Agnes hadn't just broken up with Andrew, she'd confronted him about his store. Erin had said how much he put into it, how it was his life. There was no way he'd give it up for a woman who'd just broken up with him.

"Agnes . . ."

"No, Lee." She waved the chisel between them, keeping him at bay. "It had to be done. He wouldn't stop, so I sent him that gift, made him think you were going to be there, that you'd found out about us and were going to tell Erin."

"She already knew," I said. "She saw the two of you at her house the day she was supposed to be visiting her sister."

"I didn't know that!" shrieked Agnes.

"You were still with him then. But at Andrew's Gifts, you weren't. You went there to kill him."

"No! I went there to threaten him, but not kill him. He grew so angry that he came at me. I had one of Lee's chisels with me, just in case." She sucked in a breath. "I didn't mean to do it, but when it was done, I knew it was the right thing to do. Doris has always said that these people need to be stopped, and I stopped him. Yes, I did."

"But why go after Jules?" I asked. "He didn't do anything."

Agnes eased closer. "Because he's a part of all that's wrong with this town. He dresses like *that*." She jabbed the chisel toward Dad in his overstuffed Santa outfit. "It's pure exploitation! And *you* . . ." she sneered my way. "You use his candy, sell it in your drinks."

Lee closed his eyes. His big hands were balled into fists. "I tried to protect you," he whispered, just loud enough for me to hear. "I tried to distract, to keep them from asking questions. I'm so sorry." He tensed, ready to throw himself at his wife.

"No!" Agnes, anticipating his movement, rounded the counter, chisel raised. "They have to be stopped!"

I braced myself, ready to tackle her if need be, but Dad shoved me to the side as Agnes launched herself at me. I hit the floor, shouted, "Dad! No!" just as Agnes lunged.

The chisel came down, struck Dad hard in the chest. He grunted and staggered back, just as Lee reached his wife and pulled her back. He hugged her close and refused to let her go, even as she wailed and fought like a cat about to be dunked into a bath.

The chisel wobbled from Dad's chest as he bumped up against a shelf, knocking a wooden angel to the floor. He looked down at the chisel as if surprised to find it there.

"Dad!" I scrambled to my feet. Tears threatened as I reached for my phone.

"I'm okay," he said, tugging the chisel free. There was no blood on it. "It hit the padding." He patted his chest as if to make sure. "But, boy, that's going to leave one heck of a bruise."

Across the room, Lee sagged to the floor with Agnes, who was trembling. The fight seemed to have gone out of her, but not the rage.

As I placed a call to the police, she glared at me with such malice, I could *feel* it.

For someone who was supposed to be spiritual, Agnes Komph had a lot to learn about the true spirit of Christmas.

27

Pine Hills was covered in a white fluff that was over a foot deep. In most places, the roads were closed. Plows were working them, but it would take time.

I'd already shoveled my driveway, nearly killing myself in the process. Lance took care of his and Jules's before going over to help Caitlin. We'd then shared hot chocolate, had a few laughs, and went back to each of our homes to lounge around in our pj's. My muscles were sore, but I was feeling good.

The police arrived within ten minutes of Agnes's attack on Dad. It would have been sooner if not for the snow. Lee never let Agnes go while they waited for the cops' arrival, and then, without a word, they left with them. Detective Buchannan showed up a few minutes later, scowled about the place for a few minutes, and then sent Dad and me on our way.

Laura wasn't thrilled when we got back, nor was Paul, who ended up leaving when his mom called him in to help sort through the mess. My dinner party was a dud, but that didn't mean it turned out to be a bad night. A killer was apprehended, and everyone I cared about was safe. That was all that mattered.

I yawned as I stretched where I lounged on the couch. Misfit was passed out on the floor. His newest catnip toys were strewn around him, damp from constant licking. I had a mint tea rapidly cooling on the coffee table, but I didn't have the energy to reach for it. The house was silent. I leaned my head back, content to just relax and let my snow-shoveling induced aching muscles recover.

My phone rang. I snatched it up before it could rouse the snoozing kitty.

"Hi, Dad. How are you feeling?"

"Sore." He laughed. "How are you faring, Butter-up? Have you heard from Paul yet?"

"Not yet." A deep, gnawing worry churned, but wouldn't let it get to me too much. He'd call once everything was sorted out, even if it took all of Christmas day. "How's Laura."

"She's good. She's threatened to wrap me in Bubble Wrap, but otherwise, she understands. A bad person was taken off the streets. What's a little bruising compared to that?"

I shuddered, remembering that chisel coming down. If she hadn't aimed for his chest, but his head . . .

"I just wanted to let you know that Laura and I

won't be stopping by until the weather improves. There's more snow in the forecast."

My heart sank. "Oh? But don't you leave tomorrow?"

"Actually, no, we don't. We've already cancelled our flight because of the snow. Besides, I haven't had enough Krissy-time, and well, I plan on getting it."

I grinned. "That's great. What would you like to do? Now that the killer's been caught, I don't have anything to distract me."

"Oh, I'll think of something," Dad said with a laugh. "I'll call you later and let you know what we plan to do, all right, Buttercup? We can talk about it then."

"Sure thing. I'll be here."

We clicked off. I tossed my phone onto the cushion next to me and was leaning back to catch a nap when the sound of crunching snow met my ears. Misfit's too, because he popped up and scrambled from the room, ears pinned back in annoyance.

A peek out the window and then I was running for the door.

"Paul!" He was bundled up tight as he got out of his car. His police hat was replaced by a knit cap that looked so worn, I couldn't imagine it kept him warm. "You came!"

"Of course, I did." He crunched his way over to me, accepted my hug, and then let me usher him inside. "It's Christmas."

"I wasn't sure you'd make it," I said, indicating the snow. My freshly shoveled driveway was begin ning to look white and indistinct again. "It's pretty bad out there."

"It is. But it's not bad enough to stop me from seeing you." He shed his coat, gloves, knit cap, and snow boots. The process took a good five minutes with a whole lot of grunts and muttered curses. When he was done, he heaved a relieved sigh, and then cursed. "Your gift! I left it in the car."

"It can wait," I said, stopping him before he could go through the process of putting everything back on. "Let's just sit and talk for a bit, okay?"

He hesitated, and then nodded. "All right."

Paul sat at the island counter while I put on some coffee. Tea was fine and all, but it couldn't beat the comforts of a hot cup of coffee with a cookie inside.

"I should still be mad at you about last night," said as I dumped out my now-cold tea. "You have waited for me."

ow. I really am sorry about that. You know

ughed. "Oh, yeah, I do. Chief called me as as you left the station. She warned me that you might get yourself into trouble." It always amused me that he called his mom "Chief."

"Hey! I don't have a scratch on me." Just a tiny bruise where I'd fallen when Dad had pushed me, but that was on my keister. Paul didn't need to see that.

Yet.

"Well, I'm glad you're okay. Your dad, too. How's he doing?"

"He's good. It looks like he's going to stay in town for a few extra days. With the murder, and Laura being sick for most of it, we didn't get to spend much time together."

"That's good." Paul nodded, and then thanked me when I poured him a cup of coffee and handed it over. "He still shouldn't have taken that risk. Neither of you should have, father and daughter time or not."

"But we got her," I said. "I still can't believe it was Agnes."

Paul took a sip of coffee, set his mug aside. "She ranted and raged for quite a while at the station. She was still going by the time I got there, and didn't wind down for an hour afterward."

"Wow. She *was* pretty upset about Dad's outfit."

"Lee tried to take the blame for the murder. He said he should have done more, should have stepped in and stopped her. He was trying to pr⬛ tect Agnes this entire time. He suspected sh⬛ the one who'd killed Andrew, which was ⬛ was so standoffish as of late. He thought ⬛ bully people into looking the other way."

As much as I might want to, I couldn't faul⬛ for that. Lee only wanted to keep his wife from harm. She might be a killer, might have been radicalized by Doris, but he still loved her.

"What about Jacob Callahan?" I asked.

"John apologized to him and sent him on his way last night. He seemed to understand, and since Becca offered to drive him home, he didn't raise a fuss about being detained. I think he was glad it's over more than anything."

"That's good." I wondered if I'd be seeing him around Caitlin's sometime soon. If so, I planned on checking in on him and apologizing for ever thinking he might have had something to do with the murder. "And Doris?" I asked. "From the sounds of it, it was her words that sent Agnes over the edge."

Paul sighed. "She didn't kill anyone, nor did she have anything to do with the threatening gifts, so there's not much we can do."

"She won't get into trouble?"

"I'm afraid not." Paul didn't sound happy about it. "At least legal trouble. From what I'm hearing from John, Doris might have caused enough distress for the church that she'll be asked to have her meetings somewhere else."

It served her right. I get that she didn't like how a lot of us celebrated the holidays, but that didn't give her the right to hassle us for it. Words have power, and Doris had used a *lot* of hateful words. She should be punished. Maybe then she'd see the error of her ways and would stop hounding people who just wanted to live their lives how they saw fit, though I wasn't holding my breath.

"Lena Allison is going to be doing some ride-alongs after the snow clears up," Paul said, drawing me out of my thoughts.

"With you?"

He shook his head. "With Becca Garrison. Chief Dalton met with Lena and thinks she could have a future in the department. She thought having another woman show her the ropes might help her with her confidence."

"That's great!" Though a part of me was sad.

We'd just gotten her back at Death by Coffee, and it appeared as if that return was going to be brief. "I hope it works out."

"I'm sure it will." A gleam came into Paul's eye then. "You know, it's pretty cold out there."

"It is."

"I was thinking . . ." He cleared his throat, stood. "I left your gift out in the car, but that doesn't mean we can't celebrate."

I slithered to my feet. "No, it doesn't."

"I thought maybe, if you were interested, I might go ahead and unwrap one of my Christmas gifts now." He glanced back toward the tree and the pile of waiting gifts there, before turning back to me. "But not one of those."

Heat flared through me, made my next words come out as a purr. "Only if I can unwrap one of my own." My roving eyes told him exactly where I'd start.

"Of course." He stepped into the living room. "Shall we begin?"

I didn't bother speaking. Words had caused enough trouble as of late. Instead, under the flashing lights of the Christmas tree, I let my hands do all the talking.

Talk about a Merry Christmas.